THE LITTLE ICE CREAM SHOP BY THE SEA

LIZZIE CHANTREE

lemon meringue

PUBLISHING

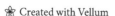 Created with Vellum

DEDICATION

With big thanks to my amazing family for their endless support. Extra thanks go to Heidi, Sam and Alice, for being such an inspiration. Hugs sent to my incredible readers. I appreciate you picking up my books, telling your friends and family about them and for posting reviews to let other book lovers know about my work. You are superstars!

ot again! Genie Grayson wanted to scream and throw her hands in the air. Instead, she stuffed her fist in her mouth and turned away. She'd thought she had her terrible phobia under control – she was a perfectly sane twenty-two-year-old – but the last few weeks had been stressful, and this was her Achilles heel. She looked around furtively to see if anyone had noticed, but there was hardly anyone enjoying breakfast in her family's seafront restaurant.

The evil seagull had dropped a lump of cheese onto her pristine outdoor tablecloth. After flying right into the restaurant awning. It had obviously been at the beer that always ended up in the gutters after a busy night at one of the clubs further down the beach.

Genie rarely admitted to having this issue, as who in the world, other than herself of course, had a problem with cheese? No one who managed a restaurant and ice cream parlour, that was for sure. Not a responsible professional who served food all day and had to be surrounded by the awful stretchy stuff that smelt like her grandad's old socks after a day on his feet.

She knew if she recited the alphabet backwards she'd be ok. She'd had years of practice. She usually got to about W, and then her pulse slowed down and she was able to take a deep breath and move on. She looked up and saw the gull sitting on the wall above the restaurant, its piercing red eyes like lasers. She shushed it away, but it just turned its back on her.

She often wondered if she had an allergy to wild animals. She'd tried to pet one at a zoo on a school trip and got bitten, then her hand had swollen up and she'd been rushed to hospital, even though she'd been fine after a few hours. She'd avoided zoos ever since. She gave the jungle a wide berth too. It wasn't too difficult from her current location on the coast of Essex, but she wasn't taking any chances. Cheese, on the other hand, was impossible to dodge. Not only did she work in kitchens, she cooked when her dad had a day off. Luckily, their bestsellers were their huge breakfasts, and plates of fish and chips.

Genie knew that if she gave into the urge to shove the offending messy table in to the road, she'd get herself in all kinds of trouble with her parents, and probably the local council. She was already on their radar for changing all the restaurant's lightbulbs to a deep shade of red one weekend, to create an ambience. She'd had a formal letter the following week suggesting she might be moonlighting as a sex worker. That was slander! She might be a bit busty, and she was down on her luck, but she was too tired to blink some days. She just plastered on a smile and worked through it. Takings really had to pick up, at the restaurant though. They needed more customers.

She had to find a way to calm down and reasonably work out a plan of action, either by talking to her mum, Milly, about their current dilemma, or by finding a boyfriend and having some hot steamy sex to take her mind off things. While she pondered that thought, she grabbed the tablecloth by the edges with a couple of forks and shoved it behind the counter into the washing basket, quickly re-covering the table with a fresh cloth.

Genie smiled brightly at two school mums who were perusing the menu but her grin dropped as she turned towards the kitchen at the back of the little restaurant. She wondered if anyone would notice if she stood in the middle of the room and screamed. Probably not.

The mums were the only two customers, and they'd already caught her cursing in Spanish under her breath as she wiped down the tables when they'd arrived. They had looked at her in confusion. She'd picked up a 'learn to speak Spanish' course at the charity shop the week previously, in the hope that she might one day travel abroad with friends. She'd also thought it might help if they ever got a foreign customer, however unlikely that seemed. But when she'd got the disc back to the house, it was a homemade knock-off copy and the only vocabulary was swearwords. She hated being conned, so she'd resolutely learned the whole tape, which consisted of about fifty phrases that all sounded mightily dodgy. They were great for easing frustration, though, as no one else knew what she was saying. She hoped. She'd looked up a few of the words, but then been worried her parents would question why she was Google-translating so many profanities. She didn't want them to start to wonder if that council letter had been spot on.

Usually, the breathtaking panorama of sandy beaches and the endless skyline across the road were enough to lift her spirits. But today she felt she might as well go and bang her head against a wall, instead of trying yet again to reason with her parents. The family business *had* to be brought into the twenty-first century. She knew she had a temper and didn't always explain things clearly without combusting into flames, but they still treated her as if she was nine years old.

All she was asking of her parents was that they let her try out a few new business ideas and a handful of new ice-cream flavours. She didn't want to reinvent the wheel. Their business hadn't changed for decades. They still had the same chairs and tables, and even the menus, that her grandad Gus had installed. Her parents' restaurant, Graysons', offered bought-in, basic puddings, but Genie had seen massive growth in big gooey ice cream desserts presented in glass mugs or tall glasses. She didn't see why they couldn't try this. They had a prime site on the seafront, for goodness sake! She could feel her temper begin to rise again. Then she remembered – their customers. She didn't want to scare them away. She twirled round to face them again with another smile.

Her parents were worried about upsetting her grandad, who ran the ice cream bar. He only offered about six flavours these days. She had spent much of her time with him and her grandma when she was growing up. Her parents had stepped in to take over the business when her grandma had died a few years previously. Her grandad had begun wandering around the small garden at the back of the restaurant and shouting at the plants, raging at the loss of his wife. In the end, they'd explained to customers that he was an inventor seeing if upsetting plants stunted their growth. It was the only explanation they could come up with for his behaviour, which was becoming more and more erratic.

Their regulars knew about Genie's grandma and understood Gus's sorrow and anger, but occasionally a new customer would start to glance around to see if there were spaces to eat elsewhere, which meant even less income for them all. Genie missed her grandma Vera terribly, as she had always let her sit with them after school. Genie would perch on a high stool behind the ice cream counter and Vera would tempt her with her latest ice cream concoction and cuddle her, while Gus served a steady stream of customers anxious to get Vera's new flavours before they sold out.

With Genie's parents selling breakfasts and lunches, and Gus and Vera on ice cream, the restaurant had worked like a dream. Then her grandma died and Genie's parents had taken the reins, working harder than ever to cover their grief. They looked more frazzled as each year passed. Genie was used to coming home from school to the empty house they lived in, up the hill, as her parents were always working. Soon, she was roped into doing her homework at the restaurant, and then it seemed a natural progression for her to help out. She'd been doing that since she could walk anyway. She loved the restaurant and was proud of her family's heritage. She needed to spread her creative wings, though, and felt that since Vera had passed away, Gus was wilting. She wanted to keep her grandma's spirit alive, and Gus needed Genie more than her parents did right now.

She spent her weekend evenings making batches of ice cream for him to sell, though he kept telling her she should be out partying with people her own age, not keeping an old man company and trying to keep his business alive. He was bored one night and bought two whippy-type machines for simple, smooth ice cream and declared that she wouldn't need to help him anymore. It broke her heart. She could see that he was trying really hard to manage alone, but he was struggling with his memories of his beautiful wife and the happiness she'd given everyone with her smile and her amazing ice cream flavours. He just couldn't replicate them.

Genie had asked him about trying different recipes, but he'd harrumphed and told her that if she thought she knew better, then she could get on with it. And besides, he'd added that there wasn't enough business to try new ideas. He liked his whippy ice cream machines and they did sell a fair amount of cones, but there was no love in the ingredients. Vera used to sprinkle chocolate chips, lemon rind, tiny bites of apple and many other incredible ingredients into her mixes to make you feel like you were eating a mouthful of magic. Your tongue would tingle and most people came back to order more. People visited from miles around to try her latest flavours. Recently Genie had decided to try to keep the tradition going. After five generations of her family running this business, she was determined to make it shine again, in honour of her grandma.

As far as she was concerned, Gus had given her the green light. She'd always worked hard for her parents and was determined to turn their fortunes round. All the shops along the seafront were looking a bit tired these days. She felt they'd get stuck in a time warp if something didn't change.

She tried to calm herself down. She chanted a mantra in her head that she'd heard on the radio that morning. It was supposed to make you feel zen, but it soon irritated her now she couldn't get the stupid phrases out of her mind.

Her parents had often told Genie she was too bossy for her own good, but then, she'd had to be. Her schoolwork had suffered and she'd failed most of her exams, because she was always helping out at the restaurant or washing and cleaning at home while her parents were at work. Her parents had despaired, but what else could they have expected?

It was why she hadn't yet found a home of her own, even at her age. Her parents had moved into her grandparents' Georgian seafront property when Genie had been just two. The house and the business were their lives. She secretly couldn't imagine living anywhere else, but she'd never tell her mum and dad that. Her grandad had moved into the annex, which was separate from the main house. He'd recently paid a man to put a fence up between the two buildings, saying he needed more privacy. Genie suspected that he wanted to be able to hide away with his grief. She felt that she couldn't express her own sorrow, as she had to keep everyone else's spirits up. Her dad walked around looking permanently grumpy and her mum often wrung her hands, which in turn made Genie anxious. Genie did the restaurant books, so she knew that they could just about scrape by for now, but how long that would last for, she had no idea. They needed something to change – and fast.

Maintaining the house, her family and the restaurant was a full time job. Although none of the whole parade of restaurants were up to date, they were still quite busy as very few bars and eateries were allowed on each stretch of beach. They rarely came up for sale, tending to stay within a family. Everybody was friends with everyone else, but the décor in each venue was old fashioned, as far as Genie was concerned, and their clientele was getting older too.

That was fine, Genie respected older people, but a few tended to sit for hours, hogging the tables, and they didn't spend much money. She'd almost poked an elderly man's eye out once when she'd thought he might be dead and was checking he was still breathing. Thank goodness, he'd woken up with a start. As an only child, she loved it when there was a mix of ages mingling around. Her dad was an only child too, so there were no siblings to help him run the restaurant. It had fallen to Genie and her mum. But since Vera had died, it felt like the life and soul of the place had gone with her.

The school mums, who were regulars and probably their youngest customers, checked their designer watches to see how much time they could spend relaxing before rushing off to pick up various offspring. It was still only 9.30am, so she wandered over to take their order and chatted amiably, as she did with all their customers, biting back her frustration.

It was hard keeping up a cheerful face with the

customers, when she knew that the restaurant's takings were down again that quarter. The quiet worry that seemed to be with her most days was starting to make itself more apparent. Even if it meant more of her mum's death stares, or her dad's rolling eyes, she was determined to turn the family's fortunes around.

CHAPTER TWO

*A*da stared out at the beautiful sea view in front of her, but couldn't really take anything in. Tears threatened to spill from her eyes, but she was tougher than that. She refused to feel sorry for herself.

Since her darling Ned passed away last year, she'd been determined to stay in the apartment they had bought together when they knew he was unwell. He'd wanted to come back home to the seaside town he'd been born in. Although it had meant leaving their friends and family behind, he yearned to wander along the sandy beaches and sit and watch the seagulls. He wanted to wriggle his bare toes in the sand and eat melting ice creams as the sun went down.

The months before he went were bittersweet. He had been at peace in his hometown, so she couldn't be cross with him for leaving her alone. She'd never lived here before, though, and the endless beaches and little shops and eateries dotted around were a far cry from her past life, full of interesting people and endless social engagements. Here she had a beautiful home, but her family lived abroad and she could not – would not – let them know how much she was still grieving, and move home. Here she felt close to Ned. She could run her fingers through the sand and picture him next to her doing the same. The joy on his face, when he'd recounted stories of his childhood in the old fishing town and told her of his summers building sandcastles on the beach and riding the waves with his friends. She remembered it so well.

They had only visited his birthplace once before. But as soon as he was diagnosed with his illness and given such a short time to live, he suddenly craved home.

To her, home was their huge house in America. Ned had been a celebrity photographer and they had moved often, but they had settled down in the States. She had adored the huge rooms with high ceilings and the warmth of the sun that eased her old bones, but here she was, in a new place, a place that wasn't really home for her.

Her sons called her almost daily, but so far, she'd refused to go back. Ned was here with her, she could feel him, even though she couldn't see his kind face anymore.

He would be telling her to get onto that plane and stay with their children, but they were busy. They had careers and families of their own. What would they want with a heartbroken old woman, wandering around their houses looking lost and frequently bursting into angry tears? They didn't need her dragging them down, when they were coping with their own grief. Ned had filled the room with his presence and people clamoured for his attention. He was one of those souls that others gravitated towards, to bask in the glow of his golden personality. She had been well used to it, though, and his gaze always found her in a crowded room.

She knew she could get through this, but she would have to do it in her own time. They would all probably demand that she visit them, or they would descend on her at Christmas, so until then, she had almost a year to compose herself and to let the outside world think she was recovering. She was an actress. She could do this. She would make damn sure that by the time her boys got here, they'd think she was coping beautifully, rebuilding her life and staying strong. She gripped the handrail of the panoramic balcony on her penthouse flat and gazed through a sheen of tears at the waves kissing the shore. She tried to feel some of the peace that Ned had found here.

Movement caught her eye on the promenade below and she recognised the young woman from one of the breakfast places along the beach. She was looking mutinous, even from this distance, stalking back and forward and muttering to herself. Her hands were bunched into fists and she was brandishing one of them at a very innocent-looking bush, before she swung a kick at a plant pot and then hopped about holding her toes. Ada couldn't help but smile. She had met the girl and her parents a few times and exchanged pleasantries, but Ned hadn't really wanted to eat out. She'd only been there alone, when the isolation had got too much for her. Perhaps she'd go there today and try and chase away her demons. If Genie – she remembered the girl's name at last – was in a bad mood, then they could be grumpy together. She might even have a little chat to the hedge as she walked past, too. It wouldn't answer back. She was pretty sure everyone in her building thought she was an eccentric recluse, so no-one would bat an eyelid to see her talking to a plant.

The little cafés and bars along the seafront were quaint and beautiful and looked as if they hadn't been touched by time, which was charming. Ada did think that they could do with a few modern touches, like softer cushions on their seats for frail bottoms like hers and maybe the odd tweak to the menus as a change from cooked breakfasts and chips. The beach was popular, though, and the street below was often bustling with people. It was just the restaurants that seemed eerily quiet. She couldn't understand why, as the prices were very low for the huge plates of food that were served. Seaside fry-ups were usually a crowd pleaser. They were too heavy for a little woman like her, though. She wished they offered something a bit healthier. Perhaps she ought to ask for a children's portion, but she always felt embarrassed to do that and ended up leaving at least half her meal.

Maybe if she went for brisk walks along the shoreline, then her appetite would return. She knew she was wasting away here. Her children would be horrified if they could see how much weight she'd lost. She always hid most of her body behind a table when they video-chatted with her. She wore a bulky jumper and stuck a smile on her face and told them she was *fine*.

She straightened her back, which ached slightly from all her tossing and turning at night. She often thought she must be searching for Ned in her sleep, as she woke up feeling like she'd done a workout. She felt the worse for it, not better. Her building had a gym downstairs and a spa, but she'd never ventured in. She used to swim every day at her old home, but now she worried that she'd pass out through exhaustion while in the pool, and hadn't plucked up the courage to risk it yet.

She occasionally wondered if she should just let herself drift off and be with Ned, but she was stronger than that. She would survive this. Brushing a tear from her eye, she turned and decided that she needed some fresh air. In fact, today was going to be the day when that huge breakfast at Genie's restaurant didn't defeat her.

CHAPTER THREE

*G*enie smiled politely at the little woman in front of her, who was becoming a regular. She had beautiful skin, and her soft grey hair was always pulled back into a perfect chignon, but her eyes were so sad. Genie didn't know her well enough to ask her if she was ok, but she could feel the unhappiness emanating from her, even though she always looked up at her with a bright smile.

Today she was working her way through a huge plate of food and had been bravely tackling it for the last hour. She had only got about a third of the way through, and looked exhausted. Genie had once asked her parents to offer smaller portions for different sized appetites, but they had told her not to be silly, their prices were so cheap and no one would want a smaller plate for the same money. Genie secretly thought they overloaded the plates too much. If they would just take two or three ingredients off the breakfasts and add them as extras, they would make much more money. People could still have a hearty breakfast, but the pound or two on each plate for beans, mushrooms, and extra toast would make such a difference to their bottom line. It would give them a chance to improve everything else.

Genie took Ada the fresh pot of tea she'd asked for and gave her a warm smile. There was something about her that drew Genie to her. She wanted to reach out and give her a supportive hug. Instead, she whipped the plate away as soon as the lady put her cutlery down and was rewarded with a grateful glance. A woman that size probably ate muesli for breakfast, lunch and dinner.

Genie looked down at her own ample hips and bulging bosom and decided that she was going to try and take her next door neighbour's dog out for a morning walk along the shore more often. She'd also try not feel so stressed that she couldn't be bothered to cook a proper meal at night. Her parents loved food that was quick and easy to whip up, but Genie enjoyed fresh ingredients and spent ages scanning new recipe ideas and trying out different flavours at home. It didn't have to take an age to make a meal from scratch – as long as it didn't contain cheese. If it did, she had to put on gloves to handle it. This often caused her to spill most of the ingredients. She'd then have to put on wellington boots to sweep up the disgusting, cheesy tendrils before they touched her toes. Genie's parents had lost a bit of weight recently, but this might have been because they were stressed out about the businesses along the seafront, rather than her delicious evening meals.

She eyed her dad's not-quite-so portly stomach. She was pleased to see he was in slightly better shape these days. He wasn't as grumpy either. Her mum, on the other hand, always made an effort with her appearance and scolded Genie about being such a slob. But Genie didn't have time to spend ages shopping with friends for the latest fashions. Besides, her clothes usually stank of grease from the fryer in the back kitchen by the time she got home, so she had given up on that years ago. She was clean and presentable at work, with her long dark hair pulled back in a ponytail to keep it away from the food (and cheese) and a fresh blouse and skirt every day. Even that seemed an effort.

She had piercing blue eyes that customers often stopped her to ask about, and long silky black lashes, which meant she didn't need much make-up. Her skin was slightly tanned from working outdoors, even at this time of year. Half the chairs and tables were inside, but the other half were under an awning. This could be swept back at the touch of a button, allowing diners to sit in the sunshine. The British weather was actually good this year, so the awning was open for a lot of the time, even though Christmas wasn't all that long ago.

Genie glanced up from a table she was clearing. Trudie, from one of the other restaurants further along, had popped her head in to say hello. She glanced around to see if they were busy and grinned a hello at Genie.

'Hey Trudie, how's business today?'

Trudie paused to say hello to Ada, which surprised Genie, as she'd thought the older lady pretty much kept herself to herself. Ada greeted her politely and then turned back to her tea.

'We're really busy,' said Trudie. 'And I've run out of milk already. I forgot to send the order today. We've got a coach party in and they're causing havoc, moving all the tables round.' Trudie smiled happily.

Genie knew she wouldn't mind a huge crowd. These businesses were used to being packed to the rafters at weekends, but being busy on a weekday and not having to pace up and down the road looking for customers was a complete bonus.

Genie grinned at the other woman's infectious smile. Everyone along the parade called her Tantalising Trudie, because her hips swayed mesmerizingly as she weaved between tables. Trudie kept Genie sane and was always dropping in for a chat with her or her parents. Genie had tried to copy Trudie's sashay once and had tripped over and almost landed face-first in the lap of one of their male customers. She'd looked up to apologise, and seen Bob from the local council office staring disapprovingly down at her, his face bright red. She wouldn't be trying that move again in a hurry.

Everyone along this parade of restaurants got on so well. It was what had kept Genie going when her own friends stopped coming to the restaurant and she had fewer people of her own age to chat to. Trudie was more her mother's friend than hers, but they still got on really well.

'Of course!' she responded to Trudie's appeal for milk. 'I'm sure Dad ordered enough and we're quiet today, so I'll grab you a couple of cartons.'

Trudie smiled her thanks and pulled out a chair and sat chatting quietly to Ada, who seemed pleased at the interruption. When Genie returned, Trudie jumped up, waved her thanks and jogged back to her own establishment, waving to Genie's dad who had just come out of the kitchen with huge breakfasts for a table of two.

CHAPTER FOUR

*G*enie rolled her eyes. Her dad inclined his head to acknowledge Trudie, but he barely made time for their customers these days.

She could remember being here when her grandparents had run the restaurant and her parents had just been helping out. The place had always been bursting with happy clients and her family stopped regularly to chat to their visitors and to find out about their lives and families.

Recently, she'd noticed that her dad had gone into his shell. He didn't chat to customers, while her mum had a constant pinched expression on her face. To give her credit, Mum did schmooze with anyone who hadn't been there before, or who looked like they might have slept in silk sheets by the cut of their clothes, but she tended to turn her nose up at their valuable regular clientele of locals.

Genie's mum Milly had been born in Cornwall, with its beautiful countryside and craggy stone buildings. But she'd grown to adore the little town and the sandy shores of Essex she had found herself in, after meeting and falling madly in love with Genie's dad James. Having said that, she did complain that the sea wasn't clear enough here and the beaches were more stone than sand. She'd been living here for over twenty-five years, but still craved the rugged shores of her home. They used to go to Cornwall each year, but since her granddad had become a liability with customers, they couldn't go. There was simply no one else that they trusted to run the business.

Genie didn't mind, as her mum's sister in Cornwall was a menace who had always tried to get Genie to plait her hair and scrub her face, and her grandparents there had never really taken to her dad, even after all these years. His family wasn't good enough for their daughter, as far as they were concerned, and they didn't waste a second telling him so, from the moment the family got to Cornwall every time.

Genie had always wanted to stamp on their toes to shut them up when she was younger, and had almost managed it once, before her dad had seen the mutiny in her eyes and quickly swung her up into his arms and carried her to look at the sea before anyone else observed them. He had tickled her tummy and told her to take no notice of them, when she was small, but now she was older she could see he was itching to do the same. She was sure he was waiting for her mum to defend him and his parentage – but she never did.

It was weird how her mum was so grumpy with her dad, but when another man came into the restaurant, she suddenly morphed into a social butterfly. As the years wore on, and the job got harder and the responsibility seemed to weigh more heavily, she only appeared to find a glimmer of sunshine in people other than her own family. She still hugged Genie and smoothed down her hair, but it seemed half-hearted, as if she wasn't really concentrating.

Her mum had loved Vera so much. She had been a much warmer and happier character than Milly's own mother, Lucille. But since Vera died, Milly had started to become more like Lucille, 'the miserable one,' as Genie secretly called her. Now Milly snapped at everyone and frowned a lot. They were all grieving in their own ways, but they weren't supporting each other, however much Genie tried to help.

Her dad didn't appear to notice and just got on with things, but Genie felt he should pay her mum more attention and then she wouldn't look elsewhere. Genie had begun to worry about their relationship and had tried to tell her dad to take her mum out and pamper her a bit, but he just said he was too tired and needed a good night's sleep for work the next day. Milly had visited her parents in Cornwall on her own a couple of times recently, but had always come back more stressed than when she went, and it had been hard to juggle the rota with so few staff.

Genie had persuaded them to take a day off a couple of weeks ago, but they'd ended up just sitting in the bar that Trudie managed for her uncle, and gossiping over a bottle of wine. They could do that any day of the week!

Trudie was her mum's best friend and when they got together, no one else got a look in. Her dad usually sat quite happily, staring out to sea, and let them get on with it. Trudie's husband had left her a few years ago, which had caused quite a ripple in their tight-knit community. Trudie had been devastated, but Genie's mum and dad had helped her through it, and Genie had been proud of them for looking after her. Recently, Trudie gave the impression that she was dating a new man, and seemed happier than she had in a long time, but she hadn't told them about it and they hadn't pushed her after what she'd been through. She was probably worried it would all go wrong again and wanted to wait before she confided in them all.

Today was a training day in the kitchen. They held one every month, and had done so for years. Her dad was their main chef and insisted she learn new skills each time they stood side by side in the kitchen, though he hadn't learnt any himself for ages. On the other hand, she regularly spent her nights watching cookery shows and tried to hone her techniques. She did give him credit for encouraging her love of food, but he had also restricted any free time she had to see her friends and have an actual life.

Her dad often tried to get her to cook with cheese, but she refused where possible. It was why she stuck to desserts. She hadn't plucked up the courage to tell him that the dancing anchovy cartoon on his apron often made her feel faint too. He'd ship her out of the kitchen *tout de suite*.

She would happily jump off a bridge on a bungee rope, or pick up a handful of spiders, but she just couldn't bear to touch some foods – especially ones like walnuts. They looked like gnarly brains. She loved to eat them, but she always tipped them into a little plastic bag and bashed and bashed them until they crumbled into tiny clumps. Nothing weird in that.

At home, she spent hours creating beautiful ice creams. She didn't want to cook bacon and eggs, she wanted edible art, something that caught the customer's imagination and tasted sublime. She'd been thinking for a while about home-made ice cream bars with classic flavours like chocolate and mint or strawberry and chocolate cream. Her efforts tasted delicious, but were a bit clunky and messy, which frustrated the hell out of her. She thought it was probably because she was always tired and couldn't concentrate, but in reality, she was self-taught and although she could bake beautifully, she didn't have the ability to conceptualise how her ideas could translate onto the plate the way she wanted them to.

CHAPTER FIVE

*G*enie's bones ached from a sleepless night. She'd been trying to think of a way for her grandpa Gus to be happy again, and for her parents to be able to take some proper time off, away from the business. She loved them all, but their constant doom and gloom was dragging her down. No-one would never be able to replace Vera, but perhaps Gus needed some company now and again. She racked her brain for a solution, but her tired mind came up blank. She'd once got him to sign up for an adult education course on computing, to bring the business up to date, but he'd got home and moaned that it was full of old people and said he wasn't going again.

She started in surprise when two of her old school friends came in and sat down at one of her tables. She went over to say hello as they hadn't been in for a long while. She pulled up a seat for a minute while she gave them menus. It was great to see someone her own age for a change. She wished she could confide her worries to them. It was hard for her to always carry everything herself, but with her parents currently living on another planet, and no Vera to confide in, she was pretty much alone. She felt the punch of loss when she thought of Vera. If only her parents could regain some of their old cheerfulness. Her dad used to have a playful side, but recent petty arguments with her mum had eroded it to dust.

She grinned at Fae, her best friend from school, and then turned to say hello to Una, the third member of the group. Fae and Una had remained firm friends and now worked together at a local travel agency, so they didn't have much time to pop in to the restaurant.

'It's great to see you here. How've you both been?' She looked at their golden skin and the sunglasses perched on their immaculate hairstyles and frowned, whilst they both looked at each other shiftily.

'Uh… um…' said Fae, biting her lip and looking at the table. Genie frowned and turned to Una.

'We just got back from two weeks in Spain.'

'Oh!' said Genie brightly, pretending this didn't sting like salt in her eye. 'How lovely for you both. You didn't tell me you were going. I wondered why you didn't answer your phones.' Genie wondered if that laser-eyed seagull was in the vicinity and hoped he'd fly over and drop food on their immaculate hairdos.

'It was too expensive from Spain,' said Fae apologetically. 'We knew you wouldn't be able to leave this place and decided it was easier not to ask you this year.' She picked up the menu and ducked her head behind it, leaving Una to explain further.

'Look Genie, you never come anywhere with us now. We know you have to be there for your family, but you do have to have your own life. We thought we'd come and see you today to say we might not be able to pop in as often.'

Genie was really confused. As it was, she only managed to get into town to see them once a week for a quick coffee. She always invited them back here for a free lunch, but they were often busy too and only ever came occasionally. Now they were telling her they were coming less. How much less could it be?

'We've been going out with a group that we met at the big new nightclub in town. The thing is, no-one really comes down here anymore. They tend to go to the other end of the beach with the modern bars and the slot machines. Why don't you leave this business to your parents and apply for a job somewhere with prospects?'

'This place has prospects!' Genie insisted.

Both women raised their eyebrows, then Una went on. 'There are so many new foodie places in the centre of town. This section of the beach, well, it feels like it's in a time warp,' said Una. Then her skin flushed as she realised what she'd said. She looked up apologetically at Genie, whose mouth was set into a tight line. Sparks were beginning to form in her eyes.

Fae grimaced and then hid her head behind the menu again. Genie stood up and pulled her notepad out of the pocket of the little apron that was tied around her waist. She raised an eyebrow to Fae and waited for her to give her order, which she did rapidly, ordering for Una too in case she blabbed something else. Genie wrote it all down and gave Fae a half-smile.

'It's not a problem. I'm pretty tied up here now Gran's not around. I understand that I work a lot of hours with my family. I'm sure I'll manage to get into town and meet up with you sometime,' she turned and gave Una a polite smile, which didn't meet her eyes. Then she marched into the kitchen to give her dad the order before she threw something at someone.

Fae had had the grace to look ashamed when Genie had mentioned Vera, as neither she nor Una had bothered to turn up to her funeral, seeming to forget that they had grown up playing on the beach beside Genie's house. Genie's gran and her mum had always welcomed Genie's friends, and they had been given free ice cream and sandwiches wrapped in greaseproof paper to take and eat on the sand, even though they often dropped them and ended up with a crunchy lunch. Now the restaurant wasn't good enough for them, it seemed.

She really wished she could add a little surprise to their breakfasts, but the kitchen was always spotless and her dad was a stickler for hygiene standards, so she'd have a hard time finding a speck of dust to put on their plates.

She sighed and rolled her shoulders whilst tilting her head from side to side. It was a trick she often used to calm herself down, but as her breathing was now coming in short sharp gasps, she was feeling more pumped up than docile. Even the fresh scent of the sea didn't alter her mood. She stepped out into the little garden behind the shop and kicked the nearest plant pot, then howled in pain at the stupid idea – the pot was full of soil, waiting to be planted up. She glanced to the end of the garden, where her granddad was often found inventing new contraptions for the restaurant, none of which ever worked. She marched over to stick her head around the door to see if he was hiding there.

Seeing him muttering with his head bent over a soldering iron, while he tried to get two pieces of metal to stick together, she smiled and finally felt some of the annoyance at her friends' lack of tact ease away. She'd always loved seeing her granddad tinkering about in this shed, but she was waiting for the day that he ever made anything useful. He turned and noticed her, then frowned and beckoned her inside. She perched her bottom on the chair next to him, fleetingly remembering that she should be inside handing out the breakfasts, but instead she laid her head on Gus's shoulder. He leaned in and scooped her to his side. 'What's the matter, cupcake?' he asked, stroking her hair.

She snuggled into him, inhaling the familiar scent of his aftershave and sighed. 'Fae and Una are outside. They just told me that they won't be coming here as often from now on. It's too old fashioned for hipsters like them.'

Gus moved back to look at her, anger blazing in his eyes. She felt confused for a moment, as it seemed to be directed at her. 'They're right, Genie. I know you keep telling me we need to update the place and you're not wrong about that, but I'm too tired to start again. You're too young and pretty to be hanging around with all of us. When I started work here it was buzzing with people. It was a great career, but lately it's hard on all of us. I'm not sure this is the right life for a young woman like you.'

Genie stood up aghast. 'What do you mean? A woman like me?'

Gus took her hand, and she didn't shake him off. 'A woman with the world at her feet. You should be with people your own age, following your dreams, not toiling away for family obligation.'

'Grandad!' Genie was appalled. 'I don't feel an obligation.' She did, but she wasn't about to tell him that. 'I love being with my family and I've never wanted to work anywhere else.'

'How will you meet a suitable young man... or woman, if you stay stuck in that kitchen with your parents and me?'

'Granddad!' Genie flushed bright red and didn't know where to look. 'For a start I'm not interested in women, but if I was, I would be very grateful for you right now. But I don't have a boyfriend because I'm too busy with my career.'

'What career? Your mum and dad have a stranglehold and won't let you have free rein and I'm a grumpy old man who's tried to keep the memory of his wife alive by refusing change.' He hung his head.

Genie moved towards him and enveloped him in her arms, resting her cheek on his whiskery face. 'If I'd wanted different choices, I'd have pushed for them, Grandad. You know me well enough. I would blow a fuse if I wanted something badly enough and didn't get my way. We've all been grieving. But perhaps we can talk about making a few small changes to the restaurant, to attract a younger customer base?'

'Genie,' called her dad from the kitchen, so she jumped and kissed Gus's nose before running back in to take the food to her friends. She actually felt a lot better now and, as she picked up the plates from the counter, she blew her dad a kiss, which made him smile too. Then she weaved with years of expert skill in between the tables, to offer her first real smile of the day to her ex-best friends.

CHAPTER SIX

*A*da leaned on the balustrade and then moved over slightly to a less flaky patch of metal. It was such a shame to see it like this, when a simple coat of paint would make all of the difference. She understood the council probably had other priorities, but surely the local community could get together and sort this out?

She chipped away at a section of paint. It separated from the railing and fluttered in the sea breeze, falling onto the sand below. She stared after it despondently. It looked so out of place on the soft grains. It had tried to nestle into the beach, but it stood out. You just couldn't mistake an outsider.

She'd tried to fit in here, and had even gone to a cards night with some of her neighbours to try and ease her loneliness, but her smile never quite reached her eyes. The gloom that surrounded her hadn't been dispelled.

The breeze smelled of salt, and then she caught the scent of chips from the little restaurants on the parade and her stomach growled. She hadn't been looking after herself recently. Ned would have been horrified, if he'd still been here. He would tell her to buck up her ideas and move on.

She smiled as she recalled his sharp wit and endless humour. He didn't suffer fools, and he'd tell her she was an idiot for wasting her life, when he'd lost his.

She'd met and fallen in love with him at such a young age and by twenty-one, she was pregnant with their first child. She'd already had a glittering career by then and having a baby didn't stop her. Ned supported her and, as he was older, he'd helped her through those first months of not having a clue what to do with their blue-eyed bundle of joy. It had been hard to fit in work and play, but Ned had made everything easier for her. He'd done that for the rest of their time together and although everyone, including her own parents, had told her she was too young for him, they'd been proved wrong. He'd been a keeper. He might have been more experienced than her, but they'd both had glamorous careers and had been drawn to each other as soon as their eyes had met. They had been with each other since that moment.

She'd forgotten how to function without him. But, back then, she had been a pretty feisty woman. She'd needed to be, to succeed in her career. She'd managed it without the help of her parents, who hadn't approved of her job either. They'd said she was too wild; too ambitious, but as soon as she'd met Ned, she hadn't felt the need to rebel anymore.

All she'd ever wanted was to make him happy. And she had. He told her often enough. She'd caught a man with a dreadful reputation as a playboy photographer, and he'd done everything in his power to make her fall in love with him. It had worked and, to everyone's surprise, they had become inseparable. When she was working, he could often be found on set, quizzing the camera crew about their setup and, while he was in his studio, she would pop in and he would light up the room with his smile and swing her off her feet, even when she weighed a ton, heavily pregnant with one of their three sons.

She smiled finally at that memory and then looked at the clear blue sky, rolling her shoulders and straightening her back. Her stomach rumbled again and she caught sight of Genie scurrying between tables. Her long black hair was dragged back in a hairband and her womanly figure was swamped. Her black skirt was the wrong length for her petite frame and cut her legs off at the widest point. Her tops hung down from her breasts and hid her waist, making her look about a stone heavier. She always appeared to be clean and presentable though, so Ada couldn't berate her too much. And she had beautiful eyes and big pouty lips. People would pay a fortune to mimic that via surgery.

Ada was used to stylists and an endless wardrobe. But it was hard to look your best if you didn't have help. And perhaps it was about time she took a reality check and worked on her own situation. She glanced down at her very loose cotton trousers, which were a soft pink, but could do with an iron. Her short-sleeved blouse, dotted with tiny dark pink flowers, was also hanging from her already petite frame. She used to feel so good in it, but now her breasts had shrunk and her arms were almost skeletal.

She had a feeling that one or all of her sons might turn up out of the blue, if she didn't start taking better care of herself. She looked over to the rows of cafés again. Her sons had all visited since their father's funeral. She knew how hard that must have been to manage, especially as some of her grand-children were still at school. She had done her best to keep them all busy and then shove them back home. She'd loved every moment of seeing them, but it wasn't the same without Ned. He had left a gaping hole in her heart and even seeing her beloved children and grandchildren hadn't closed the edges. If anything, it tore them apart further as she saw so much of him in their sons' eyes.

Turning her feet in the direction of the restaurants, she

made her weary limbs move forward. She left behind the flake of rust in the sand and decided it was time she tried to live again. It was so much easier to tell yourself this than to actually do it, though. She hoisted her old brown designer handbag over her shoulder and plodded towards the scent of chips.

She was dithering over which restaurant she would be least conspicuous in, while she looked so awful, when Genie saw her and waved. Ada baulked slightly as she had wanted to be alone, but she had little choice other than to walk towards her now. She mustered up a smile and headed over. For a lady of sixty-eight, Ada was usually very sprightly and full of life, but she almost had to drag her feet across the floor to get anywhere these days. She often felt like she was wading through treacle.

Genie offered her a bright smile and didn't comment on how scruffy Ada was looking, or how down she must appear. She held out a chair for her, grabbed an extra cushion to place behind her back to make her more comfortable and then left and reappeared with a frothy hot chocolate topped with whipped cream. Ada's eyes went wide as she took in the tall mug with chocolate oozing down the sides. 'You look like you need this,' said Genie with a wink. 'In fact, you look like you've had the same kind of day I have.' She lifted her left foot and Ada saw a small bandage on her big toe. She was wearing black flip flops and it wasn't the most demure attire.

Ada gasped when she looked more closely. Genie's toe was turning black. 'You should put some ice on that! What are you doing, running round after customers with a possible broken toe?'

Genie giggled and looked around to see if they had any other customers. They didn't, so she sat down opposite Ada and gingerly lifted her foot to rest on the chair between them. 'It's not broken. Dad's already told me off and checked it out. Mum put a bandage on it before she went to the wholesalers. She's not very good at first aid,' she joked, holding the foot up slightly. The tiny bandage began to come off and she leaned forward and stuck it back down.

'How did you injure it?' asked Ada. After a second, she gave in to the delicious scent of the drink in front of her and started spooning some of the heavenly chocolaty cream into her mouth. Then she grabbed a clean spoon for Genie and scooped some up for her.

Genie took it and was soon letting the blob of chocolate foam slide between her lips. She closed her eyes in bliss and then grinned again. 'I was in a bad mood. My oldest school friends came by. I haven't seen them in ages. First they announced they'd gone off on holiday without me and then they said they're not going to visit me while I'm working anymore, they're too busy with the posh restaurants in town. I kicked a plant pot in the garden out back.'

Ada's eyebrows shot up and she glanced into the restaurant. She hadn't realised there was a garden at the back. Now she actually looked, she could see windows into a back room and then a small garden beyond.

'These were all houses before they became shops,' Genie explained. 'Grandad's parents lived upstairs. Now the flat is a bit of a mess, and grandad invents things in his shed in the garden.'

Ada's interest was piqued. 'What has he invented?

Genie giggled and then filched another spoonful of whipped cream. 'Nothing! He's been trying for years, but nothing's ever worked. He likes to solder stuff, but it's usually more art than effectiveness. He enjoys it, though.'

Ada smiled, the first real smile she'd felt for a while, as she pictured Genie's grumpy old grandad being an artist or an inventor. She'd only met him once and he'd practically ignored her. So much for customer service!

'That wasn't nice of your friends… to come here and announce they didn't have time for you.'

'To be fair, I don't have much time for them either as I'm always working, but I did always try and meet them once a week or so, even if it meant catching up on work later.'

Ada was appalled. 'Don't you have days off?'

Genie sighed and her shoulders sagged a little, before she noticed they had a new customer. She lowered her injured foot to the floor, before pushing herself up. 'It's a family business. I've been working here since I was at school and we can't afford extra staff. We all work as hard as each other but, since my grandma died,' she paused as if to catch her breath. 'Well, Grandad's in a world of his own and the rest of us have to take up the slack. It's what families do,' she shrugged. She bent to give Ada a quick hug before handing her a menu, telling her that the hot chocolate was on the house. Then she turned to welcome her new customer.

Ada looked around her with fresh eyes and a renewed interest. Ok, the place wasn't buzzing with customers, or rammed with the high tech gizmos that she was used to in the expensive places she frequented in the States, but it did have an old-fashioned charm. You instantly felt at ease here, which was a hard thing to get right. The furniture was old but extremely comfortable, and the place was spotless. You could probably search for weeks and not find an unwashed surface or a smear of grime anywhere. The food was plentiful, too… not exactly good for the heart, with so many fried options, but it was high quality and value for money nonetheless.

She scanned the long menu and finally found something not so gargantuan to eat. She settled into her chair to sip her still-warm drink, realising in surprise she had almost drunk the whole lot without even noticing. She must have been hungrier than she thought. She looked down at her bony arms and unpainted nails and vowed that something would change today.

She also wanted to try and help Genie to find some balance in her own life. Ada had no idea how, but the young woman was far too wonderful to be working every hour of every day, however much her family needed her. Ada craned her neck to check out the other restaurants along the parade. She bit her lip and played with the edge of the menu while she tried to envisage what they would all look like with a big investment.

If they had a revamp, perhaps Genie's friends would come back and some other younger people would be tempted to try them out.

It was about time Ada chatted to her old friend Ralph again, and asked him to see if there were any investors sniffing around. Ralph had an ear to the ground and always knew what was happening in the business community. If he didn't know, then he could certainly find out. She'd never seen him fail yet. Feeling much more positive, she smiled at Genie to let her know she was ready, and placed an order for a plate of fish and chips.

CHAPTER SEVEN

*a*da's smile slipped from her face when the call came from Ralph a couple of days later. She felt bad because she hadn't been much of a friend to him lately. He'd visited Ada and Ned often when they had first moved to the flat she lived in now, but when he'd tried to drop round recently, she'd put him off. She hadn't been able to deal with any reminders of her old life.

Ralph was one of Ned's oldest friends, and he was a true gentleman. He hadn't pushed her and he'd sounded glad when she'd rung him the previous evening, even though it was more of a business call.

But now Ralph was telling her that nothing happening locally. He couldn't imagine any investors being able to put capital into the businesses there. They were all run by generations of the same family and it was practically impossible to buy one. He agreed that they would be a gold-mine if run properly, due to their location and the popularity of the seafront, but he'd visited them himself and in his view they were all pretty run down.

Ada sighed and thanked him, before promising to meet him soon for a coffee. She walked out onto her terrace and stared at the beautiful view. The waves caressed the shore and the sky was so clear and bright that it had drawn families to the beach. Children were running in and out of the waves squealing in happiness, and parents licked at ice creams, melting and dripping down their arms, while they waited for their children to return. It had only been a day since Ada had seen Genie, but she felt compelled to talk to her again. She knew she was missing her own children and it wasn't fair to lay that at Genie's feet, but what she didn't know wouldn't hurt her. If it meant more custom, then that could only be a good thing, surely?

She would have to let go of the idea of someone developing here and try and help Genie another way. She was sad that there wasn't going to be change, but maybe she should decide to abandon the idea of interfering in the business side of things, and see if there was a nice young man working nearby that she could introduce Genie to. A bit of matchmaking would take her mind off her own troubles and it was about time she had some fun. Ada glanced down at her freshly-painted nails. They were a delicate shade of pink that reminded her of the inside of a seashell. She was proud that she'd got them painted, it seemed like a little victory. Perhaps she could achieve something small each day, and begin to live again? Maybe she could even pluck up enough courage to go home.

Walking purposefully to the door and grabbing her handbag, Ada glanced at her watch and decided to go and get herself some lunch. She also remembered that she'd seen a dashing dark-haired young man the other day. He had just started working at the place right at the end of the row, and he looked about Genie's age. Ada's eyes began to sparkle for the first time in a very long while and she wondered how much trouble she could get herself into for meddling. Quite a lot, probably.

CHAPTER EIGHT

*G*enie rolled her eyes at her parents. They were acting decidedly weirdly, not that it was so unusual these days. Her dad had even started talking to the evil pigeon, who seemed to have taken a shine to her grandad's shed and was currently tidying up a pile of twigs it had dumped on the roof. If the pigeon had ideas about moving in, she'd just have to dissuade it.

Yes, Dad was definitely acting a bit shifty, and her mum had begun sprucing the restaurant up a bit with new plastic tablecloths and was wearing more lipstick. She was also talking far more to male customers, which made Genie frown. Genie had already given the salt shaker to someone who'd asked for sugar, and then she'd slumped into an exhausted heap into a chair – before realising someone was already sitting in it, trying to get out of the midday sun! Her face had flamed in embarrassment when he'd said 'oof', as she'd landed on him. It wasn't very gentlemanly of him. She didn't weigh that much… and it was his own fault for wearing colours that blended in with the stupid chair.

She chanced a glance as she rushed off, embarrassed.

Maybe he was fit and gorgeous at the very least. Her heart sank. He was about seventy and looked like he hadn't eaten for a while from the way his body sagged into the chair. No wonder she hadn't seen him. She made a note to send a doughnut over by way of apology on her way to the garden.

It was too exhausting trying to keep up with what the hell was going on with her family, so she chose to ignore it instead. Genie asked her mum to take the man in the chair-coloured clothes the doughnut while she tried to persuade her grandad to come out of his shed. She needed him, and it was about time he stopped being a recluse and helped her with her parents. Something strange was going on with them and they wouldn't say what it was.

Her grandad wasn't even interested in the whippy-type ice cream machines these days. He left that to her or her dad. She hated serving the vanilla sludge. It went against her sensibilities to offer it to her grandma's old customers, when they were used to excellence. Many of the older ones still came out of loyalty, but they only ever bought a small cone and some shoved it into the nearest bin when they thought she wasn't looking. She was sure that was why the evil pigeon was lurking around. He was probably casing the joint. She reckoned that there was a pigeon grapevine and the word would soon get out about the ice cream bin and they would be inundated by winged intruders. She clapped her hands to scare him away, but he just sat there, watching her, until she stuck her tongue out and huffed.

Genie lived with her parents in a little Georgian house on the hill behind the shops. It had beautiful views across the sea. They used to let out the flat they had above the restaurant, but now her grandad had filled it up with his ideas for inventions and pieces of wood he found on the beach. It was getting out of hand. They would have to renovate soon, it could bring in useful extra income. The flat had three bedrooms and a small lounge and kitchenette. Once again, it all looked like it was straight out of the 1950s, but she didn't have time to think about that now.

She turned her face up to the sun and stopped to draw in a deep breath. Talking to her grandad was never easy these days. She thought for the first time that perhaps she really should have more of a life of her own. She had been saving up since starting work after school at fourteen. She had thought that being around kept her parents happy and stopped them rowing as much, but recently the arguments had been getting worse. Even though their house wasn't that tiny, she couldn't help but hear their voices.

She sighed and walked towards her grandad's shed. Noticing movement to her right, she smiled and waved at the hot new waiter, Bailey, that Trudie had just taken on as part-time staff. She hoped he hadn't seen her stick her tongue out at the wayward pigeon, like a petulant child. It was out of character as she adored animals, if you excluded psychotic monkeys who bit innocent children and evil pigeons who bombarded her with cheese missiles.

Bailey was certainly a tonic to cheer a girl up. He grinned back and winked her way. Grinning herself now, she walked faster and reached the shed in a few paces, almost knocking into the doorframe. She straightened up, pulled at her blouse to loosen its death grip on her boobs, and wished she didn't have a ketchup stain on her skirt. Turning to see if Bailey was still there, and feeling disappointed that he'd obviously gone back to work, she bent down to peck her grandad's leathery cheek. The sting on her cheek told her he hadn't shaved.

'Grandad. I need to talk to you about something,' she said.

Gus looked up from the metalwork he had been soldering and scrunched up his eyes at the sun shining in from the window. He waited to hear what she would say next.

'I want to make some changes.'

CHAPTER NINE

*G*enie had persuaded her grandad to let her try and revive their ice cream business. The only hurdle now was her parents. She'd asked them to add her ice cream ideas and recipes to the menu, but her mum said no, it was too much hassle.

Genie couldn't see why. She would take responsibility for it and even pay for the supplies if it was that bothersome. She sulked and pouted until her dad finally caved, and said she could run a small concession stand, but only if she invested in it herself. She didn't mind that, as it meant all of the profits would be hers too. They couldn't argue with that. They didn't think there would be any, so they brushed it off. It seemed they were too busy to have a conversation with her about saving their business.

She had found an old compact freezer unit in the garage at home and was excited that she could finally express herself. Vera had taught her well. She was determined that it would be a celebration of her memory and not something maudlin. Vera had been full of sunshine; you couldn't walk past her without feeling warmth. Genie had been told they looked alike, with lustrous hair that fell in a curtain around their faces. Genie thought that was where the resemblance ended, though, as her grandma had looked like the movie star Elizabeth Taylor, or maybe Vivien Leigh, whilst she looked more like she'd been swept up by the wind and spat out again.

Milly had turned up her nose at the bags of ingredients Genie brought home to experiment with, but Genie ignored her mum. Milly used to be soft and cuddly, but just recently she'd become hard and brittle, like her own mother, Lucille. Her dad had smiled at the things she'd set out, and even gave her a quick hug and a kiss on the head, but despite that James hadn't offered to help, saying he was tired and having an early night.

Genie thought of Ada and how sweet and kind she was. They'd started spending hours chatting together now, and the older woman had become a regular at the restaurant. She'd told Genie a little about her own life, but seemed far more interested in Genie. Genie flushed as she realised that she'd talked about herself far too much. Ada might be years older than her, but they'd formed a special bond. Genie loved hearing about the 1950s and 60s when Ada was growing up, and she was intrigued about her family. Genie knew she had three grown-up sons but had been surprised to hear she already had grandchildren. Ada's skin was flawless. She looked amazing, and in Genie's view could easily pass for at least ten to fifteen years younger than she was. She did often have a sad look in her eyes, though. Genie could relate to that. Ada had told her that her husband had passed away, but she didn't say much more about it.

Genie was confused as to why Ada stayed on here without him, but grief was such an individual thing to overcome or to live with. Genie knew that, from the way she'd suddenly started sobbing when she'd begun making ice cream. She hadn't given herself much time to grieve, but doing what she'd shared so often with her grandma had been both healing and upsetting. She'd ended up crying in her room for hours.

That day, the ingredients had been left untouched, but today she was feeling stronger and had more purpose, as if her grandma was looking down on her and smiling. It felt right to be back creating food and her energy levels were on top of the world. She might even go to Trudie's after work and grab a glass of wine there, in the hope of bumping into Bailey. He looked about her age and although he wasn't there often, it would be nice to be introduced to someone so hot and delicious.

So far they had only waved across the gardens and said a quick hello when they were introduced. He'd been working at the time, so it had been very brief. He had short dark hair, firm arm muscles and quite a cute backside, not that she'd been ogling. He looked taller than her, as well. She wouldn't mind gazing into his eyes for an hour or two. Mentally slapping herself for daydreaming about a man who was way out of her league, she washed her hands again and began to create ice cream magic.

CHAPTER TEN

*G*enie wiped she sweat from her brow and rolled her aching shoulders. She stood back and grinned at the results of all of her hard work. It had been a lot of graft, but she still had the churning machines at home that her grandmother had used and had cleaned the freezer until it was spotless. Now it was full to the brim with tubs of her own flavour combinations, bursting with zingy zest and crunchy caramel. She'd added fresh fruits to some and meringue shards to others, and the scent in the room was heavenly.

She'd already set up on a table at the edge of the restaurant on the street. The freezer counter was on it, stocked with twelve new flavours to try. She'd had to purchase shop-bought cones from the wholesalers, but she'd made her own dreamy toppings to drizzle on top, like fresh caramel and chocolate mint, with chocolate flakes and sprinkles as well. Everything was in jars and containers. She even had her own little till box tucked underneath the counter.

For the first few hours, she sat with a big breezy smile on her face, but as the time crept past with just a few measly sales, she began to feel despondent. All her hopes and dreams seemed to be a waste of time. Then a busload of tourists arrived and, after spending ages over huge plates of fish and chips at Trudie's place, they all wandered over and formed a queue for Genie's ice cream and spent just as long deciding which flavours to try. There had been oohs and ahhhs as she'd given them samples, and they'd all tried at least two.

It ended up being a great success. But, as she counted her takings at the end of the day, she had to admit that her costs were too high. The profits she had made wouldn't set the world on fire. It was a start, though, and when her mum had wandered over to try her flavours she had held her breath. Milly took her time savouring them and testing the toppings and looked like she'd had an idea of her own. But then she pushed it aside, and just shrugged her shoulders.

'They taste wonderful, Genie. Gran would be really proud of you,' Milly smiled.

Genie almost fell off her chair in shock and went to hug her mum, who squeezed her back a bit too hard and almost popped a rib. She let Genie go, then ruffled her hair as if she was five. She was such a contradiction, one minute looking at Genie like she was the most precious gem on earth, and the next acting as if she was frustrated by Genie's behaviour.

Milly looked into her cash box and raised an eyebrow in question. Genie sighed and picked the little box up. 'There is money, but not loads. If we made it a regular feature, perhaps people would come back again and again, the way they did for Vera?' A tear appeared at the edge of Milly's eye, but she turned and brushed it away, then she straightened her back and put her hand on Genie's arm.

'I'm really proud of you, darling. I'm not sure it's worth the investment right now, but I'm glad to see you following in your gran's footsteps and I'm sure we could add a few flavours to our dessert board, if it means that much to you?'

Genie stood up and noticed for the first time how tired her mum looked and how many more lines she suddenly seemed to have around her eyes. 'I want to experiment, and do gooey frozen desserts in the day, and then again in the evening. Or keep the ice cream bar separate and run it with my own recipes. Instead of the big meals we do, we could offer desserts in the early evening, as we aren't ever busy around that time these days. We could catch the after-school crowd and make a fortune!'

'It sounds great in theory,' said her mum, propping her bottom on the nearest table. 'But we don't have enough staff for you to be galivanting off on your own adventures. We need you to wait tables, or we'd have to employ someone else. We can't afford that and you know it.' She stood up again and looked restlessly around, as if seeing how it must look to everyone else and wishing she had the answers. 'I'd love you to follow your dreams here, but without the extra help, it's almost impossible.'

Genie sighed and rubbed her tired eyes. It had been a long day. She needed to refine her costs and work out how she could do this, within the framework of her own job. They were quiet for a lot of the time, so surely she could multi-task? She didn't suggest this yet, though, as her mum did seem like she was trying to help her. Genie knew that the business was struggling a bit, as she did the book-keeping at night now too. Her parents were too tired to keep on top of it and the accounts had to be done. She knew that something would have to change soon, or those developers who always sniffed around old family businesses on prime site like theirs would swoop, and gobble them up like the vultures they were. The business wouldn't be worth too much, as there weren't that many customers, but they'd still want the shell and prime location. Genie organised her cash box and topping jars onto a tray and rolled up her shirt sleeves.

She tried to focus on what she had to do, despite feeling the start of a headache begin to throb at her temples. Ignoring the pain, she tidied away all her ice cream tubs and rinsed them carefully, turning them upside-down and leaving them beside the kitchen sink. Taking one last look at them before she left for the night, she sighed and closed the door behind her.

CHAPTER ELEVEN

*G*enie's dad James popped his head around the
kitchen door. Genie was slumped over their
accounts books, trying to figure out how they could
make more money. She'd all but given up on her ice cream
idea. It would have to wait until they could afford more staff,
which might never happen at this rate. They used to have six
people helping, but over the years they'd had to cut back.

'Could you join us in here, please, Genie?' James asked,
not meeting her eye, his face sweating. He looked so worried
that she frowned as she pulled her heavy limbs up to follow
him into the lounge. Her mum was already there, her trembling hands in her lap.

'What's going on?' Genie asked, sitting next to her mum
and taking her hand for a moment, feeling her stomach
cramp up and fear fill her veins. Her parents never had
family meeting like this, they were always at the restaurant.
If they had anything to talk to her about at home, they
usually just pulled up a chair in the kitchen and blurted it
out. What if they were splitting up?

She'd read about parents of older children holding on

47

until their kids were old enough to look after themselves before telling them that they'd always hated each other, but her mum and dad often held hands when they thought no one else was looking and she'd seen them snuggle on the couch at home loads of times, although not so much recently. They weren't ones for open shows of affection in public, but at home they always backed each other up, which told Genie they cared about their marriage and their child.

Milly began wringing her hands in her lap and Genie's stomach sunk further to the floor. She looked from one to the other, not understanding what was going on. 'Mum?' she asked.

Her dad motioned for her to sit on the armchair next to her mum. This was usually her favourite place to sit, as it afforded the best view out of the window and across the sea. Today the waves were slapping roughly against the shore and seagulls circled menacingly overhead. Genie turned away with troubled eyes and held her breath until her dad started speaking. 'Genie. You know your mum's mum, Lucille...'

'Grandma,' interjected her mum with the age-old correction. It was as if it pained her dad to use the same familiar endearment that they had all used for his own mother.

He took a deep breath and sighed. Genie noticed how tired he looked and longed for the smiling dad she used to know. 'Grandmother,' he corrected with a tight voice.

'Of course I know her. What's going on?'

'Well...'

'Oh for goodness sake!' said her mother, standing up and going to look out of the window as the skies turned grey. 'Grandma hasn't been well for some time now, as you know. She's been trying to get your father and me to come and visit her more regularly and, after losing your dad's mum... well, it's made me think I need to make more of an effort with my own parents.'

Genie was confused. Her maternal grandparents lived so far away. She'd recently been emotionally blackmailed by Lucille to visit by herself. She remembered how she'd got the train all the way there – and returned the next day, battered and worn down.

When Genie had arrived, she'd peeked through the window and seen Lucille standing up and laughing on the phone, but when she'd rung the bell and been invited inside by her grandad, her grandmother had been deathly pale and sitting in that disgusting padded pink armchair she loved so much with a flowery blanket over her knees.

Genie hadn't thought much of it at the time, but she was pretty sure that her grandmother wasn't as ill as she pretended to be. She had a huge appetite, too, and was always barking orders for someone to get up and make her a fresh cup of tea or bring a plate of biscuits, most of which she'd then eat herself.

Genie didn't know why her grandmother insisted she visited, as she didn't seem to enjoy having her granddaughter around. She just bossed her about the whole time. She thought Lucille and the evil pigeon would be well suited. Even though she didn't like the pigeon, she wouldn't subject him to more than an hour of her grandmother's company. The poor bird would certainly crave a beer after that.

She sighed and slumped further back into her own chair. She might not like Lucille much, but she was her mum's mum, so what could she say? If her parents wanted to go on holiday and spend some time with her parents, who was she to interfere? She could now understand why her mum had been so grouchy lately, and her dad so distracted.

'Ok. How do we work this out? If you need time off to visit your mum… Grandmother… *Grandma*,' Genie gulped after a death stare from her mum. 'Well, then we'll have to hire some temporary staff. I think the young guy that Trudie has working for her is quite good,' she paused for a moment while she recalled his smile and tight biceps, then shook her head to clear the image. She needed to concentrate if she was going to be able to manage without her parents for any length of time. Gus was all but useless in the restaurant now and spent most of his time in his shed trying to blow things up.

She noticed her mum and dad looking shiftily between one another. Suddenly she stood up, hands on her hips and stared them straight in the eye. 'What the hell is going on with you two? Is Grandmother seriously sick, and you're not telling me? Are you two splitting up?'

Her mum flushed bright red and gasped in shock, then started furiously pacing the room. 'You tell her, James. I'm not sure I can go through with it.'

'Through with what?' demanded Genie, catching her mum's arm mid-swing as she marched past, and stopping her from moving.

Her dad drew her back to the couch, then sat opposite her, motioning for Milly to do the same. Genie's mother sat down silently, looking like she might burst into tears. Genie quickly went and sat at her feet, holding her hand, though she now felt distinctly queasy.

'We've decided that we need to be nearer to your mum's parents,' said her dad. 'We've been near mine for years and Gus has told us that he's going to travel for the foreseeable future.'

Genie looked up in alarm. 'Grandad? Where will he go? He can't travel alone, He's not with it at the moment and might meet someone thirty years younger than him who'll spend all his money. He's not in the right frame of mind to be alone.'

'That's what I said,' added her mum with a sigh, her face losing its bright red hue as she ran her fingers through her immaculate hair. Genie fleetingly wondered how she'd inherited her dad's thick hair, prone to kinks, and not her mum's glossy blonde mane that fell in a waterfall to her shoulders. 'But he's adamant that he's a grown man who wants to be alone,' continued Milly. 'He's still in mourning, Genie, and he needs a change of scenery or lifestyle to help him to live again,' she said sadly. 'We all do. Nothing is the same without your grandma.'

'I miss her too,' said Genie quietly. She hadn't realised how staying put had made it so much harder for them all to come to terms with their loss. She mentally pulled up a visual of their accounts books and tried to work out what they could cut back on, to afford new staff. She'd have to work even longer hours, but if it meant her family came back stronger, then she'd find a way.

Genie's mum stroked Genie's soft black hair and then cupped her face in her hands. She turned her to face them both. 'We know you miss her, sweetheart, and that's another reason why we've come to this decision.'

Genie frowned and sat back on her knees, looking at her parents. What the hell were they talking about?

'Grandad doesn't want to take part in the business anymore, and we think it's right that he should retire. We aren't getting any younger, either, and this life is all-consuming. We need a change,' said her dad.

Genie tried to work out what he was saying, but all she could hear was waves crashing against the sand. 'You need a break… a holiday, you mean?'

'Not a holiday. A clean break. A fresh start.'

Adrenaline begun to race round Genie's body as she looked at her parents to see if they'd fall about laughing and tell her they were winding her up, but they just sent her a pained stare. Not that they really cracked a smile these days. They always used to have so much fun together at home or at work, but in the last year or so, that had changed. 'What about the restaurant? How can you have a fresh start? Do you mean you're investing money and bringing it up to date at last?'

Genie's mum was muttering to herself quietly and then begun looking in the bag at her feet for some hand cream, which she located and lathered on, ignoring the question, but then turned to her dad as if willing him to get on with it. When he didn't say anything, she sighed heavily and took Genie's hands in her own, slightly sticky ones. 'Grandad wants to travel and my parents aren't getting any younger. They need us and it's about time we spent more time with them.'

Genie's eyebrows shot up into her hairline and her dad looked mightily shifty. 'You can't stand mum's parents,' she accused.

'Genie! I do like them and we're worried about them,' said her dad through gritted teeth, mopping his brow with a handkerchief from his back trouser pocket. 'It's time for us to make a change while we're young enough. We won't be investing in my family business. It's been an uphill struggle for years and it's taking its toll on us all.'

Genie gasped and put her hand to her mouth. Had aliens flown in and replaced her dad with this stranger? Had he eaten some dodgy cheese? The restaurant was his whole world. Her eyes turned on her mother, who flushed again and looked at the floor. 'I'm confused. You're not investing in the business, then what are you doing with it?'

'We're selling it,' said her mother in a strangled voice. 'Before the business is the death of us all.'

Genie jumped up and faced them. 'Will you please tell me what the hell you are talking about? The restaurant has been in this family for generations.'

'Well, that's about to change,' said her mum. 'We need you

to understand, Genie. It's not healthy for a woman your age to hang round with old people all the time, or be working every hour of the day in a business that doesn't turn enough profit.'

'You won't invest, or let me invest, so how can it ever make money?'

'Throwing money at something that doesn't work isn't the answer. Your dad and I need a rest. We never see each other and the only quality time we spend with you is at work. It's not healthy for any of us.'

Genie sat down heavily on the sofa and stared out of the window at the grey skies and restless sea. 'So you're selling my family legacy? The thing I've worked every hour for after school, and failed my exams for?'

Her mum chewed her lip and gazed at the floor despondently, but Genie didn't care how petty she was being. This hurt. 'So you're moving in with that old bat in Cornwall?'

'No!' said both her parents in unison.

'We've found a small tearoom on the seafront nearby. It's got a flat above and it's a flourishing business,' said her mum.

Genie stood up again and began pacing, like her mother had earlier. 'So you're selling *my* family business to buy another business on another seafront?'

Her dad had the grace to look ashamed. 'We don't know what else to do. We need to relocate. Your other grandparents told us about the shop and flat being up for sale. It's a smaller concern than this and more manageable, plus it has lots of custom. It's off the main beach, unlike this one, but is still on the seafront. It's also modern and there's the accommodation, too. It would be a fresh start.'

'How the hell do you expect to make a go of it, if you can't even do that here?' yelled Genie, her voice filling the room. She stomped out of the lounge and into their airy kitchen and began to make some dinner for them all, pummelling some pizza dough she'd put in the fridge earlier that day. She threw some cheese on top of it – before realising what she'd done and jumping with fright. She quelled the urge to be sick and stuffed the pizza into the oven, slamming the door and almost shattering the glass. What a way to cure her phobia.

Her parents stood mutely at the kitchen door watching her antics, then her mum walked over, holding onto her dad's hand and making him follow her. They sat at two of the stools at the kitchen island and faced her. 'Something's got to change,' said her dad sadly. 'We've talked this through, over and over, and it's the only option left. We need to sell the business.'

Genie gulped in some air and counted to ten before she started yelling again. 'So you've talked about this over and over… and it seems like Grandad is in on it too, and you're all happy for someone else to run our family business, to rip the heart out of it and to trample on my grandma's memory?'

Her dad's eyes filled with pain and her mum pressed her nails into her palms. 'The decision's been made. The business is up for sale.'

'As of when? You didn't think my part in the running of the business was important enough for you to discuss this with me?' Her heart was breaking, and she angrily brushed tears from her eyes before they saw them.

'We knew you'd try and talk us out of it, and we felt this was best for all of us. A fresh start, with a new, smaller business that won't demand all of our time, and perhaps we can start to live again,' said her mum sadly.

'Where will I go?'

Her mum looked astounded. 'You'll come with us, of course! You would only have to work half the hours, and you would have time for friends and boyfriends.'

'But I don't want to leave the friends I've got here.'

'You're not six, Genie. You hardly ever see your friends

and you can make new ones. The flat has three bedrooms, so there's room for you – and Gus, when he gets home from his travels.'

'It's not home, though, is it?' whined Genie.

'It's my home,' said her mum.

'What about this house? I thought this was home?'

Her mum looked around and for the first time Genie could see that something had changed. She seemed dispassionate about the walls she'd lovingly decorated after her marriage. It was as if, now that her decision had been made, she couldn't get out of here fast enough. 'It used to be, but it's too big. We aren't getting any younger and this place is a lot of hard work.'

'So you'd rather be in a flat than a pretty Georgian house, overlooking the sea, with its own private garden?'

'We'll need money to retire on, in case the business doesn't work. The money from the restaurant will pay for the new café, but the house will be our pension.'

'So you're really selling it?' Genie was aghast. It was getting so real now. They had it all worked out. They thought they could uproot her and she'd just trot along after them. Were they mad?

'We're renting it out fully furnished for now, but we will have to sell it eventually,' said her dad, coming round to hug her, but she shrugged him off and leaned down to get the sizzling pizza from the oven. She yelped as it burnt her fingers and she quickly dumped it onto the worktop. The air filled with the fragrance of melted cheese, but her stomach heaved at the thought of one morsel touching her lips. She pulled up a stool and sat with her head in her hands. Her brain ached and she felt she'd need at least two massive glasses of wine to numb the pain.

CHAPTER TWELVE

enie decided that maybe she wanted more than two
glasses of wine, so she got off her stool and grabbed
a bottle from the fridge and a glass from the
cupboard. She could usually hold her drink quite well, but as
she hadn't been out for ages, or even had time to sit with a
glass and one of her favourite chicklit romance novels, as
soon as she took a mouthful it brought fresh tears to her eyes
and stung her throat. She choked a little and her mum came
and rubbed her back, like she had when Genie was a small
child.

Genie gave her an evil look, which made her mum recoil.

'We thought you might like the challenge of helping us
with a new business,' her mother said, getting two more
glasses and topping up Genie's so it was almost overflowing.
'It has a small window to sell ice-cream to customers passing
by. You could sell your new flavours from there.'

'I like the business we have,' said Genie stubbornly.

'Everything is so set in its ways, though. We are too young
to rot here!'

Genie was surprised to hear her mum talk about the business that way, as she worked as hard as the rest of them to keep it alive. Her brain begun whirring as she thought of what it would be like to live somewhere new. Not to have to work such long hours, maybe having time for a boyfriend, or even just one real friend. Then she shook her head as the red mist filled it again. 'I just don't want to sell this business.'

Her dad looked glum and sipped his wine.

'Dad. Why are you agreeing to this? Is Mum making you?' Genie asked.

'Genie!' scolded her mum. 'Your dad's a grown man and I'm fed up with taking the blame for everything. It's been a really tough couple of years for us and Dad wants to get away and live somewhere new.'

'Dad?'

'Your mum's right. I miss my mum, and Dad doesn't want us around. He has big plans to travel the world. He doesn't want to stay here and be reminded of what he's lost.'

Genie felt like she'd been punched in the stomach. 'What about me? He's still got me, and you guys. He's not alone.' Tears pushed themselves out of her eyes and she sniffed miserably and brushed them away with her hands.

'He needs to get away to grieve. We all do,' said her dad in a muffled voice.

'I don't! I want to be here to remember her.'

'Genie, she'll be with you wherever you are,' said her mum, holding her hand.

'I'm not going,' Genie said stubbornly.

'You'll have to,' her mum replied. 'The business is going up for sale tomorrow.'

'But it will be snapped up for a stupidly low price by a developer, and then any personality will be stamped out of it.'

'We can start a new chapter in Cornwall.'

'With *your* mum and dad telling us what to do every five

minutes, and a cramped tearoom at the end of a lane. No thanks.'

'Genie!'

Genie took a big mouthful of wine and stared defiantly at her mum. They all knew that she couldn't stand her other grandparents. If they were the reason she was losing the place where she lived and worked, then she'd hate them even more. She was sure that Lucille would outlive them all, so this was one long soap opera as far as she was concerned. Then she felt mean and chastised herself. Maybe there was something else going on here in her parent's marriage? Or perhaps they had just decided they'd had enough.

'I want to buy it,' she blurted out.

'*What?*' her parents said in unison.

'I don't want to lose the business. I've worked hard here for years and it's my heritage. I don't want the shop bull-dozed to make way for a fast food joint. I've never had time to spend any money and have been saving up for a flat for as long as I can remember. I can get a business loan for the rest.'

Genie's mum looked shocked. 'Don't you like living with us? You could have moved into the flat above the restaurant if you were so desperate for a place of your own.'

Genie's tone softened a bit, and she really looked at her parents and finally saw how exhausted they were. She suddenly felt some of the gloom lift and a buzzy feeling filled her bones.

'Of course I like living with you, and I've always been thankful to you, but I hoped that one day I might meet someone and want some privacy. And the flat is full of Grandad's junk. Obviously I'm such a loser that meeting someone nice has never happened,' she glanced down at her ample chest and hips and sighed, sloshing more wine into their glasses as all three had miraculously emptied. 'The flat above the restaurant would be too big for me on my own and

I suppose I got lazy about trying to move. I understand you want to be with your mother in Cornwall, and I even get that Grandad here needs to get away and rebuild his life, but this is where I belong.'

'Not without us,' her mum said vehemently. 'And we need to go.'

'Well, I need to stay just as much.'

Her dad looked at her sadly and then got up to leave without another word.

CHAPTER THIRTEEN

*G*enie sat on her bed in her room and tried to make sense of what had just happened. She knew she was a bit of a wuss and relied on her family too much, but other than Fae and Una, all of her old friends had drifted away. She tried to recall the last time she'd been out with anyone else and couldn't bring anything to mind. She was such a loser! She wished she could confide in Fae about how lonely her life had become, but Fae always had Una beside her these days and Genie didn't think they wanted her around.

At school it had just been Fae and her, until Una had moved in round the corner. She'd seemed so glamorous with her secret make-up stash and her knowledge of exactly what made boys want to go out with you. Genie had never quite understood what on earth she was going on about, but it seemed to work for Una. She was constantly surrounded by boys at school. For some reason she'd chosen Fae and Genie to be her new friends, when Genie was pretty sure she could have fitted seamlessly in with the cool crowd.

Genie had sometimes seem Fae looking longingly at that

crowd, but she'd never have left Genie. They'd been best friends since playschool, when Genie had stopped the nasty girl with giant pink bows in her hair from kicking Fae's toys over, which she had taken to doing regularly. Genie was one of the bigger children and Agatha, the scrawny girl with the bows and a permanently angry face, had looked Genie up and down and decided to go and pick on someone else. Agatha was always causing aggro. She had accidentally helped Genie, though. She and Fae had been firm friends ever since, both steering clear of Aggie, who had grown up to be the queen of the 'in crowd' at school.

Genie wished she had someone to lean on and the confidence to just turn up or invite herself out with the girls. Perhaps she should get a different job, where she was with people her own age? Not for the first time, she wondered if she should have tried harder at school and not been involved in the family business from such a young age. Who would employ someone with no qualifications? She'd look stupid at an interview.

She sighed and squared her shoulders. She might not have stacks of letters after her name, but she did have common sense and the experience of running a business. The problem was, she'd read in the paper that people only wanted graduates. Who would be interested in a girl who'd only ever worked for a failing family business?

What was she going to do? Her family was deserting her and the warm bubble she'd always felt at being surrounded by them had just burst, and left a sticky mess around her. What about her? Had they even given her feelings a thought in this? She'd given her life to them since she was fourteen!

Could she go with them? She knew it was time she grew up, stopped being mollycoddled, and learned to manage her own life, rather than relying on them, but this was too much. Perhaps her parents wanted time alone. Were they fed up with having to tip-toe around the house because of a twenty-two-year-old who should have her own home, instead of being able to walk around naked if they wanted to? Genie cringed at the idea and wiped her hands across her sweaty face.

Every bone in her body ached and she eased into bed and pulled the covers round her until she looked like a big caterpillar. Burying her face, too, she finally let the tears flow until she fell into an exhausted sleep.

CHAPTER FOURTEEN

enie was aimlessly kicking the side of one of their three booths when Ada walked into the restaurant. Genie hadn't felt this lonely or despondent for years and she'd even finally reached out to Fae and Una and cried and cried when she'd told them that her family were leaving, but they'd just said that perhaps it was for the best and surely she'd find lots of hot surfer dudes in Cornwall. She'd quickly dried her eyes and stared at them in wonder. They hadn't listened to a thing about her not going or continuing the business on her own, they'd just heard about moving to a surfing town. They hadn't even begged her not to go, or said they'd miss her if she moved hours and hours away. They just told her the gossip from their group and that one of them had gone on a date with Bailey, but he'd not called her back yet.

Now she looked around at the fixtures and fittings of her place and tried to work out how much of her savings she'd have to invest to bring everything up to her own standards. The figure she envisaged made her eyes water, but at least the decisions would be hers. If she had to sell up at the end of it, then she would know she had tried.

'Hi Ada,' she smiled at the woman. She'd recently begun looking forward to seeing her. After the few days she'd had, Genie needed to see a friendly face. 'What are you doing out alone at this time of night?' Genie was thinking of closing up. It was getting dark and there weren't many people out and about tonight.

'I've been on an early evening walk and then I saw you kicking that poor innocent piece of wood,' Ada tilted her head towards the booth that now looked decidedly wonky at the bottom. Genie grinned. It was nice to see actual mischief and not sadness in Ada's eyes. 'I thought I'd better come in and rescue it.'

'You shouldn't be walking around at night on your own,' scolded Genie. Ada was very sprightly and looked young for her age, but Genie still worried for her. 'I was just about to lock up, but do you fancy a hot chocolate... on the house?' Ada hesitated, then obviously decided that Genie needed company. She pulled out a chair near the front window and sat down, while Genie made them big fragrant hot chocolates. Ada laughed when she saw them. 'Do you need a sugar rush?'

Both mugs were overflowing with whipped cream and Genie had generously sprinkled mini marshmallows on top, to hell with the consequences for her bottom line or her backside, if the business was already going under. A few free marshmallows weren't going to do anything other than make Genie feel better – and maybe also make her hips an inch or two wider. Both women sipped their drinks in silence, then Ada sat back with a contented sigh, eyeing Genie over the rim of her mug of chocolate, waiting for her to speak.

Genie ran her hands through her hair, which was messier than usual. Her bottom lip wobbled. Ada frowned and waited. She put the mug down and leaned forward to take Genie's hand. 'What's the matter? I've not seen you so unsettled, other than the time you hurt your foot when your friends upset you with their thoughtless comments.' She looked at the damaged booth and then at Genie's feet. 'At least you have shoes on to protect your toes today. Do you always kick things when you're angry?' she smiled.

Genie sniffed and a small answering smile played on her lips. She looked up at Ada and saw concern in her eyes. Genie hated herself for crumbling in front of a customer, but Ada had a way about her that made you want to talk to her. 'I'm just having a bad day.'

'A really bad one, by the looks of it,' Ada said shrewdly, then turned to admire the inky blue sea outside. It was getting dark now and she seemed to be trying to come to a decision in her mind. 'Let's have a change of scenery. Sometimes that can make you feel better. My flat is just a bit further along the seafront. Why don't you walk me home and then come in for a glass of wine? You look like you need something stronger than hot chocolate.'

Genie recognised that Ada was using the fact that Genie didn't want her out on her own in the dark to her own advantage, but felt grateful that someone was actually willing to listen to her. She smiled her first genuine smile of the day. It had been hard working alongside her parents, knowing that they had been scheming behind her back for weeks, or months. She'd wanted to rant at them, but after hours and hours of going round in circles the previous evening with no clearer solution, they had all gone to bed feeling anxious and angry.

'That would be lovely, Ada, thank you. I'd happily walk you home any time you need me to, though.'

Ada just smiled and Genie could see she thought she was perfectly capable of walking herself home, but was willing to humour Genie if it made her feel better. Genie quickly sloshed the still half-full mugs into the sink and rinsed them. She took a look around at the still-workable kitchen area and back into the restaurant and felt her insides crunch up. How long would she be able to walk in here, before it belonged to someone else? She bit her lip to stem more tears and grabbed her rather worn-out handbag from the floor, getting the keys to lock up.

Outside, they hugged their jumpers to their bodies. The wind had picked up a little. They walked silently towards the other end of the beach, until they came to a fairly new block of apartments with balconies overlooking the sea. Genie had strolled past many times, but hadn't realised Ada lived here. She'd assumed it would have been one of the older buildings further up the road. This one looked like something out of a movie set and had silver balustrading and loads of sliding glass doors that you could see from the beach. Genie had often imagined that it would be like a hotel inside. Ada beckoned her in, and Genie paused in awe in the foyer.

There was a reception desk, a huge seating area with couches, and signs to a spa and a gym. Genie was confused, but Ada gently took her hand, waved to the night porters and walked them into the lift and they zoomed upwards. 'What is this place?' Genie asked.

Ada giggled. 'It's a posh place for oldies like me, or not so oldies. I've actually seen quite a few young people buying flats here recently. It's a great concept and I certainly can't complain.'

The lift doors slid soundlessly open and they stepped out onto another soft grey carpeted hallway. There was just one door, to the left. Ada got her keys out and opened the door, then stood back for Genie to enter before her.

'Wow!' Genie walked into a big entrance hall and everywhere she looked were beautifully framed views of the beach and sea. Each window was huge and had wrap-around balconies. There was what seemed like a big deck in front of her. They were in the penthouse!

To one side was a big white and grey chrome open-plan kitchen. The breakfast bar had stools facing the sea view. Behind her were doors to the left and right, which Genie presumed led to bedrooms. The worktops held pots of mint and basil and leafy plants that made Genie feel instantly at ease. This wasn't all for show, it was an actual home.

'I've never seen anything like this. It's beautiful!'

There was a dining table, positioned so you could gaze out to sea. You could see Genie's restaurant quite clearly, even though it was dark. The street-lights in front of the shops reflected restaurant signs swinging jauntily in the night breeze.

To the side of where she stood was a lounge area with a fire suspended from the roof. It was flanked by two huge, soft grey L-shaped couches, which Genie thought looked so comfortable she could happily sleep on them. She realised suddenly how tired she was, while her brain felt full to bursting.

Ada walked over to the kitchen and got two sparkling glasses from a cupboard and then opened a wine fridge to take out a bottle of white wine. Genie went to stand near the front deck. Ada pressed a button in the kitchen to open the doors, which slid seamlessly aside and into the walls. Everything was beautiful and modern, but there were also some antique pieces, and everywhere there were very glamorous photos. Genie picked up one or two and was lost for words. She wasn't an avid movie-goer, but she was sure that in a couple of the pictures, Ada was laughing and hugging some pretty famous movie stars. Perhaps she was a fan girl.

Ada handed her the wine, so Genie had to put the photos back, blushing slightly at being nosy. 'Let's go and sit on the deck, as it's still just about warm enough outside,' Ada suggested. There were two beautifully-woven throws on the outdoor chairs, so they sat on one each and Ada pulled the soft fabric over Genie's legs and settled her in.

'This place is amazing, Ada. If I lived here, I'd never want to leave.'

Ada smiled and sipped her wine, so Genie followed suit. The taste was sublime. It was cool and crisp and slightly tart. It made her salivate for more. She took another quick mouthful, finally feeling some tension leave her bones.

'Wonderful, isn't it?' Ava agreed. 'My husband used to have a little house just down the road from here and when he became unwell, his last wish was to return here.'

Genie felt appalled. She'd been wallowing in her own misery and not finding out if Ada was ok. 'I'm so sorry!'

'It's not your fault. I'm trying to move on, but I can't seem to make myself leave this place just yet either. You have to admit, it is pretty cool,' she joked.

'It's amazing,' said Genie trying to take in every detail to remember for later.

'It's a bit like a hotel,' explained Ada. 'You've seen the reception area. There's a gym and spa. It's even got its own café and restaurant. I can order room service if I don't feel like cooking. But I own my own flat. It's such a great idea. Ned didn't want either of us to have to worry about anything while we were here. It stops me getting too lonely, now he's gone, too.'

'Don't your family come and visit?'

Ada laughed. 'They video-call me all the time, and would be here every day if I let them, but they have busy lives. I'm quite content. Anyway, we aren't here to talk about me. What made you so angry that you've taken it out on an innocent piece of wood this time?'

Genie felt a bit ashamed that Ada, who was technically a

customer, had seen her lose it twice now. She was beyond really caring, though, as the business would probably be owned by someone else soon anyway. She took a big mouthful of wine and her cheeks blew out like a hamster. She decided halfway through swallowing it that she really shouldn't be such a heathen. She should savour what was very likely to be a more expensive wine than she was ever going to taste again. She tried to filter it slowly into her throat, but just ended up coughing and spluttering half of it back out onto her black trousers.

'Sorry!' she hiccoughed, her shoulders slumping and her body sinking into the seat, which was remarkably comfortable, even though it was some sort of sleek metal. 'I don't know where to begin.'

Ada patted her knee kindly and sat back in her own chair, regarding Genie with thoughtful eyes. 'How about at the start? What has happened to make a young woman who always seems like she hasn't a care in the world, at least in front of her customers, suddenly look like she's carrying the burdens of the universe?'

Genie felt like she might cry again, so she bit her lip, then winced in pain, disgusted at how pathetic she'd become. She used to be fun-filled and full of energy. What the hell had happened to her? 'It all started yesterday…' she paused for a moment and thought. 'Actually, it's been gradually happening for a while, but I was too wrapped up in grief to notice it for more than a second. I'm pretty sure my mum's had an affair.'

CHAPTER FIFTEEN

*A*da sat up in shock. That was the last thing she'd expected Genie to say. Her mother was quite glamorous and flitted about a lot at the restaurant, but she seemed to be hardworking and dedicated to her family. It just went to show that you never knew what was going on behind closed doors. 'Ok. Well, that does happen a lot, it seems, but what makes you so sure? Have you seen her with someone else? Has she told you about him?'

Genie looked out at the shoreline. She was a sad sight. Her eyes were red where she'd obviously been crying earlier, and her usually reasonably neat hair was scraped back anyhow in an elastic band. Her blouse had food splotches on it and her nose was pink, too. Ada wished with all her heart she could do something to help.

'Mum's been dressing differently, she's always snapping at Dad and now she wants to move to be nearer her own parents in Cornwall. I think she's got a fancy-man there. Why else would she want to move?' said Genie, who looked like she was clenching her teeth. 'Though why Dad would follow her, if she's got a boyfriend and he hates her parents, I don't know,' she said, while picking at her nails in her lap.

Ada let out the breath she'd been holding. 'So you don't know that she's been unfaithful?'

'They told me last night that they've been planning to sell my family business for a while. We've had that place for generations, but all of a sudden she can't bear to be away from her own mum, who is pretending to be sick and emotionally blackmailing her to move nearby.'

Ada tried to make sense of Genie's garbled explanation. She didn't know what it meant, but understood that Genie's whole world was crumbling around her.

'It's so unfair. I don't want to move. My grandad's going travelling and they've bought a tiny tearoom in Cornwall, with about forty covers and an in-situ manager. What about my legacy? I've worked at Graysons' since I was fourteen and Grandad has never been anywhere further than Norfolk! He always said why did he need to go anywhere else, when he had all this on his doorstep,' Genie gestured towards the endless shoreline.

Ada got up and pulled Genie to join her inside on the couch, as the wind was picking up. When they'd got comfortable again she could feel anger flare inside for the upset Genie's parents had caused their only child. She was sure they must have good reason, but for now, she was really cross! 'So they didn't include you in their decision to move, or to sell your family business?'

'Nope,' said Genie glumly. 'I'm not going to move to a flat with my parents and run a tearoom in the middle of nowhere. This is my business too. I've told them I'm buying it and I'm not taking no for an answer. Plus the tearoom already has a manager. I'd be the kitchen staff!'

'Did they agree with you in the end?'

'Nope.'

'So what are they going to do?'

'They're still going. They've had their offer accepted on the tearoom and flat. I do understand that Mum needs to be nearer her parents, however awful they are, but believe me when I say that after one hour she'll be running for the hills. I don't know what Dad's thinking. Maybe she's got another man there, but then why take Dad?'

'Did you ask him?'

'Not about Mum having an affair. That would crush him. He just said that after losing his own mum, he appreciated Mum's parents more and he understands her need to be near them. She'd moved here for him and left her friends and family, and now it's his turn to give up his life for her. I just don't get it! He hates it there, he hates my grandparents. My grandmother, Lucille, is a dictator.'

'But I guess he thought he'd have you there to support him?'

'I'm not leaving my family restaurant. I've been telling them for years that it just needs a revamp. They won't listen. So I'll buy it – and show them.'

Ada paused for a moment. 'But how will you cope without your family?' Ada knew how hard it was to be far away from those that cared about you. She'd done it, but Genie wasn't like her. She spent practically every waking hour of her life with her family.

'I'll cope,' said Genie defiantly.

'Oh, Genie. I'm so sorry that you're going through this and I'm cross at your mum and dad for putting you in this position. How can they expect you to just pack up and leave something you love so much?'

Genie's eyebrows shot up and her mouth fell open. 'How come you understand that, when they don't?'

'Perhaps they don't have a choice. If the business isn't doing well and they don't have money to invest, perhaps a smaller place and a flat is all they can afford? If your grandmother Lucille is unwell, however much of a complete horror she sounds, then I can understand their need to move closer, especially if your dad's dad is moving away too. Are you completely sure you don't want to go with them and see what it's like?'

'I know what it's like. My grandmother insisted on taking me to the café they've bought the last couple of times I've visited. Now I know why. The old witch knew about this too. The café is nice and it's on the end of a promenade by a beach, but it's nothing like here. It's all new and shiny, while this place has history.'

'What can I do to help?'

'Nothing. No one can help. I have some money saved. I've been putting a little money aside each month for a deposit on a flat of my own, for years. I'll have to get a business loan for the rest. If I rent out the flat above the restaurant, it's doable. I might not have qualifications, but I've been running that business for years,' she said heatedly. She took a sip of her wine and seemed thoughtful for a moment after her outburst. 'The problem is that Graysons' hasn't been making very much money for a while now, so the bank might not be prepared to lend me the money.'

She rested her face in her palms, with her elbows on her knees, facing Ada. 'I can understand it, but I've wanted to invest in the place for years. It's got so much potential and we used to make loads of money. It just lost its mojo after Grandma Vera died. I really want to make it into an ice cream bar, like it used to be. Smaller emphasis on breakfasts and lunches, but go all out for gooey chocolate iced desserts and flavoured cones, or lollies and so on. The place used to be buzzing, and it could be again.'

Ada jumped up and clapped her hands, almost upending Genie and sending her sprawling onto the floor in surprise.

'I want to help. I'll go in with you!'

'What?'

'I'm bored, miserable and I can see why your parents let you run the place. You've certainly got an affinity with your customers.'

Loads of ideas whirred round Ada's brain and she felt a glimmer of joy fill her veins for the first time in ages. Now she'd had the idea, it seemed like the answer to her own prayers. 'You'd have free reign to do your ice cream idea, but we'd also have to see a business advisor friend of mine called Ralph. He's a real dish and was such a good friend to me and Ned, when he was alive. He handles all of our overseas investments and he's actually local to this area. It's how he and Ned met. They went to college together, albeit in completely different fields of expertise. I think they started chatting in a bar over a beer.'

Genie seemed dazed and was mute for a moment before she shook herself and stood up, brushing at the food stain on her blouse. 'Overseas investments?' She looked completely bemused by what that could mean, but began trailing her eyes around the room, as if to try and work out who Ada actually was and why she was offering her a lifeline. 'You can't be serious? I couldn't take your money.'

'It's an investment, and it would make an old lady very happy. I have lots of money and want to do something productive with it. I won't risk anything I can't afford to lose.'

'I think you should wait and speak to your friend Ralph. There's no way he'd let you invest in a business you know nothing about. Plus, I never thought of partnering with someone outside my family. It might be a bit weird.'

'I can understand that, but I know you, Genie. We've become closer since I've been here and I consider you a friend. I see how hard you work and I also see that the restaurant has a prime location and could be really popular. I think you've been stifled. I'd be happy with a minority shareholding and you would be the boss.'

Genie's mouth hung open. Ada guessed that no one had seen potential in her before. Her parents were just too damn busy thinking of themselves. That same anger burned in her stomach and she was determined that she would help this young woman, whatever it cost her.

CHAPTER SIXTEEN

*A*da's friend Ralph was busy the following week, so Genie spent the next few days trying to sort the problem out for herself. She worked even longer hours than ever, and then sat at the desk in her room with figures buzzing around the pages until her eyes were tired. Some nights she had to prop her head up with her arms, until she gave up and fell asleep at her desk. Her body protested and ached afterwards.

She was determined to keep out of her parents' way, if she was such a bother to them. But she would do whatever she could to keep the business in the family. In the end, though, she couldn't see a way forward on her own. She pleaded with her parents to reconsider.

She did have her back-up plan of Ada's offer, but how serious could that be? Ada knew nothing about the food industry as far as Genie could see. Nor did she want to take money from a woman who should be spending it on having fun, not on a business that had seen better days, even if it did have potential.

After another row, where Genie felt like she was about to

combust in flames, she realised she felt bewildered by Milly and James's behaviour. Her parents were steadfast, though. They kept pleading with her to join them and saying that they would always be there for her, but refused to change their plans.

Why Cornwall? Genie wondered. It was beautiful, but so was the coastline where they were. Why leave their seafront home? And how could they think that she would just drop everything and follow them? Then she remembered that she didn't have anything to drop. No friends, no boyfriend. She'd picked up a book at the library about being a business owner, and now she threw it down in disgust. She decided that she would start being better at living the life of a young woman in her prime, and try and be less of a loser who couldn't make friends or keep them.

She'd turn the business around and make it so successful that everyone would want to know her, then she'd meet a hot man that made women gasp his name when he passed them. He would only have eyes for her, his fiery but stunningly gorgeous and definitely-not-fat girlfriend. That reminded her, she needed to stop eating leftovers and to start cooking fresh meals again.

She was so depressed that she actually didn't care if she went near cheese anymore. She had started leaving little blocks of it out for the evil pigeon, albeit via the end of a fork. She still couldn't touch the stuff. The first time the pigeon had watched her with wary eyes until she'd retreated into the kitchen and then gobbled the whole lot in one go. She'd made the blocks much smaller and now he flew down and picked one up before landing back on the garden wall. Sometimes he dropped food in mid-air and she nearly got hit in the face. She was sure they were friends now and he wouldn't do that on purpose. She'd read somewhere that it was lucky for a bird to poo on you, but she wasn't taking any chances and had worked a way to run, flick the cheese or scraps and do an about turn in twenty seconds before the bird even realised she was there most of the time.

She thought fleetingly about what her life would be like if she did move to Cornwall. It was such a stunning part of the country, but her grandparents were there, and that marred her view of it. She felt tense the minute she stepped across the county line and usually had to stop for a double expresso to give her the energy to fend off their nagging about her clothes, which were always wrong and her hair, which was never styled properly. She wished she had a 'Cornwall grand-mother' force field that Lucille bounced off when she stepped within ten feet of Genie.

Stop being so mean, Genie berated herself for being unkind to her own flesh and blood. Then she shook that feeling off. Lucille deserved it for being a complete witch. Because Vera had been such a cuddly grandma, whose face lit up whenever she saw her only grandchild, Genie always felt confused around her mum's mum. Why didn't she smile with joy when she saw her? It was always more of a grimace as if she was causing trouble again. And about what? Genie had never quite worked it out.

She pictured the endless beaches of Cornwall and tried to visualise herself amongst the hot young surfer dudes and gals. She shivered. If she tried on a wetsuit, someone would probably call the RSPCA and report a beached whale.

She glanced forlornly at her appearance and decided that today was the day she would start to smarten up. She had curves, and knew she didn't have a problem attracting men. They always chatted her up at work or when she was on a rare night out with Fae and Una. Admittedly, the ones who winked and asked her out at work were usually over fifty and had a limp, but it might get to the point when she actually considered dating an older man. Not that old, but perhaps she needed someone with a bit of life experience. All the young men she met seemed at bit dull or arrogant to her, so she gave them a wide berth.

Maybe she needed a sugar daddy who could help her run the place? She curled up her lip in disgust. She'd drive him up the wall with her temper and the poor old sod would probably keel over in shock if she undressed in front of him. Good job that idea didn't appeal to her. She wanted to do this on her own, or maybe with a little help from her guardian angel Ada.

She got up and eyed herself in the mirror with disgust. She grabbed her boobs and squished them together, wishing they weren't so gargantuan, but they sprang back into place. She looked down at them and arched her back, wondering if she should wear lower cut tops to attract more custom. Then she scratched that idea as most of her customers were over seventy and she'd probably give them a heart attack. Then she'd have less custom than ever!

She vowed to stop being such a slob and to work off the extra curves. She didn't mind having wide hips and big boobs, but she currently looked like she was carrying a life belt around her middle under her clothes. She stuck her tongue out at her reflection and sucked her stomach in.

Immediately, she saw the old Genie and she almost kicked the plant pot by the window in frustration, before remembering how that had ended up last time and going to sit down again, looking out at the sea. It was still warm outside and a sea breeze was wafting through the open window. Stars were twinkling in the inky sky and white boats were bobbing up and down on the water. All was calm outside, but indoors she felt tumultuous. Her stomach had been churning for days and she was sure her blood pressure must be through the roof.

Her mum had begun packing up the house in the

evenings, even though they hadn't agreed on anything yet. She just said she'd seen a programme about how much happier people were with less clutter around them at home. She'd ordered a skip and had laid a tarpaulin out next to it. She'd begun chucking anything and everything into the skip, with useful items on the plastic sheeting to be taken to the charity shop.

Genie had wanted to scream and stamp her feet, but this would just prove how juvenile she still was, so she'd actually sorted out her own bedroom one night to prove a point, but was now missing half of the things she used regularly that she'd thrown out in a fit of pique. She swore and moved the plant pot out of her eye-line, behind her bathroom door. Genie wouldn't be surprised to find herself chucked on the top of the skip, the mood her mum was in. She was trying to appear extra sunny, but then Genie would catch her standing looking out at the horizon, her hand pressing on her breastbone as if her heart was beating too fast.

Genie almost wanted to run over and hug her to find out what the hell was going on, but then her own heart hardened and she left her mum to wallow in her own misery for the stress she was causing everyone else, by deciding to abandon her business and her only child.

CHAPTER SEVENTEEN

*M*illy was in the flat above the restaurant. Her nerves felt like they were strung out across the room. The flat had three bedrooms, so it would cost too much for Genie to stay in, she had been right about that, even if by some miracle she did find the money to buy the business.

Milly sighed and shoved a book into the box by her feet with unnatural force, then winced as her hand smacked painfully against its spine. If Genie kept being so stubborn and refused to come with them, then she would need the income from the flats to keep the business ticking over. She would then have to pay rent on a one-bedroom flat. The thought made Milly cross, but Genie was a grown woman and she was as strong-willed as hell.

Milly kept asking James if they were doing the right thing. Her appetite had vanished. But they'd said the words out loud to Genie about leaving, and the world hadn't caved in around them. Milly had been looking for a way out for a while now and recent events had almost made the decision for her.

She knew Genie was confused. Milly herself was too, but she'd had to make a call or lose her marriage. The fact was that James had finally given in and realised that she meant what she was saying – something had to change. They were working themselves into the ground for very little reward and barely spent any quality time together.

Then Milly had found out how unwell her mum was and, since losing Vera, she couldn't bear to lose Lucille, however hard work she was to be around, however much she'd even set out to ruin Milly's life. James's behaviour lately had cemented her decision. She'd been forced to take action before all their worlds came crashing down around them. Poor Genie was totally devastated, but Milly's heart was broken and she had to get away.

Her parents weren't getting any younger and they needed her around. There was of course the other reason they were leaving, but James didn't know about that yet. She prayed that he would be strong enough to understand. If she got him away from here and they had more time to be together, maybe they could rebuild that bond they used to have. And, once they got settled and Genie saw how good the new business and lifestyle could be for them all, then Milly prayed that she would follow them there.

If Genie did invest in the seafront restaurant – and Milly thought that highly unlikely – then she would soon run out of money. She'd end up being forced to sell to a developer. They'd already had two offers from local firms but, despite hating the idea, Milly knew they would give Genie a chance first. Hopefully she'd see the error of her ways after she'd tried to raise the finance. Then they could all pack up and move together. Milly got up and steadied herself on a chair, as her legs nearly gave way. The walls felt like they were closing in on her. She wished she could talk to Vera over a coffee like she used to.

Sighing and rubbing her hands across her tired eyes, Milly picked up some boxes of Gus's weird inventions and put them in the corner, ready to recycle. It was hard to believe but she would even miss his mad inventions and hoarding tendencies. Hopefully he'd come back from his cruise with a lighter heart and would decide to join them in Cornwall. It would be another reason for Genie to change her mind. Milly was prepared to do everything it took to have her precious daughter by her side. They'd have a new business, away from all their problems, and perhaps they could be a proper family again.

Milly had to ignore her hurt pride and her burning desire to start stamping her feet and screaming at people at work who she was supposed to be able to trust. If she gave way to her impulses, there would be no hope at all of Genie being able to continue the business. Above everything, Genie was Milly's priority. But she knew how her daughter felt about her right now. Milly's whole world had crashed and burned lately, but she would stand tall and show she was nobody's fool before making those that had hurt her pay a heavy price.

She closed her eyes for a moment and her stomach clenched. It was a frequent feeling these days. It covered up some of the burning anger and hurt she felt. She wanted to scream at her mother at the injustice of what she had done and then scream at James for not being there for her when she needed him. She wanted to defy her mum by staying in Essex, but she knew she couldn't do it. Their reasons for leaving were too strong. Milly hoped that gamble she was taking would pay off and that Genie would follow them to Cornwall. And Milly also hoped that her own mum didn't have the power to cause total destruction again. For now, Milly had to play nice and pretend she was happy with the move, but if Lucille didn't keep up her end of the bargain, there would be hell to pay. Milly wasn't the meek child she had once been. She was a grown woman with a family to protect. It was just horrific that the person Milly was protecting them from was her own mother.

CHAPTER EIGHTEEN

*a*da sat on her hands in Ralph's office to stop herself from jiggling about too much. She hadn't been this excited for ages and, although she tried not to pin all her hopes on the young woman who sat facing her across the table, she couldn't help but want to grab onto the first time she had felt alive for months. She'd gone over and over the idea of investing in a new business at her age, and decided *why not?* She wasn't that old and she had lots of experience running businesses, so what did she have to lose? Money, she supposed, but she had oodles of that. And what was the point of it, if it didn't help her to have some fun?

She looked across at Genie, who seemed a bit pale. She kept gnawing on her bottom lip, which only succeeded in making her mouth look even more plump and exotic. Ada didn't know where she got her Latin looks from, but it was those piercing blue eyes that set her apart. Perhaps that was an Essex trait? Ada sent her a reassuring smile while Ralph, who was looking mightily dashing in a blue suit with a crisp white shirt and patterned tie, had his head bent over the file of figures they had given him a few days before. He tapped the pen in his right hand on the desk in concentration.

'The numbers are good,' he announced, looking up and giving them a warm smile, his eyes twinkling. 'I would advise that Ada has a forty-nine per cent shareholding and Genie has fifty-one per cent.' He seemed to notice that Genie was about to protest, as they were investing the same capital. He held up his hands to halt her words. 'It's easier that way. You always have to have a boss. That way, one person has the final say. You know the business inside and out, Genie, so it wouldn't make sense for Ada to have a majority shareholding.'

'But…'

'It's only a couple of percent, Genie and I had to argue with Ralph about it. It's your family business, so I would be happy with an even smaller percentage, but he didn't agree. I'm not doing this for the money.'

'But what's the point of doing it, if it's not for the money?' asked Genie, putting her hands on the table. She frowned. Her face was a little flushed, but her eyes were bright and enquiring.

Ralph began getting papers out of a briefcase that was by his feet on the floor. Ada smiled at them both. 'I have faith in you and think you'll make us money, Genie, but for me, this is the first thing that's caught my interest since Ned died.'

Genie was surprised that Ada was being so candid. 'Don't you want to be in control of the business?'

'No, dear. I want some fun! I don't need the responsibility at my time of life, but for you it will be a challenge. It's your family business. I'm happy to be a silent partner. I've asked Ralph to add that to the contract, but I'd love to help out if you need me. I've been in business before with my Ned. When it comes to the wire, one person needs control, not two. You know you can make a success of this, with a little freedom and a cash investment, and I think so too. I quite like the idea of being a sleeping partner. I can sit around and drink coffee, or eat your new ice cream flavours all day and get fat, and you can scurry around looking after everyone.'

Genie looked sceptical, as if she couldn't envisage Ada sitting still for long anywhere, but she leapt up and came round the desk to envelop Ada in a big hug.

Ralph gave them a copy of their new contract to sign. It made them partners in a new venture called *Genie's*. All they had to do now was make an offer on her parents' restaurant, and hope that it was accepted.

Ada felt sad for Genie in one way, but was excited at the same time. Genie seemed to need a new challenge. She had to untie herself from her parents' apron strings and show them what she could become. If they didn't see the potential in their daughter, then Ada could. The girl was strong and wilful, but she worked hard and was as genuine a person as Ada had met for a while. Ralph had taken an instant liking to her and he was already protective of her. He'd made sure the deal was fair.

Genie had no idea of the effect she had on other people. It must have been from growing up surrounded by different generations and personalities, because as far as Ada could see, she could charm honey from bees if she set her mind to it. Ada had seen how determined she was about her business, and was glad Genie had found a way to keep it without her family's help. It was their loss and her gain. Genie had made Ada feel more than just a widow who'd lost her way, and for that she would happily have invested in a hundred businesses. She wouldn't tell Genie that just yet, though, as knowing her, she'd have ideas to buy up the whole parade. Ada didn't quite have the energy for that.

Ralph stood up and took off his suit jacket. It instantly softened his appearance and made him look more approachable. If Ada hadn't known him so well, and hadn't seen the way he used to laze around at their place in the States with Ned, drinking beers from the bottle and roaring with laughter, then she might have thought he was austere and a bit scary. Now he came and linked arms with both her and Genie and told them he was taking them to their restaurant to buy them both lunch, before they had to cook it themselves.

All the tension in the room disappeared at that, and Ada could see that the excitement in Genie's eyes now matched her own. This was going to be so much fun!

CHAPTER NINETEEN

*G*enie couldn't relax over lunch. She felt like she'd been unfaithful or something, by meeting Ralph and Ada behind her parents' backs. What choice had she had, though?

Although her insides felt like they were on the high seas, she also welcomed a new warm feeling, because she was having lunch with two new friends who were behaving more like family than her own parents at the moment. She was a little nervous about giving a share of her heritage to someone outside the family. But she'd had meetings with so many banks in the last forty-eight hours. None of them would invest in a business that was losing money, even with her ideas and financial projections, and with an investment. She had heard you could borrow money from anywhere, but unless she took out a loan with outrageous interest, no one was prepared to back her, except Ada.

Surely it was better to keep some of the restaurant in the family? Plus Ada had very kindly put a stipulation in the contract that Genie had the right to buy it back for market value in five years. Better to have part of her business than lose all of it to a stranger, like her parents wanted. This way, if she succeeded, then she could buy Ada out for a nice sum and both of them would be happy. Genie saw movement out of her eye and noticed her mum leaning out from behind the back door, trying to look inconspicuous, which in turn made her more obvious. If she leaned over any further she'd headbutt the other side of the doorframe. Genie frowned. What the hell was she doing?

Realising that she was trying to work out who Ralph was, Genie beckoned her over to their table. This was the first time Genie had taken a meal as a paying guest, and she was really enjoying having everyone run round after her for a change. She could get used to this and vowed to hire sexy waiters as soon as she made money, so that she could take time off and enjoy the view. And not just the one of the sea!

There were no other customers in the restaurant, so Genie asked her mum to call her dad out of the kitchen and for them both to come and join them. Milly hesitated, but called out to James nonetheless. They all sat around, her parents with fixed smiles on their faces, as Genie did the introductions.

'Mum, Dad. This is Ada, as you know, and this is her lawyer, Ralph,' she said gesturing to her new friend.

'Lawyer?'

Genie's dad shook Ralph's hand but looked as bemused, as did her mum.

'Ada is my new business partner. Ralph has drawn up a contract which we think is a fair offer for the restaurant. We know you need a quick sale and I can only afford a certain amount, so although it's not a huge sum of money, it is a good offer for a business that isn't making money anymore.'

Genie's mum gasped and covered her mouth in shock. She looked angrily at Ralph and Ada. James stood up quickly and his chair toppled and hit the floor with a thud. 'What the hell's going on here?'

'Dad,' said Genie, taking his hand and making him sit back down. 'Before you jump to conclusions, read the offer. I know it's probably not the usual way of making a business sale, but Ralph is an old friend of Ada's and he isn't charging us for his time while he's out of the office,' she winked at him to ask him to play along, before turning imploring eyes to her parents. She wanted this with all her heart and she hoped they could see how much it meant to her.

'You've both shown me how serious you are about moving, and that it has to be done with speed due to Gran's health.' Genie clamped her teeth together for a second and tried to control her breathing while she thought of her grandmother joking with her friends on the phone. Her mum looked even more worried.

'But we really thought you'd change your mind and come with us.' Her mum looked like she was about to faint.

'I told you that I wanted to stay. With Ada's investment, I can see how I get on, doing things my own way. I've learnt so much from you both, but I'm a grown woman and I don't want to move away from my home.'

'Surely your home is wherever we are?' A lone tear escaped from her mum's eye and she angrily brushed it aside.

'I need to stand on my own two feet for a while and I'm not ready to move. As the business expands, I'll be able to take time off to visit you more often.' Seeing her parents exchange glances about how likely this would be, when they all worked every hour they could from morning to evening, Genie felt tears well up in her own eyes. 'Just take a look at the contract. Get your lawyers to read it over and if it seems fair, then I beg you to sign it. It means you can set your plans into motion and I can start mine.'

Ada and Ralph didn't interfere with the exchange and

seemed to sense that they should stay silent, but Ralph did clear his throat, stand up and offer his business card to her parents, before shaking their hands and motioning to Ada that they should leave the family alone to talk about their future. Ada leaned in and gave Genie a quick hug, which made her mum's mouth set in a thin line and Genie jumped up to see them out. When she got back, the three of them faced each other over the table.

'We've decided to rent our house out for now,' said her mum quietly.

'I thought you needed the capital?'

'We do, but I had a bad feeling that you might not join us and I want something to come back to. The rent will go towards saving for somewhere bigger for us in Cornwall, instead of the flat above the shop. We can always sell the house later when we have all decided if we've made the right choices.' She got up and hugged Genie fiercely, and Genie bore the pain until her mum let her go and her dad pulled her into his arms too and kissed the top of her head.

'Perhaps we should stay here?' he asked her mum.

'How can we? My mother is ill.' She gave him a strange look and turned to go into the kitchen where Genie heard her switch on the kettle, the universal cure for all ills. Her dad's shoulders slumped, but he sat back down and began reading the contract Ralph had provided, looking like a man about to go to the gallows.

CHAPTER TWENTY

*A*da was feeling quite smug. She'd been for a long walk along the beach that morning and had actually spoken to a couple of people from her building. Ralph had invited her to dinner, but she wasn't ready for that yet, even though they had been friends for years. She understood that Ralph had always had a soft spot for her, but had never over-stepped the mark. He knew how much she and Ned had loved each other. He'd always looked out for her.

She'd been surprised to find out he had offices near to where she now lived. Ralph travelled a lot, as had she and Ned, so they'd regularly met abroad, but she recalled Ned and Ralph sitting over dinner and telling her the story of how they'd met in their first jobs after college. Both men were born near to the seafront she'd just walked along, and she supposed it made sense for Ralph to have offices near his roots. The building he was in looked modern and new. Ralph was always upgrading everything. He had never married, but often brought girlfriends with him on his travels. He used to tease Ned over what he was missing, but Ned would just give him a knowing look and sweep Ada into his arms for a theatrical kiss, which would make Ralph laugh and walk off in disgust. Ada always batted Ned away, but she'd adored how open and honest he was.

She wasn't sure how she felt about Ralph being so near all the time, but she supposed she was the one who had sought him out. She had originally assumed it would all be done via phone or the internet. Obviously she was happier to see him in person. It was actually good to converse with someone other than family who reminded her of Ned.

She was now finding it easier to cope with the pain of loss. The business with Genie had reignited her fire to see something succeed. She was surprised at how much she wanted the young woman to show her family that she was more capable than they realised. She supposed it stemmed back to her own parents telling her not to marry Ned at first, as they'd thought he was too old. They had tried to make that decision for her, by banning contact. Thank goodness she'd been strong enough to stand up to them. They couldn't have loved Ned more in the end. It went to show that parents didn't always get it right. Their hearts had been in the right place, though.

She wasn't sure she could say the same for Genie's parents. There was something not quite right there. Her mum seemed shifty and her dad looked like he'd given up. Genie's grandma Vera sounded like an amazing woman and, from Ada's own experience, she could understand that grief made you do some strange things. She was testament to that, sitting on her own in a huge penthouse flat on the other side of the world to most of her family. The decision had been right for her, though. She just knew that Genie had some-thing special that her parents couldn't see. She had determi-nation and she wanted to succeed, even if it meant wrenching herself away from her family. She was also as stubborn as hell! What normal twenty-two-year-old would put every penny they had into a failing business, just because they wanted to keep the family name afloat?

Ada had a plan to help them both in other ways too. Genie would need a place to stay and the penthouse was big enough for them both to live in and not bump into each other for days. They could plan the business by night and help with renovations by day. She just had to work out a way to persuade Genie that it wasn't charity, but good business sense. It might help them both not to feel quite so alone.

Ada had several grandchildren of her own, and one or two around Genie's age, but she had already fallen in love with this wilful woman. Genie reminded her of her younger self. Ada grinned as the doorbell rang to tell her Genie had arrived and she rushed to bring her inside. She wondered if she should tell Genie she thought of her as family already? It might scare her away. But the reason Ada had wanted to help was because she already loved her like a granddaughter.

Genie looked flushed and beautiful as she walked into the apartment. She had been there a few times now and was comfortable enough to wander into the kitchen and begin making them both a strong coffee. They found it hilarious that they both liked to start the day that way.

Genie looked at her suspiciously when she didn't speak for a moment. 'You look like you're plotting something shifty,' she joked.

Ada couldn't help the wide smile on her face as Genie waited patiently to be let in on the secret. 'I've been thinking. We're going to need the rent from the flat above the restaurant and I already have ideas for that.' She ignored Genie's shocked look and hoped she didn't feel railroaded, but Genie needed a partner who was going to help her at first, then step back and let her run the place.

Genie held up her hand. 'Hang on. We haven't even signed the deal yet.'

'I know, but if it goes through, we'll need the restaurant up and running as quickly as possible to bring in capital. If we forward-plan, we can make it seamless.'

Genie frowned and Ada could imagine the cogs of her brain whirring, trying to work out if this was a good idea or if she was being out manoeuvred.

'Do you know Bailey?'

Genie's eyebrows shot up into her hairline. 'Bailey? Yes. He works for Trudie.'

'Well I was talking to his mum and dad the other day. They came in to collect him from Trudie's. They need to move locally and are looking for a three-bedroomed flat. We're going to need staff. Bailey will be living with them. It could be ideal. What do you think?'

Genie rubbed her temples and downed her coffee, then looked disappointed that it had all gone. 'It does make sense, I guess. I had thought of him, as he's casual labour at Trudie's, but I'd have to see if she minds first.'

Ada loved the way Genie made such fast decisions and didn't stamp her feet or get in a huff. 'It was your idea. Do you remember telling me about possibly taking Bailey on part-time? Well, when I spoke to his parents, it seemed like too good an opportunity to miss. I didn't say anything as it's your call, but he would be handy to have around.'

Ada dug Genie in the ribs and she laughed out loud as Bailey would certainly look good anywhere. She recalled his firm muscles and long legs. 'How come he's living with his parents? He must be younger than I thought, then. I've seen him with his little brother.'

'Not everyone can afford their own places these days,' Ada winked at her, because at twenty-two she was still living with her own parents. Genie had the grace to blush.

'What do you think about moving in with me for a while? I thought it might be a good way for you to save money on rent for the first crucial few months, then you will have a bit of breathing space to look around and find the right home.'

Tears welled up in Genie's eyes and she sniffed. Ada leaned forward and hugged her. 'What's up? Do you hate the idea?'

'It's not that. I've been so shocked about all of this happening, I hadn't really given much thought to where I'd live. I kind of thought that I'd have to stay in the flat at first, but I also knew I should be renting it out. It has just started to gnaw at me a bit. I'm used to living with other people. I know I need to grow up a bit and I'm buying a business, for goodness sake, but I feel pathetic sometimes. Everything in my life has changed in the last two weeks.' A big fat tear splashed onto her arm. 'It's almost like I'm living in a parallel universe. Someone has taken my parents and replaced them with mean aliens.'

Ada smothered a laugh at the drama of it all and walked over to grab the fresh croissants she'd had delivered that morning, one of the benefits of having a concierge. Genie smelt the air and perked up a bit, offering a wobbly smile as Ada placed the plate in front of her with a jar of fresh strawberry preserve and a block of creamy butter. 'Let's have some breakfast while you think about it. You don't have to decide now.'

'I'm supposed to be on a diet,' said Genie morosely.

'Who said you should lose weight?' Ada eyed Genie's soft curves and anger flashed in her eyes.

'Me.'

'Oh!' Ada laughed, pushing the food further towards her. 'Well, if you are dead set on it, then you can use the gym and swimming pool here if you do move in. Although I don't know why you'd feel the need, you're beautiful as you are.'

Genie's mouth hung open, just as she was about to take a huge bite of the crumbly patisserie which she had lathered with jam and butter while Ada was talking. 'There's a pool too?'

'Yes. Residents can use it for free whenever they want.'

'I'm moving in,' said Genie, biting into the crumbly croissant and sighing in bliss.

CHAPTER TWENTY-ONE

*T*he next few weeks were a blur of talking the formal offer through with her parents' lawyers and having it accepted by them. Genie had been secretly hoping her parents would jump out from behind the door in the soulless office where they had all met and tell her they'd been joking. It would have been nice to laugh until their bellies hurt about the prank they'd played on her, pretending to sell the family business – but today it was real. It would take a while for the formalities to go through, but it seemed that they'd done one of the quickest business deals in history. She'd even hoped that her grandad might turn up and offer her some money to keep part of the business, or her dad, but neither of them had.

It made her sad to realise how much she had relied on them. For the first time she actually felt so bad about all the stress she must have caused them, by throwing their plans into disarray and not going with them.

Her parents were supposed to be leaving in two weeks, to find a place to rent in Cornwall, but she had told them she could manage without them now as custom was so sparse. They had originally spoken about letting the chef who worked with her dad go, even though he was a hard worker and had been with them for years. They just hadn't been able to afford him. Now, without her parents' wages, she could keep him on.

Suddenly it was final that they were leaving. It made it harder for her to see them every day, not knowing when she would see them again. They'd be busy with their own venture and so would she. Tears blurred her vision and she had to keep taking deep breaths and close her eyes, trying to focus.

She was glad that they had at least decided to rent out their house, so they could come back if they wanted to. She was determined to show them what the business could have been, if they had believed in her enough. She wanted to make them beg her to let them come back and be part of the family business again.

They had now begun to clear the house out, and Genie felt like a walking scarecrow – except with big boobs. She could feel that she'd lost weight, and actually missed her wobbly bits. They'd kept her warm at night. She probably hadn't lost that much, it was just a few weeks, but she felt like she'd been on a starvation diet, or one of those boot camps where they screamed at you to jump out of bed at 5am and then force-fed you carrots. She'd taken to pacing the floor until the early hours of the morning, until she fell into a fitful sleep

Her mum had sat her down a couple of times and seemed like she had the world on her shoulders. She kept bursting into tears and hugging Genie. If it was so hard to leave, why go? Genie thought she was going to tell her about having another man, but she'd always baulked at the last minute and spoke about something inconsequential, like cancelling the milk or which suppliers she should drop and which to keep. It was all so confusing.

Her dad seemed to have accepted his fate quietly and, without Gus around, it had been so hard. He might be grumpy now, but he was still a light in her life and she missed his warm hugs and whiskery face. She even missed the weird things he made in his little shed. He had packed up and left with glistening eyes and a promise to call her regularly.

Now she smiled sadly and got up to find another packing box. Her jeans felt looser and she pulled on the old black belt she'd taken from Vera's wardrobe after she'd died and tightened it, vowing to Vera that she would make this right somehow and entice her parents and granddad to come back to her and their heritage. She would save it for them all, and they would thank her for it… she hoped. If not, then at least she had tried her best and not given up and just walked away.

She filled another box without thinking what she was putting in it and remembered that Ada had offered to come round and help her sort out what to put in storage and what to send to her flat. It would be weird to live somewhere else after all this time, but it would be worse to be rattling around the house on her own, she supposed. She couldn't really believe that she was packing up her family home, helped by a pensioner she'd only just met. She sniffed and rubbed her tired eyes, scraping her hair back into a messy ponytail.

None of her friends had offered to help her when she'd mentioned she was moving, or had given her a shoulder to cry on, though they knew how much her family meant to her. They'd just said how exciting it was to be moving out and getting away from her family.

But she loved her family. If they knew anything about

her, then they should at least know that. She collapsed onto her bed and let the tears flow. She grabbed an old teddy bear that she'd found when she was packing and buried her face in his soft chest as she wept.

CHAPTER TWENTY-TWO

*A*da was biting her lip and concentrating hard on the page of figures in front of her when she heard Genie come in. The girl had moved into Ada's flat a week previously, but still always sloped off to her room to give Ada privacy. Ada sighed and rubbed her temples, looking out across the calm sea and taking a lungful of the crisp, salty, sea air that was coming in through the open sliding doors to the balcony. She asked Genie to turn on the radio and a hauntingly beautiful song filled the room. Ada wanted to ask her to play something a bit more upbeat, but the song seemed to fit Genie's mood these days.

It had been an adjustment for Ada to have a young person around again and she'd worried at first that Genie would be aghast at how boring her life had become, but Ada felt like a butterfly that was just waking up from a not-so-restful sleep and suddenly she wanted to test her wings and shake some moves!

She'd tried making home cooked meals for Genie, but she was an atrocious chef and burnt everything, so Genie had laughed and they'd had to resort to calling the concierge for take away meals, as Genie was too tired to whip up a meal after a long day. Ada could see how much the young woman was missing her family, now her parents had moved to Cornwall and her grumpy old grandad had locked up his shed and gone travelling.

Ada felt a bit sorry for anyone going on the cruise he'd booked as the old man could freeze water. He had made it very plain that he thought Ada was an interfering bat for helping Genie. She'd raged in turn that he was a misery, going galivanting and deserting his only grandchild. She had hung her head in shame when he'd yelled at her that he'd purposely not helped Genie. He'd wanted her to go out and make new friends, and move away from the all-encompassing and sometimes suffocating life of a family business. Ada hadn't considered that the family was making the move for Genie's benefit. Maybe now that had all backfired because she'd poked her nose in.

She wondered if she'd latched on to Genie as she missed her own rambunctious grandchildren. She'd had a video call from her eldest grandson, Calvin, the previous evening and had to tell him to go and put on some clothes. The boy was too good looking to be wandering around in just shorts and nothing else, however hot it was in America. Girls had always fallen at his feet and she felt it was improper to make them all suffer by having him prancing around like a peacock.

He was so like his father, Ada's son Taylor, and his grandfather, Ned. In fact all of her sons were devastatingly handsome, but Calvin's mother was a model. Although Ada had felt some reservations at her first meeting with Sasha, as she was so quiet, Taylor had gone all out to win Sasha over. It was a bit like history repeating itself, as they had both been quite young. What could Ada do, as they had been so obviously in love? She almost felt sorry for what she'd put her own parents through, but it had all turned out fine in the end.

Sasha was a complex woman. She was smart and beautiful, but also one of the kindest people that Ada had ever met. People wrongly assumed she would be a complete witch, as she was a supermodel and had the world at her feet. But she had a gentle soul. She had managed to build an incredible career and hold off the swathes of men who'd tried to woo her, until she'd met Taylor.

They say it's always the quiet ones, though, as Sasha made Taylor work hard for her affection. Ada saw the love they had for each other. Sasha was an amazing mum too. Calvin and his siblings were lucky to have such devotion. It had made them a little spoilt, and Ada sometimes despaired at their antics.

Especially Cal. He was incorrigible! He had made a multi-million pound business from a small investment, and then got ahead of himself. He was an incredible chef and in great demand. He had invested his own money in a huge restaurant in a hot spot in town. It had been an instant hit.

Suddenly, he had found himself the darling of the industry. Paparazzi followed him everywhere. Ada had tried to warn him about expanding too fast, but he hadn't listened. Within the first year he'd overextended and gone bust. He was currently licking his wounds at her place in America. Although she loved him dearly, she'd like to have him actually listen to her experience occasionally and not be quite so gung-ho about his life.

Ada sighed and then grinned. She couldn't stay mad at Cal. It was impossible. He had his mum's sweet nature, but with an edge, plus those good looks and his dad's easy charm. It was a killer combination. She didn't stand a chance. One smile from her grandson, and he got his own way.

Ada was surprised at how quickly Genie's family business

was changing hands, but she supposed that a private sale had far less paperwork attached, making it easy for the changeover to go through. They had sat up long into the night, and Ada felt good to have aching bones from working hard and not just through sitting still.

Ada was determined to bring in a younger crowd to the rebranded restaurant, for Genie's sake. She needed to be around people of her own age. This was one thing Ada and Genie's granddad did agree on. If he'd taken the time to talk to her about it, and not just shout in her face, Gus would have realised that there were other ways to find new friends for Genie and to help her grow. He'd seriously underestimated his granddaughter and how much her heritage meant to her. As an only child, Genie was lonely and the business was part of her. She couldn't give it up without a fight.

They had decided that they would begin with small changes. They would start with the ice cream idea, as it was almost summer and Genie had confided one night that she wasn't sure that she could take any more change. Ada had given her a warm hug and tried to help her feel some excitement about how much they had already achieved, in such a short space of time.

They had employed a packing company to clear up the house without telling Genie's parents – they had left earlier than expected due to a sudden health scare with Milly's mother, which had turned out to be a false alarm. Ada felt that it might have done them all a favour, though, as now there wouldn't be any drawn-out and tearful goodbyes. It had been fast. A bit like ripping a plaster off a partially healed wound.

Ada walked over to the kitchen counter and began to set out ingredients. Genie had begun to fill her nights with flavours and textures as she blended new ice creams and worked out her aggression and sadness at her family by pounding fruits and herbs together, and working the mixes until she had the perfect combination. For the first few days she had stuck with some of the recipes Vera had made. Then she had turned her nose up, saying she hadn't got it just right.

She had spent a day rooting through cupboards at the restaurant until she'd unearthed Vera's secret book of her special flavours. Ada had helped her look, and had even been on her hands and knees, trying to see if it had been used to prop up a table, as it didn't seem to be anywhere else, but then Genie had wandered in with it, as if in a daze, with smears of dirt on her nose. The place seemed to have gathered dust since her parents had left and Ada knew that the time was right to do the refurbishment.

Genie hadn't wanted to shut the restaurant down, so they had compromised on closing for three days, Sunday to Tuesday. They had planned in advance exactly what they were going to do. Ada had much grander plans for a big re-launch and opening party, but Genie still needed convincing. She felt they should just change gradually. The poor girl had had to fight for the smallest change with her parents, but now she had free rein, she seemed to be floundering a little.

Looking up, Ada saw Genie had changed into jogging bottoms and a grey T-shirt. It looked like Genie really hadn't been looking after herself lately from the curve of her hipbone, which was now visible where she'd lost weight, and the chipped nail polish on her hands.

'If we are going to be cooking again tonight, you need to clean off that polish and put some of the love you put into your ice cream into yourself.'

Genie looked down at her hands in shock. 'You're right. I can't cook with chipped nails. I should know better than that.'

Ada sighed. 'I wasn't trying to scold you. I can't wait to

taste the flavour you are trying tonight. Plump cherries and some of those creamy toffee pieces that you made last night.'

Genie went to the bathroom and came out with scrubbed nails. Her hair was pulled back from her face with an elastic band and she looked like she'd splashed her face with cold water to add some colour to her cheeks.

'If we keep trying all of these ice creams, I'm going to get fat, but at least you'll stop looking scrawny.'

Genie did raise a smile at this, looking at her still-ample bust and thighs. 'Sorry if I've been a bit of a grump lately, Ada.'

'You haven't!'

Genie gave her a knowing smile. 'I have, and it stops today. I'm fed up with feeling maudlin and I'm ready to stop wallowing. We've got a business to run and I want Mum and Dad to wish they'd never left.'

'You want them to wish they'd listened to your ideas, before giving up?'

Genie looked up in obvious surprise at Ada's insight. 'I want them to want to come home, but I also want them to wish they hadn't left. Is that awful of me?'

Ada sadly took Genie's hand and squeezed it. 'Of course not! It means you're human. Well then. Let's make the business so successful that they won't be able to resist coming back.'

'You wouldn't mind?'

'Genie. They are your parents and of course you want them around. I don't have a problem with them coming back if that's what you decide. I agreed I would sell you the business back in five years anyway. If that moment comes sooner, then we can work it out at the time. For now, this is keeping an old woman from going insane.'

They both grinned at each other, eyes sparkling now. Genie looked like a weight had been lifted from her shoulders. She grabbed her apron and searched the cupboards for one for Ada. Gingerly offering her the dancing anchovy one her dad always wore, she ignored the surprised look on Ada's face. Ada took the proffered item as if it were gold plated.

Putting it around Ada's neck and tying it up behind her back, Genie rested her head on the older woman's shoulder and Ada stood still and enjoyed the moment.

It hit home suddenly how much she missed her own family and she thought perhaps she had been harsh on them, keeping them away from her, when maybe they might need to be near her too.

Being around Genie and her boundless energy and enthusiasm before she'd been dealt this blow, made Ada want to recapture some of that *joie de vivre* herself. It was time to start living again. Picking up her phone and making a decision later, Ada decided she should let the rest of her family know what she had really been up to. Perhaps they would stop worrying that she was alone all the time now, and feel happier getting on with their own lives.

CHAPTER TWENTY-THREE

*G*enie and Ada stood back and looked at that they'd achieved. The walls of the rebranded restaurant were sparkling white and the new sign saying *Genie's* swung softly in the breeze. The font was slick and modern, but with a scrolling typeface that almost looked like it had been drawn by a professional calligrapher. The lettering was white against a deep blue background that seemed to change hue as you walked by and made you feel like it was born of the sea. It worked well with their new waterside theme. Genie had wanted to keep the name of the restaurant, but both Ralph and Ada had advised against it. Everyone locally knew Genie and would still recognise the family name. Genie did seem to enjoy a fight and had argued about calling it Vera's. Ada had liked the idea and was touched by the sentiment, but this was Genie's business and not her family's. However much Genie had adored Vera, Ada said she felt that it was right for the restaurant to be named after the strong woman who was bringing it back to life.

Ada and Genie were now the proud owners of a sixty-seater restaurant on the seafront. They had managed to persuade Ralph and his two sons, who were visiting from London, to help them. Genie had almost swooned over them, as they were so gorgeous. She'd also taken on Bailey, her first staff member, even before they had opened their doors for the first time. It felt scary to be employing someone without discussing it with her parents, but when they had called to chat, which they did almost every evening, she held off from sharing too much for some reason.

It had turned out that the little boy she had seen with Bailey was actually his son, which had made her almost spit out her drink. Bailey was only nineteen! She had asked him a little bit about how he would manage with a small child, as she didn't have any experience of hiring staff with children. She'd usually left that to her mum. Bailey seemed competent, so she tried not to get distracted by his arm muscles, and concentrate on being a good business owner. She was professional and not a mollycoddled twentysomething. She needed to put her big girl pants on and make some decisions. A couple of months ago she might have banned cheese from her restaurant, but today she didn't care. She was getting stronger every day and the evil pigeon had seemingly decided that this was his new home too. He watched over the renovations with his beady eyes like a sergeant major inspecting his troops. She had even begun to enjoy his company.

Ralph's sons had taken off their shirts in the warm sunshine and helped lift all the booths out so that they could paint, do a deep clean and then decide on their new layout. Genie hadn't known where to look, with so many muscles to gaze at every time she turned round. When the eldest son, Toby, had winked at her, she'd almost passed out in shock and had to fan her face with their new menu cards. Who knew such beauty existed? She'd liked to have taken a quick snap on her phone with the sea in the background to prove these beautiful men had actually been helping her, but that would make her a complete weirdo.

She'd also have loved for Fae or Una to have walked past while Genie was laughing at one of Toby's endless jokes as he hoisted a heavy table into his arms and walked across the room as if it weighed nothing more than air. Then they wouldn't think she was such a sad loser.

It was hard work, as her parents had refused to change anything for ages. She'd had to move pretty much everything. She'd kept costs low by hiring someone local to paint a mural of the beach along the back wall. She'd then added tonal blue accessories rather than the old floral ones, and moved the tables to create a much more welcoming impression.

Ada had persuaded someone to squeeze them into their schedule and work on their rebrand, and Genie had got the same expert to design their new menus. Genie had assumed Ada was asking another old friend for help, but then the sharp-eyed girl had seen the invoice one evening when she was looking at their accounts and had been shocked. The friend owned a major design company. He had only charged them a nominal fee, though.

Genie didn't know how Ada did it, but she came up trumps every time. The design was so feminine and beautiful, but part of Genie felt that if it really represented her, it would have had flames and a dented flowerpot.

She had tried really hard not to become angry with Ada if they disagreed with anything. She was used to a brick wall of silence when discussing anything with her parents, but Ada sat down and listened to her ideas, often taking notes in a sparkly little notebook she kept in the new pink handbag she'd treated herself to last week.

She'd also bought Genie a new workbag in a subtle sea blue tone as a gesture of their partnership and Genie had hugged her and cried. Her own parents had sent her a card and her mum had a frame made for her with all of their names on the A4 sheet inside it, which had made her sob for hours, before she'd brushed herself down, fetched a hammer and hung it proudly on the wall by her ice cream bar. The only blot on the gift was her maternal grandmother's name, which made Genie scowl each time she passed it. Luckily her mum had obviously asked for that name to be quite small, so if Genie only looked at it fleetingly, she could pretend it wasn't there.

Genie found that Ada was so reasonable that she couldn't get mad at her, and she also discovered that she herself was listening more and starting to behave less like a wilful child. She did feel a bit guilty about the times she'd been cross with her parents, then quashed that thought as it had often been their own stupid fault.

Genie stepped back and looked at herself in the mirror. She'd come a long way from the messed-up girl who'd worked for her parents. Gus was happily sunning himself in Spain and had actually called and sent her a postcard, her mum and dad had settled into their new roles and were already talking about coming home for a visit, and Ada had turned out to be her best friend. It didn't matter about their respective ages. They just fit together.

Ada walked in wearing a swishy pink silk skirt and a cap-sleeved cream blouse, with a kitsch ice-cream brooch that made Genie laugh out loud when she saw it.

'What is that?'

Ada giggled, before pinning a similar one onto Genie's top. 'I found them on the Internet. I think we could sell these too. Perhaps even get our own made, with *Genie's* underneath.'

'I love it! What do you think?' Genie did a twirl for Ada.

'You look beautiful.' Ada gave her a big hug and stared

113

into the mirror with her, her smile wide and her eyes sparkling. The dress Genie wore was sleeveless and showed off arms toned from years of carrying plates of food. It was a warm blue, swooping wide across her chest and clinging to her curves. The pattern criss-crossed her bust and waist, accentuating her figure. She looked so sexy, with the hair straightening treatment that Ada had insisted she try, and her freshly painted red nails looked glossy and healthy. To one side of her hair was a sparkling slide with crystals glinting in the sunshine.

'Are you ready for our grand opening party?'

Genie took a deep breath and smiled, but it didn't quite reach her eyes. 'I wish Gramps and Mum and Dad were here,' she said. Ada hugged her fiercely and Genie felt tears brimming in her eyes. She bit her lip as she didn't want to ruin the skilfully-applied make up that Ada had done for her earlier.

'I wish my family was here to see this, too,' Ada said, brushing a stray tear from under Genie's eye and gently touching her cheek. 'We did a very quick turn-around. We could have easily picked a date when they could have come, but you didn't want to make Gus leave his cruise early. And then your grandmother had a nasty turn yesterday, so your mum and dad had to go back and stay with her. They were on their way. You know they'd have been here otherwise.' Ada picked up a lightweight summer sweater and folded it over her arm. 'They wanted to be here for you. Your grandma can't help being unwell.'

Genie's eyes narrowed and her mouth set in a thin line, and then they both burst out laughing. They had spent many nights over a bottle of wine discussing how many ideas Lucille could come up with to interfere with their lives. She'd called several times and demanded that Genie give up her 'silly' idea and move to Cornwall with her parents. She'd played the sickness card, and even tried emotional blackmail, saying her mother cried all the time without her. Genie's mum always sounded fairly happy when she spoke to her, so she knew this wasn't true. The old bat.

Genie straightened her back, put on some fresh red lipstick and then tucked it into her new silk handbag. Snapping the decorative clasp shut, she held out her elbow for Ada to link arms with her.

They took the lift down to reception, where Ralph, Toby and Bailey were waiting. Two of Toby's friends were being amazingly helpful and agreeing to be waiters for the night, even though Toby had been busy at work all week and none of them had much idea of how to wait tables.

Ada had roped them in, to Genie's embarrassment. She'd promised them all free food, not wages for the night. After sampling Genie's new recipes, they had all agreed! Seeing their faces as the lift doors opened, and hearing the appreciative comments on how beautiful the ladies were, Genie felt on top of the world. Not only did she have five gorgeous men and a new best friend to escort her to the opening of her fledgling business, they had finally managed to get it ready this morning after days of panicking that the paint wouldn't dry or the booths wouldn't be sanded in time. It had all come together. The restaurant now literally looked like you had been swept off the beach and deposited in a watery wonderland.

As they approached the restaurant, they could already see a crowd outside. Genie had invited all her old friends, and Ada had also put an announcement in the paper and had leaflets made, which she'd asked Bailey to deliver around town.

Genie hesitated for a moment, nervous. Supposing they all laughed at her or thought she looked stupid in her new clothes? What if they didn't like the way she'd moved the furniture to make it more sociable, or the secret back room they now had for her brand new idea of ice-cream teas?

But Ada was at Genie's side and didn't let her falter. The room had fresh fabrics and painted walls, but it also now had four different-sized tables with mis-matched chairs they had scoured the house and flat for. Each was beautiful in its own right and gave the room charm. The walls had undulating waves painted all over them, looking out to distant views. The mural artist was a master of her craft and Genie could easily have sat for hours gazing at the walls, pretending she was in a watery paradise. Genie hadn't wanted a white and grey box, she'd wanted a reflection of the coastline, to remember sunny days with her grandma and to show the world how beautiful this idyllic spot in Essex was.

Everything in the new restaurant sang of glamour and chic coastal style. With Ada's help it looked like something out of a movie, with booths along the right-hand side, reclaimed tables in the main space and a counter, also to the right. The kitchen was still behind this as they hadn't needed to change it, which had made a huge difference to their budget. There was a gap between the counters where you could see the new back room, but to the left of that as you looked in was Genie's pride and joy: her new ice cream bar.

She was starting with thirty flavours but was bursting with ideas for more. She had a bank for toppings and hot and cold sauces, and she had plans for her own waffle cones and ice cream bars. There was room in the centre to queue for ice creams and on either side were five small tables for people to sit and enjoy the view and savour their treats. To the right, just before the booths, were ten other tables for people who wanted food and gooey ice cream desserts. They could choose from the fresh or frozen cakes in the big counter, and just stop for tea and cake, or go all-out and have something from the scaled-back menu of daytime meals. She had picked the ones that had worked well for her family for years, but made them smaller in most cases. You could still buy fish and chips or the big breakfasts at *Genie's* but you could also pop in for a smaller bite.

Genie and Ada both looked at the crowd and grinned at each other. This was what they had planned for and now it was here, they might as well enjoy it. Seeing Fae and Una hovering on the outskirts of the crowd and feeling her heart swell that they had taken the time to turn up for her, Genie enjoyed seeing their heads craning to watch as she walked by, looking drop-dead gorgeous, with so many hot men on her arm. Genie wanted to rush over and ask if they liked everything they had seen so far, but with Toby's hand on her arm and Bailey's smiling face to her side, she just gave them a quick wave and then wafted past to open the doors and let everyone inside.

She hadn't wanted to do any ribbon cutting or speeches, as the ice creams should do that for her. She just needed her insides to stop churning and for the night to be a success.

As everyone surged inside her glittering empire, she tried to steady her nerves. She motioned for the boys to get a move on, for her chef to hand out food samples and she herself got behind her ice cream bar to begin selling her concoctions. The ice cream was the only thing not free tonight. If people wanted to try them, they had to donate any sum above a pound to the local sea life charity box on the counter. Genie knew how much they struggled for funding and, as they had always supported her, by putting her business cards in their window and now her shiny new leaflets on show, she was proud to be able to give something back – if anything sold. If it didn't, then she'd got fifty pounds from the cashpoint and would stuff that in the charity box to try and save her embarrassment. Seeing a crowd forming at her bar already, and watching Toby effortlessly flirt with all her customers, she grinned and leaned in to listen to her first order.

~

*a*da rubbed her sore feet and then hitched them up and put them on the seat next to her. She moved her head slowly from side to side to ease the ache that had set in. The evening had been an incredible success. Una and Fae had had their eyes out on stalks, but had sloped off after a couple of hours to meet their friends. They hadn't invited them to come along for Genie's big night, though. Genie ignored the pang of pain around her heart, as they had persuaded the last customer to leave at 1am – and it was a stranger. The group of helpers all collapsed into chairs. Ralph brought out three bottles of champagne and some flute glasses, which had tiny waves around the base as if they were spun from air, they were so delicate.

'Where did you get those from?' asked Genie with a laugh, taking a glass and then looking in awe at the fine stem as if frightened she might break it.

She looked rosy-cheeked and her face was alive with happiness for the first time in a long while.

'I snuck them in earlier, while you were both getting ready. They're a present from me and the boys.' Genie's mouth dropped open into a big O and Ada was stunned too.

'We can't accept them. They're so beautiful. They'll get broken.'

'Of course you can. I know you are thinking of catering for special clients in the back room and we thought something a bit different that went with your glamorous but time-less theme was called for. If they get broken, so be it. They are for you to use.'

Genie turned the glass and light spiralled across the

surface. Ralph filled hers, then did the same for everyone. 'I know you didn't want to make a speech, Genie,' he cleared his throat and looked around. 'But I for one am very proud of what you've achieved here. Even though I haven't known you for that long, I'm amazed at what you've done here tonight and I wish you success with your business.' Genie's eyes filled with tears and she blinked them away and jumped up and hugged Ralph, then Bailey and everyone else, especially Ada.

'To *Genie's*', said Ada, holding up her glass.

'To *Genie's*,' everyone repeated, raising glasses and sipping the sparkling liquid, before they all slumped back into their seats, grinning at each other again at a job well done.

As they all walked home, Toby grabbed Genie and pulled her into the bushes while the others walked on without noticing. He gave her a thorough kissing, and then grinned and pulled a business card out of his pocket and pushed it into her hand. He kissed the side of her throat where her dress dipped low and then sighed and reluctantly led her back onto the road behind the others, as if nothing had happened. Genie was stunned to silence and probably looked gormless, so she quickly rearranged her face, as if handsome men passionately kissed her every day of her life.

She gave him a cheeky wink and grabbed his hand as they hurried along to catch everyone up. She could feel the fizz from both the champagne and the kisses buzzing through her veins, and she knew that this was one night that she wouldn't forget... ever!

CHAPTER TWENTY-FOUR

*M*illy was seething. Her mother had done it again! They had been an hour into their journey back to see Genie and to support her on her big night, when her dad had called to say her mother had had a fall. They'd rushed back, but Milly instantly knew it was a ruse. She'd then sent James off to call Genie and explain the situation to her. Then Milly had confronted her mother, and demanded to know what was going on, before she blew a fuse and started screaming at someone.

Her mum had actually cowered away in her bed, but Milly didn't care. She knew something was up. She'd worked out her mum wasn't as ill as she was pretending to be, just as Genie had always tried to tell her. Between what James had done, and now her mother's manipulation, she felt like her life was in ruins. Milly had been emotionally blackmailed by an evil old woman, but that was going to stop, right now. Her mum had got her there by promising she would help Milly come to terms with her past, but so far, as usual, Milly was on her own.

Milly and James had signed the papers for the new business and flat, and it did feel good to have a smaller business that was already successful. It was also far enough away from her mother, just out of walking distance. Milly hadn't met all the staff yet, as two were on holiday, but they would be back soon and she would re-interview them for their posts. Their CVs were exemplary, so Milly couldn't see why there would be a problem.

The business and staff ran the café so well that Milly and James could try and rebuild the trust he'd smashed to smithereens when she'd caught him kissing her best friend Trudie. Who knew what else would have happened, if Milly hadn't found out? It was the reason he'd agreed to follow her to Cornwall, and the only condition she would stay with him to try and work things out. Trudie, like the coward she was, had immediately booked herself a month long holiday to visit family. It was a good job because if Milly had seen her, she would have grabbed her by the hair, dragged her down the street and very loudly told anyone who would listen what a tramp she was.

Milly had raged and cried and tried to protect Genie from what he'd done, but in the end James had been the one to persuade her that it was a good idea for them to leave and start afresh. Her mum being ill had galvanised them into action, when in fact she had been prepared to leave James. Milly knew that Genie was confused and probably blamed her for all this, but she was determined to make a new family business for them all and hoped that would persuade Genie to join them again.

Milly pined for her child so much that her heart ached. She even missed her temper tantrums and colourful swearing when she was annoyed. How she hadn't broken a toe in all these years from kicking defenceless plant pots, was beyond comprehension.

Hearing her mother cough, Milly tried to reign in her anger and turned to face her. 'Well?'

Milly was shocked to see tears in her mum's eyes. In all the years she'd known her, she didn't think she'd ever seen her mum cry. She brought many other people to tears, but never spent an ounce of extra emotion on anyone. She was cold and uncaring. Milly was sure it was why she and her sister had never bonded properly. They were too busy competing for her mother's love, which never seemed to come without conditions.

'It's time you knew the truth.'

'The truth about what?'

'The truth about what happened when you were sixteen.'

Milly's face turned white and she grabbed onto the nearest chair for support. 'I know what happened when I was sixteen.'

'No, Milly. You don't.'

CHAPTER TWENTY-FIVE

*O*ver the next few weeks, Genie was upset that she barely heard from her parents, but she didn't have too much time to worry about it as she was rushed off her feet with her ice cream, making new recipes at night and selling out by day.

Genie was reminded of the days when people had queued for her grandma's ice-creams, as there was now a steady line for them from about eleven onwards. The breakfasts were also selling well. People often lingered to enjoy a speciality coffee from Genie's big new machine that whizzed up perfect cappuccinos and lattes in no time.

Genie's latest idea was to put a tiny block of ice cream into people's saucers alongside their coffees. It was a way of testing her recipes. People seemed to love the fresh hit of ice and then the creamy smoothness of their coffees. They were a bit like a delicious ice cream-filled chocolate. Customers had begun to ask if she could make selections of them for dinner parties, to wow their guests after the meal. Genie was tempted, but for now knew she had to concentrate on her normal ice creams.

They had set up the back room for ice cream teas, but Genie was reluctant to open that up just yet. She needed a way to keep the ice creams from melting and was still scouring the internet for exactly the right thing to help. For now, she'd just have to stick to serving the ices when they did open.

She had employed Bailey full time and he and his family had moved into the flat upstairs. He still made her hot under the collar every time he looked at her, but she was his boss now and she tried to keep it professional.

She had been surprised to find out that his son, Liam, was already three years old. Bailey's parents looked after the little boy during the day while Bailey worked, and they were together at night. Genie was impressed to see a young man take on such responsibility. He was kind, a hard worker, and just needed a break – and for someone to give him a job where he could be nearby for his son. Bailey was ecstatic with the new arrangement and told Genie it took the weight of the world from his shoulders, which almost brought a tear to her eye and made her want to kiss him.

Bailey went over and above his pay grade to make sure everything was perfect for every customer. He was an absolute gem. Genie discovered he'd dropped out of school to look after his son, before his parents had stepped in. As a result, he hadn't passed his exams. But he was a fast learner. She didn't have any qualifications either, but here she was, a business owner. If she could do it, so could Bailey. He needed someone to invest time in training him and to give him a chance – and not fantasise about licking his body every time he walked past. Genie told herself she really should get out more. She was a professional and not the kind the council had suggested back when she'd added a few red lights to the restaurant.

She enjoyed seeing Bailey's smile every day and they had

become friends, with a frisson of something else always under the surface. She felt she was too old for him anyway, being twenty-two to his nineteen, but they'd both had to grow up early and this gave them a common bond. He'd told her how exhausting his life had been, learning how to change nappies and dealing with teething and toddler tantrums as a single parent, but he was surviving. Genie hadn't pried about his son's mother. She hoped he'd trust her enough to tell her sometime.

Trudie had returned from her holiday, tanned and even more glamorous than ever, and had been in a few times to ask if Bailey was free to work, which he wasn't. She always appeared sad these days and asked after Genie's mum and dad a lot. She had been really close to Milly, so Genie could understand how she felt.

Trudie had bags under her eyes, probably from too much partying, which she disguised with slightly heavy make-up. Genie made time for her, even though she was often rushed off her feet. That's what friends did for each other. Genie's eyes had been opened about the people working along the seafront. She'd always got on well with them, but she now understood that she had more friends than she'd ever realised before. It didn't matter if they were different ages. They looked out for each other and she could rely on them, as they could rely on her. Who needed the Faes and Unas of this world, she kept asking herself.

Her life fell into pattern of working furiously during the day, with barely time to draw breath, and nights spent with Ada, developing recipes and chatting about their business. Ada teased her about how Bailey's eyes followed her around the restaurant like a lovesick puppy, but Genie brushed it off. She didn't really have time to sleep, let alone start a new relationship with a younger man, however sparkly his eyes were when he offered to make her a cup of tea, or how firm his muscles looked when he picked up a table to move it for her.

Genie loved hearing about Ada's family, but mostly Ada changed the subject as if it hurt her. Genie had spoken to Ada's husband, Ned, once in the restaurant, but felt the couple didn't need anyone else and were in their own little bubble, so she hadn't disturbed them. Now she understood more, she felt so sad for what her friend was suffering, missing the love of her life.

Genie realised Ada needed to heal for a while. She felt worried about how she would cope, if Ada suddenly decided that this life was too mundane for her and jetted back home, but for now she was clinging onto her and didn't want to let go, however selfish that seemed.

Despite this, Genie was much stronger lately and she was fizzing inside about how successful they had become in a short space of time. She recognised that she couldn't rest on her laurels, though, and that things might quickly change once the novelty wore off. She intended to be inventive, like her grandad, but hopefully in a much more successful way. She would concoct new flavours and treats for her customers and entice them back time and time again.

Genie loved being with Ada, but even she couldn't fill the gap her granddad and parents had left in her life. Her parents used to call every night, but recently they were too busy. Her mum was distant and Genie could once again feel that there was something she wanted to tell her. If Genie hadn't been so exhausted from her own worries, then she'd have probed further, but for now she had to leave it.

Her dad invited her to visit and sounded like he was almost pleading with her. She did smile at that because he was probably wishing he'd stood up to her mum and Lucille and stayed put. It was his own fault for being such a pushover and Genie felt the anger that she tried so hard to keep a lid on bubble up inside. He sounded like he was missing her terribly, but she wanted him to suffer for what he'd put her through and she wouldn't make it that easy for him. She couldn't go right now anyway. She would make them wait and experience a little of the pain she'd lived through.

She'd told him how well she was doing, but perhaps he assumed it couldn't be true, after all the tricks he himself had tried and failed with. She would show him! He'd sounded really disappointed when she pointed out she couldn't leave the restaurant. But it was time she let them get on with their own lives. It was also time that she began to truly live hers.

She pictured Toby and Bailey and realised that, not only did she have a viable business all of a sudden, but her romantic life had become a million times more interesting too. Perhaps she had overlooked the fact that men might actually like her looks and figure before. Maybe men liked big boobs and bums, and she didn't need to be stick-thin to attract someone? She had never seen herself as sexy or a man magnet before, but now she grinned to herself and stuck out her chest, giggling at the thought of men vying for her attention. She was a serious business owner now and men would never take precedence over that, but perhaps she could find time for a few more of those delicious kisses – and maybe even reboot her sex life!

CHAPTER TWENTY-SIX

*G*enie rubbed sleep from her eyes and gingerly eased out of bed. Making new stock all night and selling it all day was taking its toll. She'd almost yelled at Bailey yesterday at the restaurant for dropping a tray of ice cream but had bitten her tongue and gone outside and yelled at the evil pigeon instead. He'd squawked and pooed all over the shed roof in protest at her waking him up from a deep sleep.

She'd turned around to see a gorgeous pair of big brown eyes staring intently at her over the gate. Bailey's son Liam was on his tippy-toes and holding on to the fence they'd put up between the restaurant and the flat, so that they both had a small square of garden. She'd grinned and tapped his nose before his grandma had come outside and scooped him up into her arms with a grin and a kiss on Genie's cheek. They had become like one big family over the last few weeks and Brenda had even offered to pop down and help if they needed her when her grandson started his play group. He'd wanted to give Genie a kiss on the cheek too and Genie smiled at the memory before lugging herself up and throwing on a grey vest top and fitted jogging bottoms.

She was actually quite pleased as she slid them on. They used to be tight, but now they skimmed her hips and lovingly clung to her curves in a comfortable way. She knew that although she was always tired, she looked like a regular woman now and not someone who had been dragged through a wet hedge backwards and then spat out by the sea. These days she was groomed and felt quite sexy in her figure-hugging uniform of blue jeans and a red chequered blouse that she often tied under her ample bosom.

She had never dreamt that the ice creams would sell so well, so quickly. She had planned with Ada that they would build the custom up gradually, but already there were queues out of the door. Genie needed to upscale fast or face angry customers. They were already talking about taking on another member of staff and opening up the back room. Genie was worn out, but exhilarated. It was the stuff of dreams, and she was finally living hers. She could imagine Vera looking down on her and smiling and that made her determined to keep up the momentum.

She was too tired to go out with Una and Fae, though she was desperate to make more of an effort and see them regularly out of the work environment. They had popped in once after the opening and she'd been pleased to see them, but as soon as she'd sat down for a second at their table, they had grilled her about Bailey, giggling behind their menus and batting their eyelashes at him. He'd smiled back and Genie had beckoned him over and introduced them, but he'd been the epitome of professionalism. He had said hello, welcomed them to *Genie's*, and then taken their order, whisked the plates off the next table and disappeared into the kitchen. He'd probably hidden there for a while and rolled his eyes at their blatant ogling. Genie felt offended for him and then winced, as she recalled drooling over him herself on more than one occasion.

Genie's stomach had ached again. She'd really wanted to impress her friends. Not with her hot staff, but with how much she'd achieved on her own. They hadn't seemed to notice her dazzling new design layout and short but incredible menu. They didn't ask to try her ice creams. All they did was wink yet again at Bailey before going home. Genie had gone from trying to impress her parents by being the perfect child, to trying to impress her friends by being the perfect businesswoman. Neither worked, it seemed.

But she couldn't be downcast, walking into the kitchen of Ada's penthouse flat and smiling at the beautiful sight of the sea kissing the shore. There were already a few joggers and early morning swimmers out there.

She moved towards the counter to make some coffee, and then stopped in her tracks, her mouth dropping open in shock before she snapped it back up, her cheeks flushing. Coming out of Ada's room was a half-naked Adonis!

Genie didn't know where to look but her eyes were practically scanning every muscle. It would be impossible not to. Genie knew Ada was lonely and had promised her to start getting out more, but not like this.

Genie fleetingly wondered if he was a gigolo and mentally pictured her bank balance for a second to see if she could afford him, then stamped on her own foot to stop her thoughts from being so outrageous. She yelped in pain and he grinned perfectly white teeth at her. She needed to sit on her hands to stop them reaching out to him. She hadn't known men like this existed. She was pretty sure she was panting audibly as she stood there.

She rushed over to the kitchen table to put space between them, then realised this wasn't a good idea. It cut off the view of his lower half and made him look naked! He was still smiling at her and she blinked and wondered if she'd drunk more than she realised the previous evening and was hallucinating a fantasy that she had never even known she was capable of dreaming up.

When he moved towards her to take her hand, she shook her head to try and clear it. Then a red veil of anger filled her vision at him for taking advantage of an old lady. Surely he must be after her money, with that massive age gap? She ignored his hand and raised her eyebrows in question about why he was there, but that just seemed to amuse him further and he then began opening cupboards to find cups and tea and flicked the switch on the kettle as if he owned the place.

'Would you mind putting a T-shirt on?' she asked very politely, through gritted teeth.

He halted in reaching around her for two mugs that were sitting on the counter top, and his arm brushed across hers. The hairs on her forearm stood up and she jumped, trying to move back without falling off the stool she had pulled out and plonked her bottom on.

'Does my chest offend you in some way?' His soft kissable mouth was wide and smiling and his eyes were sparkling into hers, but she narrowed her gaze and pressed her nails into her palms to stop thoughts of reaching out to touch his tanned skin. He hadn't backed off and she needed some space. He was far too sure of himself and she didn't like it one bit. Poor Ada!

She drew in a breath and steadied herself on the stool, then slipped down and stood in front of him, chest to chest. 'Not at all,' she said, looking at his pert nipples and then raising her eyes back to his. 'I just thought you might be cold?'

He laughed and turned to walk back to the sofa, picking up a worn blue T-shirt thrown on the back of it. He pulled it over his head. His muscles bunched as he did this and she tried not to be caught staring, but her pulse was racing as if she'd just worked a twelve-hour shift.

The kettle clicked off and he walked over to make the tea, pouring hot water into the mugs and looking round for the fridge. She smugly enjoyed watching his search, as it was hidden behind a tall fitted cupboard. 'Want one?' he asked her.

'No thanks. I'll wait for the coffee to warm up.' She motioned towards the percolating coffee pot and went to sit back down. He shrugged his shoulders, located the milk and took the two mugs of tea back into Ada's bedroom, closing the door behind him. Genie was fuming. How dare he use an older woman that way? There must be a good thirty years or more between them.

Genie eyed up a big plant pot outside on the deck with a tall leafy shrub inside it. But she thought better of it. She had really tried her luck with kicking things. From now on she was going to behave like a lady and not take her frustrations out on innocent greenery. If she was this worked up by a few admittedly smoking-hot muscles, then maybe it was about time she got a real boyfriend, and not one she'd just imagined.

Genie sat with her hands round her scalding coffee and watched the clock on the wall. She'd have to get ready for work soon, but she'd be blowed if she'd leave that predator in with Ada. After thirty minutes of restlessly staring with laser eyes at Ada's bedroom door, she wondered if she could train her evil pigeon to poo on command. Then he could fly above, and target the gigolo as soon as he left the building. She sighed quickly, washed out her still-full mug and left it on the draining board. Taking a glance out to sea at the view that had soothed her soul earlier, she scowled and stuck her tongue out at it. Then she stomped into her bedroom and slammed the door, which was unsatisfying as it had an expensive soft-close fitting, so it just swooshed shut.

She thrust her legs into her jeans and grabbed a fresh blouse from her mirrored wardrobe. She fleetingly thought how fired up she looked and remembered how she used to fight with her mum and dad. She'd quite enjoyed the odd battle of wills and if this man, however sexy he was, thought he could just turn up and hoodwink such a wonderful lady as Ada, then he'd have a battle on his hands. A couple of piercing blue eyes you could drown in and lickable skin wouldn't be enough to win over a stalwart singleton like Genie, however randy she might suddenly feel. In fact she hadn't realised how desperate she was, or how much of a dried up old prune her friends must see her as, until right now. She'd show him. She'd show them all.

Picking up her bag and checking her phone to see what time it was, she gasped and realised that she'd have to jog the short distance to work if she wanted to be there on time. Then she remembered she was the boss, with staff to open up for her. Still rushing along, she left Ada a note asking her to meet her at work as soon as she surfaced from bed. As she left, Genie listened out quickly for any disgusting rumpy-pumpy noises from Ada's room. Feeling like a voyeur she shut the door behind her, pressing the button for the lift and trying to focus her mind on her day's work and not that glorious behind she'd seen in those fitted jeans.

CHAPTER TWENTY-SEVEN

*A*da arrived at work, flushed and with a twinkle in her eye, but Genie was rushed off her feet with the tail end of their breakfast orders and now it was practically lunchtime, so there wasn't a moment to chat.

Ada saw how manic it was and took over so that Genie could get back to the ice cream stall, which had just begun to fill up. They were offering new sweet lunches of waffles with crispy bacon and maple syrup, and brioche with eggs.

Everything Genie did was made without additives, and they had a range of gluten free, vegan, and specialist dishes that were fresh and organic. Most people with food intolerances could eat them. The new menu turned out to be so popular that she'd had to make the decision that morning to employ someone on a part-time basis to serve the food, while she concentrated on the ice cream stand.

She was still determined to make her own cones when she had time, but for now she'd bought in ones that were similar to her idea, but without the swirls and sprinkles. People seemed to love them anyway. She wanted to add a patisserie range too, but she couldn't source all of that now.

The business was evolving into a hip and happening place to be, and she was bursting with pride.

As soon as they could afford it, she wanted to offer gooey ice cream sundaes with decadent cakes for high tea. She'd also have low fat options with yogurt and reduced sugar, so that her customers didn't feel they had to hold back from treating themselves to what she'd already heard them call 'a slice of heaven'.

The yummy mummy crowd had begun to visit during the day and then come back again after school with their children for an ice cream and a play on the seafront. There were lots of pretty benches along the outer edge of the shoreline by the sea, so that mums and dads could watch their children playing on the sand and sit and enjoy a takeaway coffee or ice cream from *Genie's*.

She'd ordered branded takeaway cups with her logo, and enjoyed seeing people amble along chatting while sipping from one. The restaurant was almost bursting at the seams with customers already, yet there had been relatively small changes so far – a lick of paint, some elbow grease, a new logo and a streamlined menu.

She lifted her head to smile at a group of customers and overheard them comment on how much more welcoming the venue was now, and how good the food was, too. She felt proud but still cringed inwardly at how her precious family business must have appeared recently. Perhaps they had all looked as tired as the décor. She felt an ache in her heart as she pictured her parents opening the doors to their little café in Cornwall, and staring at a different sea view, perhaps with some of the renewed vigour that Genie felt. She pushed the thought aside and stood up straight. Now was not the time to be weak, when she had customers to serve and a gigolo to eject from her flat.

When she finally managed to grab her breath and rest her

aching back on the doorframe of the kitchen, she looked around at her happily-chatting clientele and wished with all her heart that her parents could see the restaurant now. Hearing a familiar laugh to her left, she saw Ada sitting having a tall glass of iced tea with some customers. Genie grinned as the older woman charmed them all. People loved her.

They had decided Ada would be front-of-house when she was there. The role of hostess was perfect for her. It worked like a dream and she had them eating out of her hand. She was a natural people person. Genie began to fret a little as, if Ada's charm bought in more people, they might be in trouble. They could barely cope with the customers they had. They needed a new chef, but she wanted one who could bake and so far she hadn't found the right person. She could also open up the back room, but that would just mean more work.

All the restaurants along the stretch of road next to *Genie's* were benefitting from their extra custom, as Genie sometimes had to turn away business. She hadn't seen much of Trudie, but when she had, Trudie was still missing her mum and dad, and asked about every detail of their new lives.

The other restaurant and shop owners were grateful for the increase in footfall and some had even begun their own refurbishments and slight adjustments to age-old traditions, whilst still keeping the ethos of their business. Very gradually, the tides were changing and everyone was well aware of the part Genie had played in their improved fortunes. They made sure she knew she was part of the wider family, even though her parents had deserted her, and said they would all be there for her no matter what, unlike her own kin. She winced every time someone told her that. She knew they meant well, but they might as well shove her on the floor and kick her in the ribs.

Their support made Genie glad one moment and sad the next. She did appreciate them, but not a single one of them had listened to her before, when she'd tried to reason that all of the restaurants needed to make changes. For now she'd just have to be grateful that it had happened, even though it often felt like the weight of responsibility for all of them had dropped squarely on her shoulders.

CHAPTER TWENTY-EIGHT

*A*da really enjoyed chatting to customers and feeling useful again. The hulking great surprise she'd discovered on her doorstep last night had also made her feel re-energised and full of mischief. She hadn't expected to see him so soon, but now that she had, she felt that she could face her past again.

As soon as the last customer left, Genie sat down next to Ada in the booth and propped her feet up. She was wearing black flip-flops and her toes were painting a daring red. It matched her uniform checked shirt and jeans. With her dashing new haircut and trim figure from all of the rushing about she was doing, she could give the movie stars of the 1940s a run for their money in the glamour stakes. Either that, or she looked as though she should be lounging on a chaise lounge being fed grapes by cherubs while someone painted her.

Genie didn't quite have the demeanour of the women in Rubenesque paintings, though. Ada had had to tell her off for swearing in the kitchen, when she'd dropped a batch of cakes. She wasn't as quiet as Ada had first thought and it had been lucky that it was early morning and the customers hadn't heard Genie's colourful language.

Ada was never quite sure what language it was. It sounded Spanish, but Ada was pretty sure that Genie didn't speak another language. Genie wasn't used to being this busy and they needed more help. Ada knew what had happened to Calvin and didn't want Genie to have to go through that too, although Cal's suffering was his own stupid fault. He should have listened to her advice, but he was too far in by then, and it was inevitable, she supposed.

Bailey came out of the kitchen and placed a foaming hot chocolate with a generous dollop of sprinkles in front of Genie. She beamed a smile up at him in thanks and Ada enjoyed seeing Bailey grin back, eyes sparkling, before going into the kitchen to begin washing down for the night.

'I think you've got an admirer.'

Genie frowned and looked around, then her bright blue eyes fell on the hot chocolate. Instead of the girl of a few weeks ago, who would have fallen off her chair and flushed bright red, Genie now shrugged and smiled, taking a spoonful of cream and sighing in pleasure as the flavour hit her taste buds.

Genie licked her lips and went to take another mouthful, before stopping and thinking. Then she stared at Ada, as if trying to work something out. 'We need a new staff member... and I've been working up the courage to find the right way to bring up the sex god in our kitchen this morning.'

Ada's mouth hung open in shock, but then she burst out laughing and clapped her hands in glee. 'I've got the perfect solution! My sex god can help us out.'

'What?' said Genie with a horrified look on her face.

'He's a patisserie chef, and it would mean he could spend more time with me. You look like you've swallowed a fly,

Genie,' she said happily. Genie's face paled. She was staring over Ada's shoulder, so Ada turned to see what had caught her eye.

Genie put her hand on the table as if she was about to jump up, but the sex god they'd just been discussing reached Ada first and kissed her cheek warmly, eyeing Genie with amusement. Her cheeks, from being pale, were now suddenly flaming. He settled himself down next to Ada, uninvited. Ada was just so glad to see him. She threw her arms around him and hugged him hard, kissing his cheek. How she'd missed him, even though he was a ball of uncontrolled energy. He was so like his father.

Genie suddenly seemed like she was about to blow a fuse and Ada couldn't help enjoying herself. She could only imagine the thoughts going through her head. Ada saw Genie accidentally-on-purpose kick out at the 'god' under the table. He squeaked in surprise but then grinned at her wolfishly, trying to turn on the charm. Ada chuckled. That wouldn't work with Genie. She had little sense of self-worth at the moment and would assume he was playing her.

Meanwhile, Genie rudely ignored the newcomer. Ada reasoned that the poor girl was a bit confused about men at the moment. She'd probably decided Toby was only after one thing, and that Bailey was too young for her. In fact, the two men were just a few years apart in age, and both were so charming. But now Ada had complicated matters by throwing the 'sex god' into the mix. She smiled to herself. *This really was all so amusing.*

Toby had actually phoned to speak to Genie a few times, but she'd been too busy to return his calls. Ada would have to give her a stern talking-to. She appreciated they needed to work hard here, but there would soon be enough staff to cope with Genie having a life of her own – and if she didn't pay attention, it might walk on by.

Genie leaned across the table and whispered to Ada that working with the man in front of her wasn't a good idea, and they couldn't afford him in the long term. 'Afford him?' Ada was confused now. 'He'd do it for love, wouldn't you, Calvin?'

Genie almost spat out her drink and a gleam came into Calvin's eye as she coughed. He swapped seats and slipped an arm around Genie's back to pat and then rub between her shoulder blades until she shook him off. He looked like he was really enjoying this, the naughty child. 'For you, Ada, anything!' he said to her. 'It looks like a good business you've bought into.'

Genie gasped in horror that Ada had told him private details about their deal and her cheeks flamed even more. Ada was confused by her reaction, but Genie hissed across the table to enlighten her. 'You want to bring a total stranger into the business?'

Ada looked from one to the other. 'Calvin told me you'd met this morning?'

'Oh, we did…' he smiled into Genie's eyes, and she looked like she wanted to kick him again.

'We passed each other in the kitchen when he was half-naked and coming out of your bedroom,' said Genie pointedly. Ada took a minute to digest this and then burst out laughing. She'd have to warn him about Genie's temper. Calvin seemed to find this highly amusing too.

'Oh you've made my year,' said Ada. 'You think I have enough energy for a man like Cal? He's my grandson, but I'm guessing from the fact you're upset and he's enjoying himself so much that he didn't tell you that?'

Genie almost choked on her hot chocolate this time and Cal sat back and enjoyed the reaction, then picked up her hand and patted it patronisingly, as if she were a dog. Ada could see now that Genie had been pushed far enough and that if Cal didn't cut it out she'd get up and bite his ass.

141

'Look,' said Ada after she'd finished her third bout of giggles. She'd tried so hard not to laugh but she just hadn't been able to stop. 'You've always dreamed of making this place your own, and we're already full to capacity. We're getting there, but we need more help – and Cal's a trained chef,' her eyes pleading with Genie to give it a try. Her shoulders still bobbed up and down. It must be the release of tension, finally having someone from her own family around and finding she was actually enjoying it. But she was also desperate for Genie and Cal to get on. The way Genie was looking at him, it was a wonder he didn't burst into flames right in front of them.

CHAPTER TWENTY-NINE

*G*enie felt mutinous, then doubtful as her eyes narrowed at Ada and Cal. Would someone this beautiful want to spend his days up to his eyeballs in flour? Plus the restaurant was fairly small, and he'd fill the whole kitchen with his masculine energy. Even Bailey seemed like a midget in comparison.

Genie had visions of him muscling in and her being pushed out. Perhaps he was a beach bum or a rich mummy's boy. If he was Ada's grandson, then one of her sons was his dad. Genie tried to recall which it was, then realised it must be the one who'd married the supermodel, as this Calvin looked to be in his mid to late twenties. And he was also gorgeous.

She tried to stop staring, but he still had an arm behind her on the back of the booth and the hairs on her neck were standing on end. Her temper flared. She could see how much this meant to Ada, but she wasn't about to be outnumbered. 'I'm in charge here, so he'd have to accept minimum wage and do an interview. If he's good enough, then we can consider it.'

Cal exchanged glances with Ada and they both sniggered like children, which made Genie even madder. She took a calming breath and purposely banged back into his arm, making him jolt in surprise. Then she turned and glared straight into his eyes. Surely he was mega rich, like Ada, used to living on yachts and drinking sunbeams caught by angels. 'Why would you want to work in a little place like this, if you're a trained chef? It's not a tourist hot-spot, or full of supermodels. It's not very glamorous.' Ada gave her a reproving stare for being a bitch and Genie had the grace to hang her head for a moment. But it was his fault for turning up here and rocking their perfectly calm boat.

Ada spoke for him. 'Cal told me this morning that he's decided to stay around for a while. Isn't that exciting?'

Genie was stunned to silence. She'd assumed he would only be around for a few weeks maximum and this would be a temporary arrangement. Then she'd never have to set eyes on his pretty face again. For some reason he really got on her nerves. It must be his smug expression, or the way he seemed to know what she was thinking before she did. It was so annoying. 'Uh... not really. Where will he stay?'

'In the spare room.'

'He's moving in?' Genie jumped up, knocking his arm onto his lap. He was blocking her exit from the booth, so she tried to climb over him. Then she realised he might enjoy that a little too much, so she shoved his shoulder, which he didn't move. Then she pointedly glared at him until he sighed and finally let her out. She stood shakily at the end of the table. 'I can make myself scarce and give you some privacy. I'm sure Gramps wouldn't mind if I stayed at his place until he gets back from his cruise.'

'No,' said Ada and Calvin in unison.

'Don't let me intrude,' said Cal. 'You were living there first. But it means I can keep an eye on you both,' he said smoothly, but Genie sensed an undertone to his words. She frowned and then she had a light bulb moment. He thought she was ripping off his grandmother and he'd flown in to protect Ada.

Genie wanted to stamp on his feet. How dare he assume that without even knowing her? Then her anger subsided a little as she realised she'd definitely thought the same of him. If he needed a job so desperately, then something had gone wrong in his life. Well, if he thought he could muscle in and take her family business, he'd better think again. She smiled evilly at him and his eyebrows rose, but he didn't comment.

Ada got up and clapped her hands again. Genie hoped that wouldn't become a habit. 'It's all settled, then. We can go back to the flat and make plans.' She kissed Genie's cheek and patted her arm and then said she was going to talk to Bailey about locking up, before he went upstairs to look after Liam for the night.

Genie's eyes followed Ada's progress, and as soon as she disappeared from view, turned back to Cal. He wasn't laughing now. 'Why did you call her Ada this morning and not Gran?'

'She said Gran makes her feel old, plus you didn't seem to know who I was, so I thought I'd try and work you out.' He stood up and towered over her five foot seven inch frame.

He leaned down and whispered in her ear, his warm breath caressing her neck. 'I'm watching you.'

She looked up and her gaze didn't waver from his. 'I'm watching you too. Don't think you can waltz in here and take over. This is my family business and I own it.' For some reason he seemed to find this quite funny. *The git.*

CHAPTER THIRTY

*I*t was a Monday and their only day of rest, but Genie was in the restaurant kitchen with Cal. It had been an uncomfortable night knowing he was in the room next door, probably naked. As much as she didn't want to imagine him stripping off and sliding between the fresh cotton sheets, her mind seemed to have gone off on a tangent of its own.

'Right. You'd like to work here as a pastry chef? We have a chef for the daily menu, but I can't run the ice cream bar on my own. We need to get the cost of supplies down and increase our patisserie selection.' She waved her arm across the ingredients she'd put out, some of which didn't belong together at all, but she wanted him to fail.

He looked at them and grinned at her, as if he knew what she was up to and would play along for now. She snarled slightly and told him to get on with it. She'd already asked him about his credentials when they'd spoken over coffee earlier that morning. He'd worked for a man with a funny name that she kind of recognised, but would have to search for on the internet. It wouldn't have been cool to do that in front of him, so she pretended to know who he was, but tried for an unimpressed air, so he wouldn't think the job was in the bag before he'd even shown her his cooking skills.

He had said he'd been unemployed for a year, so she felt much happier about the awful wage package she could offer him, even mentally taking a little off it. She would be doing him a favour, it seemed. He obviously couldn't get work where he lived.

She wandered around aimlessly, leaving him to cook, but then amazing fragrances wafted into the restaurant and she felt like a sniffer dog looking for a bone, as her nose led her straight back into the kitchen where he was pulling a selection of pastries out of the oven. She tried to control herself, but she must have made a noise. It was probably her teeth grinding. He looked up and they locked eyes for a moment. He placed the hot tray on the oven top and the picked up a bowl he had already begun to prepare with a delicious-looking nutty cream.

Calvin found a spoon from the counter top and dipped it into the mixture, scooping some up and offering her a taste. It seemed churlish to refuse. He was there for an interview, after all – but why did everything feel so sexual with him? She leaned forward and he put the spoon to her lips. The flavour almost made her groan out loud. The cream slid round the inside of her mouth while the nutty pieces, which had been caramelised, left a crunchy, sugary dust on her tongue. She swallowed and her eyes automatically went to the bowl to see if she could try some more. The air was filled with a sweet and sticky tang which made her even keener.

He laughed and filled the spoon again while she licked her lips and grinned back for the first time that day. 'What do they taste like?' she asked, pointing to the pastries and dainty little macaroons.

'I haven't filled them yet. They're too warm...' Before he

could finish his sentence, she had edged round him and bitten into the flaky pastry and was sighing in pleasure. She scooped up another spoonful of cream and jammed that into her mouth too, while his mouth dropped open in surprise.

'These are delicious,' she said through her mouthful of food, forgetting they were mortal enemies for a moment. 'Why are you here? Other than the obvious fact that you think I'm conning your grandma out of your inheritance, of course.'

Calvin spluttered on the mouthful of her ice cream he'd been filching from the freezer. 'Why are *you* here?' he countered, looking puzzled after tasting her flavours.

'This place has been in my family for generations. My grandparents made it their own, but now it's my time to shine,' she said, wanting to yell at him to mind his own bloody business. He was the one being interviewed, not her, but she had to tread carefully as he was her business partner's grandson.

'Where are they? Your parents and grandparents. Why aren't they still running the place with you?'

Genie scowled at him and he had the grace to look like he wished he hadn't opened his mouth, but he put the ice cream tub back and stood before her, his glance piercing.

'My Grandma died and my parents moved nearer to my mum's mum,' she said blandly, willing him to shut up.

'Why would they leave a family business? Ada said it was failing, but why did they leave you?' He seemed genuinely confused.

Ouch! Her temper ramped up a notch. 'None of your business. This is supposed to be a formal interview.'

'Maybe you scared them away with your bossiness?' he joked. 'It was a formal interview until you scoffed half of my work before it was finished. Look, have I got the job or not?'

'Do you honestly want a job here?' Genie looked at the remaining tray of baked goods longingly and wished she could sweep them all into her bag to eat in bed. At least some good would have come of this disastrous day then.

She felt uncomfortable being in close proximity to this man and she was sure he'd crept closer while she was eyeing up the cakes. She could almost feel his warm breath on her cheek and she pushed against the solid wall of his chest to gulp in some air and then wished she hadn't touched him, as it felt so good. She wondered if he'd notice if she slid her hand down to cup his backside and she bit her lip to stop that train of thought and winced in pain as she bit down too hard.

Cal paused for a fraction too long in his answer, but then caught her hand and pulled her nearer to the patisseries, to pass her one. 'I think it'll be fun.' He tilted the pastry to her lips and she had no choice but to bite into it and sigh. His eyes dilated as he watched her and she decided she might as well enjoy herself. She made a blissful mewing sound and took another bite, before he pinned her to the work bench with an arm either side and gently brushed a crumb from the edge of her mouth, his thumb touching her lips and making them open in surprise.

Genie's pulse began racing, but instead of leaning in to kiss her as she half expected, Calvin just tucked a stray hair behind her ear and turned to begin clearing up, as if nothing had happened.

She felt like she'd been holding her breath for an hour and quickly moved away into the restaurant to calm herself down. She'd really thought he was going to kiss her, but he had just been playing with her. He was probably used to woman throwing themselves at him. He'd soon find out that she had claws.

Genie wished again that she had female friends to turn to for advice about being in the vicinity of a sex god and staying sane, but she was alone as usual – and the best defence was to stay the hell away from him.

CHAPTER THIRTY-ONE

*C*al tried to regulate his breathing. He'd humoured her and done her silly baking test, but he'd got bored and played with her a little.

What he hadn't expected was the way his body responded when he was near her. When he'd had her pinned to the work bench, he'd wanted to duck down and taste the tiny dot of cream still on her lips. He'd held himself off as he knew it was a bad idea. His gran liked her and she seemed happy here, even though he was going to break it all up and bring Ada back home to the family. That was the plan he'd made with his parents and he intended to honour it. They'd done so much for him in the aftermath of his business failing. He'd felt ashamed, but they'd made him dust himself off and carry on. He'd taken some time out travelling, learning new cooking skills from far-flung places. He'd ended up in Australia, but had finally realised that it was time to go home. He'd sort out this mess with Ada and help her see she would be far happier in America.

He knew he'd overstepped the mark when Genie's big blue eyes had filled with tears. He had only done the interview to try and find out more about her, but now realised there was a bigger story here. He hadn't seriously wanted the job. He was a professional chef and he couldn't remember the last time he'd worked in a kitchen this small, although looking round he'd been surprised at how well equipped and clinically clean it was. He'd found most of the tools he'd needed and had gone all-out to impress her. His plan had been to seduce her with his body until she trusted him and told him what her plans were with his gran. It seemed that offering her a few pastries would work even better. So much for his boyish charm.

Ada was really vulnerable at the moment after losing his granddad, and Cal felt the usual kick in the guts every time he pictured Ned's laughing face or recalled the low timbre of his voice. His granddad had always ruffled Cal's hair and gently punched him on the shoulder in jest, even though Cal had been bigger than him for years.

Ada had told him that Genie's grandmother used to run this place and made incredible ice cream. From what he'd seen and tasted, Genie had the same gift. The restaurant could be a goldmine. It was situated in a perfect location and, if she got the concept right, then she would be set up for life. It looked like she was heading that way already. Her parents were mad to have let it get so run down and then left it, whatever the reason. This didn't excuse Genie for brow-beating his grandmother into investing, though. She'd taken advantage of an old woman who was grieving, and he intended to make her pay somehow.

He had initially thought about ruining the business, but now he was here, he could see that it was going to be successful. So why not help his gran to make money out of it? Genie was probably too stupid to know how to make serious money. He could change all that. He'd learnt the hard way from losing his own investment. Then the restaurant would be too much for her, and she'd beg them to buy her out. Ada could sell the building and make a fortune. It was prime real estate.

He'd have some fun making Genie pay for using his gran first, though. Her fitted tops and sashaying hips begged his eyes to follow them, and now he couldn't stop. It was beginning to get on his nerves. Living with her and smelling the scent of her hair every day didn't help either, as he was sure she lathered it in coconut, which made him salivate while his hands itched to reach out and touch her. But he couldn't. Sleeping with her would just make things messier. He wasn't about to move out, though. He'd make her want to leave first.

He would back off, but he was determined to find out why her family had left in such a rush. Now he checked where Genie was. He saw she had wandered into the garden behind the shop. She was talking over the fence to a little boy of about three or four. Her face had lit up and her eyes were sparkling as the lad showed her a shell he'd probably found on the beach. There was a pigeon sitting on the shed roof and it seemed to be leaning in and listening to their conversation, which was weird. He tapped out a number on his phone, never taking his eyes off Genie, and quickly explained to the person who answered what he wanted them to do.

∼

A week later, Cal sat down in shock. It was his own fault for digging into things that were none of his business, but it was too late now. He knew. He had the report on his lap and he was sitting in his room in Ada's penthouse, looking out at the skyline but not really seeing any of the surfers happily enjoying the summer sun, or the parents walking hand-in-hand while their kids ran along the beach in front of them. He wondered how much of this Genie knew. After spending every day with her over the past week, and finding out that they actually worked really well together, he'd been so busy that he had kind of forgotten the phone call he'd made.

He understood now why her parents had suddenly upped and moved away. It wasn't as simple as a poorly grandparent. He was holding onto something that could potentially destroy Genie's relationship with her family, and now he didn't know what to do with it. This wasn't what he'd planned. He'd wanted something simple that would make her want to leave. This was something he couldn't have envisaged. Now he'd either have to pretend he'd never seen these papers, or find a way to tell her. She'd hate him – then she'd hate *them*.

Everything was in this report. The way she'd worked in the restaurant from the age of fourteen, how she had no qualifications, but knew the business inside and out. How she didn't have many friends, but was kind to everyone. How dedicated she was to her family, and how they'd suddenly disappeared. Maybe they hadn't quite vanished from her life, but considering how close they had all been, she must be completely bewildered by the sudden change. Now he knew why. Her mum had a lot to answer for. He wondered if Genie's dad knew?

The problem was that now he had this information, he didn't know whether he should tell her. She'd blame him and say it was all his fault somehow. He knew what women were like. His last girlfriend had pinned everything that went wrong in the relationship on him, but she'd known from the start that he was a busy guy with lots of responsibilities. He sighed and tried to ease some of the tension in his shoulders. For now he'd have to keep it all to himself, and hope her parents caved in and told her.

He glanced up as Genie came into the kitchen. She looked

super-cute in cut-off jeans today and a new blouse that had the letter G woven all over it. It was quirky and quite cool. She was gradually becoming more confident and he couldn't help but follow the swing of her hips as she bent to pull some mugs from the cupboard below the main counter. Man, he needed to get laid!

She turned and batted her baby blue eyes at him, smiling like she had a secret. His insides churned and all he could think of was backing her into the counter and plundering her mouth. His own mouth went dry and his pupils dilated but she didn't seem to notice. He could see that she was excited about something.

'What is it?' he asked. 'You had too much caffeine this morning? You're usually like a bear with a sore head first thing.' The light dulled in her eyes and his guts pulled tight, but he was annoyed with her for looking so pretty and for working alongside him as though she only tolerated his presence, but could dump him at any time.

They worked like a dream together and the business was buzzing. He had so many ideas for improvement already. He'd not been there long, but it was easing his soul, being back in a kitchen, however small-scale it might be compared to what he'd been used to. He took a step toward Genie and she held her ground and thrust out her chest slightly, which made the fabric strain across her ample chest. He took a gulp of air.

She raised her chin and looked at him suspiciously. 'I know we're busy, but can you lock up for me tonight?'

His eyebrows shot up into his hairline as he hadn't expected her to ever trust him with the keys to the place. They'd been too busy to really argue much and every night they were exhausted from their new routine and fell straight into their own beds. He was supposed to be making her fall for him, to get her away from Ada, but he wasn't used to working flat out any more and the early starts and late nights were taking their toll.

'Why can't you lock up?'

'I can, but Toby, Ralph's son, has just called and asked me out to dinner and I'd like to go.'

Cal's mouth formed an O and he leaned against the counter as adrenaline began to buzz round his system. He hadn't planned for this. Ada had told him that Genie never went out and didn't have a life. He was counting on that, to be able to keep an eye on her. He didn't want another man influencing her at this early stage. But it looked like he didn't have much of a choice right now. 'I can do that. I didn't know you were seeing each other.'

'We're not… yet.' She said happily and almost skipped out of the kitchen to pick up her handbag.

CHAPTER THIRTY-TWO

*G*enie was in a world of pleasure. So this was what everyone meant about having a life!

She'd never wanted to take time away from the business before, or been able to, but now she was actually making money. She had more customers than she could have handled alone, but with Cal there, she could step away if she wanted to. He had already reorganised the kitchen to make it more efficient and advised her on her recipes. She'd resented this at first, but eventually decided that she might as well exploit his expertise, even if he was here to cause trouble. He'd finally admitted that she had a flair for flavours and asked questions about her life and business.

Genie knew he was protecting his grandma, but if he thought he was coming in to take over, he had another think coming. She was the boss and he would soon come to learn that. She hadn't broken away from her whole family and gone out on her own through being a little mouse. She was a lion – and he'd learn the hard way if he thought he could play with her. Her own dad had tried giving her gentle advice on how to run things, but she'd been managing the place for years and wasn't about to listen.

She was beginning to feel more like her old self, where she took command and was pro-active. If only she'd found this confidence earlier, she might have persuaded her parents to stay, she sometimes thought. But they had promised to visit soon and she was looking forward to showing them what she'd done.

Her mum's voice sounded over-bright on the phone and Genie wondered if living so near Lucille was making her wish she was back home. Lucille had sent Genie a couple of letters advising her to give up her silly idea of running the restaurant on her own and to come 'home' to her family.

Letters! Who sent them anymore? But the fact that her grandmother knew Ada's address made the hairs on the back of her neck stand tall. It was a bit creepy. Genie had gone out of her way to be evasive about where she lived. She didn't want Lucille to visit and start picking holes in Ada's living arrangements. Not that she'd ever visited before, but it would be just like her to turn up now and force Genie to return with her. It was only when Genie remembered Lucille was pretending to be ill that she realised she was safe from a 'royal' visit for now.

She'd run into town and bought a beautiful dress in the sale. Now she held it up to her chest, looking at herself in the mirror. Her hair shone and was curled around her face. She'd placed a little diamanté slide to one side and it glittered in the light. The dress was fitted across her bust and clinched in at the waist, but then fell to her knees. She'd gained much more confidence in her appearance since living with Ada and listening to her subtle style tips. Genie now realised that wearing tops that hung from her ample chest actually made her look a lot larger, while the stretchy ones she'd changed over to accentuated her smaller waist. The soft blue tone of the dress made her skin glow and she'd put on lashings of mascara so her eyes looked sooty and seductive. Toby wouldn't know what had hit him tonight. She was ready for some fun and he was the man to have it with.

~

*T*oby had met her in the foyer of the building and they'd had a lovely time, but for some reason she kept picturing Cal's face, and his surprise when she'd said she was dating. It put a damper on her evening and, although she had laughed in the right places and Toby had escorted her home, something was missing. She couldn't quite put a finger on what it was.

Now he put one arm on the wall next to her before she stepped indoors and lowered his head to capture her lips, sliding his other hand along the skin of her arm and making it come alive. She tilted her face towards him, as she'd enjoyed her kiss with him on the restaurant opening night. But as she moved she felt cold air on her cheek. She jumped away as the door opened and Cal stood before them. He gave a tight smile to Toby, who looked confused and stepped back, but politely shook Cal's hand as he glowered at him.

'Uh… Toby, this is Cal. Ada's grandson.'

Toby let out the breath he'd been holding and smiled warmly. 'Great to meet you, Cal.' When he realised that no one was moving or inviting him in, he glanced between them, kissed Genie's cheek and told her he'd call her in the week, a frown appearing on his forehead as he reluctantly walked away.

Genie pushed past Cal and stomped into the house. 'Well, that was embarrassing. What the hell did you do that for?'

'I was looking out for you. Who knows what that guy was thinking?'

Genie threw her hands up in exasperation and began pacing the lounge. 'He was thinking about kissing me! He's Ralph's son and he's a gentleman.'

'He didn't look like a gentleman. He was about to paw you!' Cal was frowning and he was also pacing the room. She had the fleeting thought that they should put on some gym clothes and do a proper workout. She stopped walking and faced him.

'Stop acting like my big brother. I've never had one and I don't need one now!'

'I'm not your brother,' he ground out through gritted teeth. 'Plus, you have no clue about dating.'

She stormed up to him and jabbed a finger into his chest, her eyes blazing into his. 'He was going to kiss me, and would have if you hadn't interrupted.' She looked around the room. 'Where's Ada?'

'Ada's at a friend's flat, downstairs, for a late dinner. She's decided to get out more. Stop trying to change the subject. You know when a man is going to kiss you properly, and that wasn't it. He looked like a seagull about to take a bite out of you.'

Genie thought of the evil seagull and winced. 'Oh, sod off.'

He laughed and pulled her into his arms, making her squeak in surprise, the breath knocked out of her lungs as she was pressed to his chest. 'You need practice to get it right.' He dipped his head and captured her lips with his, whilst her world tilted sideways. She grabbed on to him and then her anger flared again. He was playing with her and trying to ruin her life. Her pulse ramped up a gear and she slid her hands down to his backside and heard his intake of breath. Never taking her lips from his she leant into him and let him know she was in control by sliding her hands from his backside to his back and under his T-shirt. He broke away and stared at her, eyes full of lust. He reached out for her again just as the front door opened and they heard Ada talking to someone on her mobile phone. She was laughing and saying that yes, she had got home safe, before she snapped the phone shut and stared at them, curiosity in her eyes.

Genie was standing looking out to sea and Cal was staring at her and looking ruffled. 'Have you two had a fight again? You look stunning, Genie. Doesn't she, Cal?'

Cal ignored her and moved to the kitchen to make them all a coffee. Ada tutted at his rudeness and went to twirl Genie around to check out the dress.

'I've been out for dinner with Toby,' said Genie, following Cal to the kitchen and trying to regulate her breathing. If Cal thought he could play with her then he'd catch fire. She grinned and hugged Ada who was beaming from ear to ear. 'I heard that you went out too?'

Ada had selective hearing for a moment and just picked out the bit of conversation that meant they weren't talking about her. For now Genie let it drop, but she had a feeling that Ada might be starting to live again too.

'I knew Toby would ask you out after he pulled you into the bushes and kissed you on our opening night,' Ada said confidently.

They heard Cal crash and bang some cups in the sink and a light of mischief came into Ada's eye. Genie looked Cal's way and enjoyed the fury on his face. Then she mock-gasped and held her hand to her face. 'I thought no one saw us! I had no idea what he was going to do.'

Ada giggled, walking over and taking a coffee from Cal as he seemed to have decided to stay mute behind the counter. 'Well, it was pretty obvious to everyone else. He didn't stop talking about you all night.' Cal took a big mouthful of the scalding coffee and then coughed as he tried to force it down his throat. Ada happily slapped him on the back. 'It seems like you have a couple of admirers now.'

'What?' said Cal and Genie in unison.

Ada looked innocently at them. 'Well, Bailey is pretty smitten, has been for a while. And now there's Toby, too. A girl can never have too many suitors, Genie. It's good for the soul.' With that she kissed Cal's cheek, waved to Genie and went into her room, softly closing the door behind her.

'Bailey?' demanded Cal.

'What about him?'

'He's 'smitten'?'

'How the hell would I know? I know nothing about dating...' she parroted, marching towards her bedroom. He followed her and she had time to turn and satisfyingly shut the door right in his stupid face.

CHAPTER THIRTY-THREE

*G*enie had the hangover from hell the next day. She rarely went out or had time to drink and her body just wasn't used to it. She felt grumpy from tossing and turning all night over the comments Cal had made about her being useless with men, and she also kept reliving his kisses, which had blown her mind. How she'd managed to stay focused when she could have easily been swept up into his arms and bedroom, she'd never know. She was sure she'd have regretted it in the morning, so she was relieved that Ada had come in when she had and broken up the party.

Genie tried to ignore him at work but it wasn't exactly a huge space. There was a staff of five now. There was the chef, plus Bailey, a new part-time waitress and herself and Cal. She spent a lot of time restocking and helping waitress tables before the lunchtime ice cream rush.

Cal was annoying her already. He'd woken up super smiley and had been so polite at breakfast that she'd narrowed her eyes at him while he'd blown her a kiss. She'd childishly stuck her tongue out at him, but he'd grinned and winked back. He was infuriating. She'd thought he would be sorry and embarrassed this morning. It seemed like he'd spent the night making new plans and she had no idea what they were.

She soon found out when he kept 'accidentally' brushing against her at every opportunity. It was driving her crazy. It was subtle, but he'd go to pick up a cup the same time as her and brush her arm or hand, or his hip would touch hers and she would have to stop what she was doing to move past him. She was getting flustered and she messed up a food order, which was going too far.

She marched up to him, grabbed his hand and dragged him into the back garden behind the restaurant and into the shed. She hadn't been in here recently and for a moment she stood stock still in shock, the anger leaving her body in an instant as she saw the dust covering her grandad's inventing tools. Cal looked around too and, when she realised they were still holding hands, she flung his away.

'If you wanted to get me on my own, you could have just asked, rather than dragging me in here,' he joked. 'What is this place?'

Genie flushed and turned to face him, the anger flaring again. 'It's my grandad's shed. Look. You kissed me last night to poke fun at me and I kissed you back to show you not to mess with me. Today you're still playing games and it's affecting our work. Back off!'

Calvin's eyes were alight with mischief. She should have seen the warning signs. She'd been living with him for a short while and he caused havoc every day. He moved closer and took her hand again. 'I didn't kiss you to poke fun at you, I was trying to teach you a lesson about how to get men to kiss you. I'm happy to give you lessons in seduction, if it would help?'

Genie's eyes narrowed and she very nearly ground the heel of her foot into his shoe. 'Piss off.' She stared up into his eyes and then backed him into the little workbench, so that they were touching hip to hip. 'I might be a novice at dating, but I learn quickly. I'll ask Toby if he can bring me up to speed.'

Cal growled and slid his hands around to her backside, mirroring what she had done to him the night before and she squeaked in surprise.

'Toby's not right for you. You need a real man.'

Genie summoned all her willpower and pushed him away. He let her go, but his eyes were burning into hers. She coolly looked him up and down. 'Best I go and find one then.'

Cal stared after her as she left him standing in the shed. She wiped away the sweat that had formed on her upper lip with the back of her hand and tried to regulate her breathing. It would be so easy to fall for a man like Cal, but her heart had been broken into a million pieces by her family. If she gave anything to Cal she worried that she'd never recover.

CHAPTER THIRTY-FOUR

*I*t had been a tense couple of days for Genie as Cal was still playing up. One moment he tried to get her to confide in him and acted as if they were the best of friends, the next moment he was teasing her and trying to make her blush. He hadn't put the moves on her again and she was feeling annoyed and confused.

She was beginning to like living with him, as he made her tea and brought it in to her in bed in the morning before work. At first she'd been embarrassed and pulled the sheets up to her eyeballs, but now she kind of liked the company. That morning, she'd even shoved over and let him climb in next to her, much to his surprise. He hadn't needed asking twice, though. Unfortunately Ada had chosen that moment to come in, and had rapidly backed out apologising. Genie had rushed after her, but Cal had looked smug. She'd wanted to slap his silly face after that, as she'd felt really awkward with Ada that day. She assumed that had been his plan all along and felt stupid for falling for it.

He'd mentioned that morning that he was going out with friends in the evening. What friends? Surely he hadn't been here long enough to have made any? He was always either at the penthouse or working. She hated the burning feeling in her stomach when she thought of him meeting other women. He was so handsome that she was surprised that they didn't have groupies hanging around in the foyer of their building. He was in the kitchen most of the time, but if anyone did catch sight of him at work, she could count on them asking who he was or coming back the next day to see if he was there. It was good for business, but for some reason it annoyed her.

Genie looked up as Trudie came into the restaurant. Her eyes were red and hair was a bit of a mess, which was unusual for someone who took such pride in her appearance. Genie caught Trudie's eye. She seemed relieved to see her and turned and walked towards her, her head bowed. Bailey glanced at Genie with a worried frown and she signalled for him to take over her tables, as it was quiet at that time in the morning. Putting an arm around Trudie, she guided her to one of the back tables by the ice cream bar and sat her down, pulling out a chair next to her.

Bailey came over and put a hand on Genie's shoulder, placing two steaming mugs of coffee in front of them. She smiled her thanks and realised that she hadn't paid him much attention since Cal had arrived. She vowed to rectify that today. As he turned and left, she took Trudie's hand and felt how cold she was.

'Trudie? What's the matter?'

Trudie brushed her hair out of her eyes and sniffed. Then she straightened her shoulders and tried to smile. 'Sorry for landing on you like this, Genie. I've been feeling a bit down and I usually come and talk to your mum. I really miss her, and before I knew it my feet were bringing me your way. I don't expect you to listen to my problems, though.'

Genie gave her a quick hug and sipped her coffee, which

was delicious. 'What's the problem? I might not be Mum, but I know she'd want me to be here for you while she's away.'

Trudie started sniffling again and wiped tears from her eyes. 'You're such a good girl, Genie. How they could leave you, I'll never know.'

Genie felt the punch to her stomach that always came when someone felt sorry for her since she'd been dumped by her family. 'They seem really happy where they are,' she said sadly.

Trudie's eyes filled with tears again. Genie knew what it felt like to lose your best friend. Una and Fae hadn't bothered to come back to the restaurant, even though it was buzzing with customers now, although Fae had sent her a couple of texts saying well done. She bet if they saw Cal they'd be in all the time. The one message she'd had from Una was to ask if Bailey was single. Genie hadn't bothered to reply.

Ada walked into the restaurant and saw Trudie sitting with Genie and her mouth set in a thin line. Genie fleetingly felt annoyed. What did Ada have to complain about? Genie was on her feet for ninety-nine percent of the day, a ten-minute break wasn't going to kill anyone. It was the first time that Genie had been bothered at an intrusion from her business partner and she didn't like the feeling.

Perhaps she'd been too headstrong and should have waited to raise her own finance. It had all fallen into place, but for the first time she wondered if she'd been taken advantage of. Ada was now the proud co-owner of a popular business in a prime location. She'd been so sad and lonely that Genie hadn't considered how sharp a businesswoman she was. Knowing her better now, she realised that Ada wouldn't have come near this investment if she'd thought it would fail.

Ada walked over purposefully and tried to usher Genie out of her seat, which immediately made her want to plant her feet and stay put. Trudie was her family friend and she was the owner of the business. If Genie wanted to swan around and chat all day, she now had enough staff to cope. But Ada was having none of it. She was surprisingly strong for such a tiny woman and she linked arms with Genie and practically dragged her over to Cal. 'You're needed here in the kitchen, Genie,' said Ada firmly. 'Cal said he had a new recipe idea for your ice cream cones and he was too embarrassed to ask you to test them,' she looked pointedly at Cal. He looked confused, until he saw Trudie. One look from his gran and he nodded, led Genie away and began grabbing ingredients out of the cupboards.

'Trudie'll be fine,' Ada reassured Genie. 'Don't worry. She's probably having a bad day, that's all. I'm feeling a bit tired, so I'll go and sit with her if that's ok?'

Genie suddenly looked more closely at Ada to see if she was looking frail, but she'd been conned one too many times by her own grandmother and saw straight through it. Ada needed to practice her lying skills.

Genie had seen Trudie looking upset a lot before she'd been away and was now determined to find out if she was ok. Trudie didn't have many friends either, but the shop owners were all quite close and she knew they were sad about her parents leaving their little community. It wasn't just Genie who was missing them. Perhaps she should organise some sort of get-together where she could give them all regular news about how her parents were doing.

She had thought her parents would contact Trudie and the other shop owners themselves, but they hadn't. That in itself told her how little they must all mean to them. Otherwise, how could they have just cut and run the way they did?

CHAPTER THIRTY-FIVE

enie was trying to keep her eyes open and focus on the movie she'd been watching. She was sprawled on the huge grey L-shaped sofa in the lounge in some little shorts and a vest top, as it was humid outside. Stars were twinkling in the sky and she had the sliding doors to the deck wide open so that the evening breeze could drift in. She'd tried to sit with a new romance book and a crisp glass of white wine earlier, but even that hadn't kept her attention for long. She kept glancing at the door. Cal was out for the evening and Ada had gone to bed early.

Ada had been spending a lot of time in the restaurant lately and was fabulous with their guests. She knew them by name, when Genie could never remember them all, there were so many regulars these days. Genie was still feeling unsettled by the way Ada had taken over and chatted to Trudie earlier on. Genie made up her mind to make time for Trudie at some point soon. She would sit her down and find out what was wrong. She was pretty sure it was more than just missing her mum, Milly. Perhaps her old boyfriend had got back in touch, or let her down again?

She heard the front door open and quickly pretended to have fallen asleep in front of the TV. She opened her eyes suddenly as something trailed itself across her stomach, on show via the slight gap between her shorts and top. Cal was crouched down next to her, moving the tip of his finger across her bare skin. She pulled herself into a sitting position and dragged her top down, but that just made it pull even tighter across her chest. And now she was almost bumping noses with him.

She rubbed sleep from her eyes in the hope he'd back off. He rested on his haunches and looked at her. His eyes were sparkling and his cheeks were slightly flushed, while his hair was a bit messy. Her eyes narrowed. She pictured a gorgeous woman running her hands through his hair and plying him with alcohol. Anger flared and she stood up, making him fall back onto the rug behind him. She stared at him dispassionately. 'Do you always have to walk around half-naked?' His chest was bare and she saw that he'd obviously come in and dumped his shirt on the other couch. He probably would have thrown himself down right where she'd been feigning sleep, if she hadn't already been lying there.

He beckoned her to come and sit on the rug with him, so she sighed theatrically and moved to the edge of the couch, primly crossing her ankles and not touching him. He squinted as if he were trying to remember what he was supposed to be doing. She sighed and slid to the floor in front of him.

He picked up one of her feet and started massaging the sole, which made her almost purr in pleasure. He didn't seem to realise what he was doing, and kept rubbing. She was glad she'd spent an hour soaking in the bath beforehand and had lathered herself with scented cream, or her feet would have been dusty from sitting on the deck earlier. No one had ever rubbed her feet before. She was on them all day and they often ached, so she couldn't quite drag them away.

'Does my naked chest bother you?'

She looked at his chest, her mouth suddenly dry, and then met eyes which were challenging her own. 'Not at all,' she lied. 'I just thought you might be cold.' She looked at his pert nipples and grinned, before he touched the arch of her foot and she closed her eyes in pleasure. He picked up her other foot and began to ease the tension from that. It was such a weird place to be sitting, almost in his lap when he was half naked, but she couldn't pull away now, as it was embarrassing enough. Perhaps he had a foot fetish and he'd start to lick her toes next. She ignored the tingling between her legs, pulled her foot out of his hand and lowered her knees to the floor.

'How was your evening? You look like you've been dragged through a hedge.'

'Like you were?' he said.

'Touché!'

He sighed and rubbed his chin, which had a slight shadow of stubble and looked mightily sexy. 'I met a few new friends for drinks.'

'What new friends?'

'You're sounding jealous, Genie,' he teased, standing and then grabbing her hand to pull her up too.

'I'm not jealous,' she said, knowing she sounded it. 'But you're working for me – and I need you to be focussed on work and not on floozies.'

'Floozies?' he grinned, slipping a hand around her waist under her top, making her skin prickle. He guided her over to the breakfast bar so she could sit while he began to make coffee. 'You make me sound like a super-stud. I never date more than one woman at a time. Who needs that headache? It was a fun night, though.'

When he didn't elaborate, she huffed unattractively and sipped the coffee he handed her without saying thanks.

'Look, I've been thinking about the restaurant. I've got some ideas that might help.' Cal said, running his hand through his sandy hair, which made it look even more as though he'd just been ravaged. Her mood didn't improve.

'I'm the boss. I have enough of my own ideas. You work for me. Ada is the one with the shares and until that changes, or I'm dead, you'll have to get used to it.'

Cal frowned and plonked his coffee on the worktop where it sloshed over the rim and onto the surface, leaving a black mark that he didn't bother to mop up. 'I know we wind each other up, but it's because you fancy me,' he joked, giving her a disarming smile and waiting for her to jump up and declare that he was wrong.

Embarrassment and rage filled her veins, but he had no clue who he was playing with. She wasn't some naïve schoolgirl. She might be a bit of a loser and not that experienced with men, but she was a grown woman now and did know how to handle an egotistical male. She'd been dealing with them all her life – entitled customers who were always right. She took her time and slowly looked him up and down. 'You're right. I do fancy you, but you work for me and I don't date my staff.'

Colour suffused his face, but then he threw his head back and laughed. He moved towards her, but she danced around the kitchen units and headed towards her bedroom. 'I could really help you with the restaurant, if you let me,' he called after her, but she slipped inside her room and closed the door, resting her body against it, her heart beating wildly, listening out to see if he'd follow her. She kind of hoped that he would, but after a few minutes, she caught her breath and slumped down onto her bed.

She was lucky enough to have a huge window in front of

her bed with views out across the water towards the restaurant. Tonight she pulled the vertical blinds closed, so she'd feel cocooned in the beautiful serene space. It wasn't like her old room, where she'd had her belongings spilling onto every surface. She was a guest here and although she was gradually becoming more relaxed, it still felt like a hotel and not a home.

Her laptop was by her pillow, so she opened up a new tab. She glanced around furtively, then huffed out a breath. *Idiot!* She was in her room, no one could see her. So she typed Cal's name into the search engine slowly, and scrunching up her nose while the browser took its time to search. The page was suddenly flooded with photos of Cal and she berated herself for not having done this before. She always got references for staff members, and also checked their online presences, but she'd been stressed. That was thanks to her family leaving and then having such limited contact with them. She'd let a few things slide.

Ada had vouched for Cal and she hadn't really had much choice but to employ him. He had the skills – and she'd been desperate. She grinned at the thought of Cal's face, if he could see what she'd just done. He was so full of himself, cockily telling her how to run her own restaurant, when she could do it with her eyes closed and her hands tied behind her back. It was what she had been born to do, food phobias aside.

She rapidly scrolled down the articles and clicked them open, her eyes scanning the pages. Her stomach ached and her face flamed. The bastard! Not only that, but Ada hadn't been truthful, either, and that hurt like hell. She swung her legs over the side of the bed and propped the computer on her knees. She began to read the articles in more detail. He was famous!

The third article she read was the most in-depth and it had pictures of Ada. They were all bloody famous! Genie knew Cal's mum was a model, but she wasn't just any model, she was a supermodel. His dad was a movie producer.

No wonder they never visited. They probably had staff for their staff. Ada had been a star of the screen while her husband had been a highly regarded celebrity photographer. Even Genie had heard of him! She hadn't tied the two names together, but of course she knew who he was. She didn't go to the movies much and Ada hadn't worked for a long while, but Genie had probably seen some of her films – and now she was living in these people's house. Genie cringed with humiliation.

Ada wasn't famous in the UK, so that explained a lot, but her husband certainly had been. He was a local boy who'd done well. He'd grown up on the road the restaurant was on. Everything slotted into place and her heart broke. Did Ada want to steal her family business and build one of her own? Was this the only way she could do it, by befriending a lonely girl who'd just been dumped by her family? Another thought struck Genie. Her family had upped and left just as Ada had entered her life. Had Ada orchestrated the whole thing? Genie threw the computer on the bed and ran into the en-suite to throw up her stomach contents into the toilet.

She placed a hand on the sink and tried and failed to reach the taps. She gave up and sank down on the bathroom floor, groggily trying to recall what she'd read about Cal while she dragged her hand over her sweaty face. He'd been a millionaire, but had over-invested and lost everything. *What the hell was he doing here, then?* He'd intimated he was protecting his gran from Genie, which she kind of respected, but Cal was in hiding. People were looking for him in America. No one probably expected him to turn up in a little seaside town in the south of the UK. But if he thought he was going to sweep in and start again with her family business, then he would soon find out no one should underestimate a small angry British girl from Essex.

She wiped her mouth with the back of her hand, leaned on the towel rail to lever herself up and turned on the shower, walking into it fully clothed. She let the freezing water wash over her body and numb it to what she had to do. She would succeed and she'd make them both wish they'd never set eyes on *Genie's*. They had been playing with fire and now they'd set everything alight. She was no fool and it was about time she began behaving more like a boss and less like a friend. Her business would be a success no matter what, and she'd bring her family home.

She decided that she'd get to the bottom of whatever had made her parents leave and get them back working alongside her if it killed her. If it meant shipping in her other grandmother and grandfather so they could check up on them and their health, then they could live in the flat above the restaurant. If they were desperate. She pulled a face, deciding that she wasn't that generous – actually, they could stay in Cornwall.

Wishing she had a very big glass of wine, but not wanting to go back into the kitchen, she scanned the pages online again, flushing, her heart racing and her palms beginning to grow clammy. She glanced around to make sure Ada hadn't appeared out of nowhere. Then she gulped in some air to slow her breathing down. She quickly wiped the computer's browsing history.

How could she have not known about Cal? It seemed that he was a celebrity chef back home. He'd lost everything when he'd over-reached. He must be licking his wounds. Now he was living in the same penthouse flat as her and his ex-Hollywood film star grandmother. If she'd told anyone, they would never believe her. She picked up her phone and then despondently threw it down on the bed beside her. Who did she have to tell anyway?

CHAPTER THIRTY-SIX

The next morning, after a tumultuous night's sleep, Genie decided that she would face Ada and demand an explanation. If Genie had been so wrong about her, then she should just put her cards on the table and draw battle lines without hesitation. They would understand after today that she was aware of their plan and she wasn't going anywhere. She took a deep breath and felt some of the old fierce Genie return, finally!

Seeing Ada chatting happily to some new customers, Genie inclined her head towards the beach. 'Ada, I've got a couple of new flavours to show you. Have you got a minute to sit with me on the sand?' If Ada was surprised to be asked to leave the restaurant during the day, she didn't show it. *Ever the actress*, thought Genie with a growl.

Ada nodded and finished her conversation, going to pick up her bag that was behind the counter. Genie scooped some of the recipes she'd recently finished into small tubs and picked up two spoons. She was proud of these flavours and didn't really want to waste them on Ada, but she needed an excuse to get her away from the restaurant. Bailey was in today, as was their regular chef. Cal was in the back, baking a batch of tiny cakes that she had asked him to get on with. They were so intricate that they would hold his attention for hours. He'd looked surprised when she'd asked, but he'd just nodded and begun taking ingredients out of cupboards and got on with the task without a word, as if he could sense from her taut responses to his banter that morning that she wasn't in the mood to joke.

As they crossed the road at the little zebra crossing, Ada linked arms with Genie, which wasn't the easiest thing when you had hands full of ice creams samples. Genie pressed her mouth into a thin line and tried to smile. They sat side by side and Genie slipped off her flip-flops and ran her toes through the sand, trying to calm her racing mind. She didn't know if she was doing the right thing, but this would fester and destroy her if she didn't put a halt to it now.

Ada took one look at the tubs that Genie handed her and dug her spoon in. The ice cream was a mixture of raspberry, white chocolate and chilli. It was smooth and delicious, but had a slight tang at the end, which made your tongue tingle.

'It's delicious!' Ada took another spoonful, but then frowned. 'If this had a bit of a crunch somewhere, it would be the best ice cream I've ever tasted.'

Genie sighed, knowing Ada was right. She thought the same thing, but the crunch she'd wanted to add was tiny macaroons to go on the top. Every time to tried to make them she'd failed. They ended up looking like flat nipples. She needed Cal, but was loath to give him the challenge. She knew he'd manage it flawlessly.

Ada took the second flavour from her and tried that, sighing in bliss. 'This one is perfect.' She turned to face Genie, shielding her eyes from the strongest rays of the sun with her hands. 'Something's troubling you today, isn't it?

Don't you trust me enough to share any worries with me now? Aren't we like family?'

Genie wanted to jump up, stamp her feet and shout that no, they weren't family. They were just business partners and that was all they would ever be, but she bit down on her bottom lip and waited a moment for her pulse to stop jumping around. She hated storing up bad feeling, which was why she usually kicked something or ranted for a while to release the tension, but she couldn't do that now.

She'd had to grow up in the last few months. She watched the sea wash in and out across the sand. Small children were squealing and dancing in and out of the surf. Taking a deep breath she looked at Ada. Ada seemed worried, but was waiting for Genie to speak and Genie thought how deceptive appearances could be. Ada looked like a lovely elderly lady, with her soft swishy blonde hair and gentle face, whilst inside she was a schemer and a liar, and Genie was about to call her out.

'I looked Cal up on the internet last night. In fact, that led to articles about all of your family.' She didn't say anything else, she just left it open to interpretation, and waited to see what Ada would say.

Surprisingly, Ada just threw her head back and laughed. 'Oh my! I'd assumed that you did that ages ago, Genie. That says more about your character than you know.' Then she stopped laughing and stared into Genie's eyes, frowning. 'That troubles you? Why?'

Genie shifted uncomfortably in the sand and she tried to work out if she'd gone wrong somewhere. Why wasn't Ada mad at her snooping?

'Cal's business went bust. He's broke, he needs a new venture and it looks like he's set his sights on mine.'

Now Ada's mouth set in a grim line and she put the ice cream tub she had been gradually eating down beside her on the sand, folding her arms across her chest. Now she looked angry, and Genie wanted to stutter and apologise, but she'd been through too much and wasn't about to be messed around. Not even by a little old lady with fiery eyes.

'Tell me I'm wrong, then?' Genie said fiercely.

'You're wrong. You can't always believe what you read in the papers.'

Genie did feel a bit stung by that – shouldn't she know better than to judge people? She had no qualifications and wasn't accomplished, but she was a business owner and certainly not stupid, although on paper she probably looked that way.

'What's he doing here, then? Other than getting in my way,' Genie snapped.

Ada gave her a stern look and Genie's skin warmed up, colour filling her cheeks. 'I know you've been good to me, Ada, and I haven't felt so lost with you here, but I'm not deserting my family business for anyone. if I'd have wanted to give it up, I've have gone with my parents.'

'And you don't think I know that?' Hurt showed in Ada's eyes. 'You're making assumptions based on what you've read. I thought we trusted each other? It's why I gave up my career. I was fed up with people assuming they knew me from reading a few lines in a newspaper or gossip magazine.'

'I thought we trusted each other, too.'

'I do trust you,' said Ada.

'Just not enough to tell me the truth about your family?'

Ada sighed and stared out to sea for a moment, collecting her thoughts. 'I'm sorry if you feel that way. I guess I'm used to everyone either knowing about my family or delving into our past. Being here has been like a breath of fresh air for me. No one cares who I was in a past life.'

'Why would you want to hide the fact that you're a famous movie star in the States? I know your flat here is amazing, but you have an incredible life in America. Don't you miss it?'

'I miss Ned,' said Ada with such sorrow that tears immediately sprang to Genie's eyes. 'If I went back there, everything would remind me of the life we had. Here I feel free. I'm not being chased by photographers and I can enjoy the memories I have about our time here, without people judging me for grieving in my own way.' Genie took her hand and Ada looked down at it as if in a daze. 'I'm gradually coming back to life here and you're a big part of that. It's not about the business for me. It's about you, Genie. You've begun to heal my soul. Nothing can replace Ned, but you've eased the loss.'

Genie felt tears slide down her cheeks and she quickly brushed them aside and pulled Ada in to a hug. 'I'm sorry.'

'It's ok,' sniffed Ada, her eyes glistening as they drew apart. They were still holding hands, but Ada broke the connection and smiled suddenly, a glint in her eye. 'Let me tell you about Cal. Not the Cal you're read about in the papers, but the real man.'

Genie leaned back on her elbows in the warm sand and tilted her head towards Ada. 'This I can't wait to hear.' She hoped they were all coping okay without them at the restaurant, but found she was too wrapped up in Ada's story to care too much. She had a warm feeling in her heart, where earlier she'd felt only rage. She realised how much she and Ada had come to rely on each other and the thought scared her a little. Everyone she cared about seemed to disappear from her life at the moment.

'Cal was such a precocious child. He was, and still is, adored by us all, as he's so damned charming. He learned that trick early on and it's worked well for him. Don't get me wrong, I know he can be a pain in the backside, but he's a good boy. He's such a talented chef. He went to school and studied hard for years. It's his passion and he has a gift for making incredible food from few ingredients.' Ada stared off into the distance while she spoke. 'His popularity exploded and he made the most of it.' She paused while she watched two small children running along the beach, the breeze making their hair trail in the wind. They were laughing and dipping in and out of the surf, while their parents walked behind them, holding steaming drinks that were in *Genie's* branded coffee cups.

'He bought a restaurant after working for many top chefs and, although we advised against it as it was too soon, it flourished. We had to agree that he'd got the formula right, but then he got carried away and overextended too quickly. He wanted to build on the momentum, but cash flow became a problem. He lost everything. The press had a field day and he came home to be comforted by his family. The media hounded us all and, although we didn't want him to, he went travelling to make them leave us alone.'

Genie watched one of the children topple into the water as she tried to balance on one foot and show off to her sister. Her mum rushed forward and brushed her down, but luckily the water wasn't deep. The girl's sister and dad found it mightily amusing once they saw she was unhurt. Genie couldn't help but giggle too, then adjusted her face to mirror Ada's stern expression. She tried to imagine Cal as a sexy suit-wearing business owner in a flashy restaurant, and not a hulking great man in jeans who worked in her small kitchen.

'He had lots of women throwing themselves at him and he did enjoy that for a while.' Genie flinched, but saw Ada watching her carefully. 'All of my family are famous, Genie. It's the world my kids grew up in. Cal's dad is a movie producer and his wife was a Calvin Klein model before she married my son.' She giggled then. 'Can you believe my grandson is named after pair of pants?'

She laughed heartily and Genie joined in. 'What?'

'Not really. He's named after her idol. She was totally in awe of the designer and has always said he inspired her career. It's fun to wind Cal up though.'

'No wonder you don't see much of them, if they have lives like that.'

Ada sighed and eased herself back on the sand, clearly enjoying the warmth of sun on her face. 'I used to travel a lot with my husband. He was a celebrity photographer who ran a big stock image site, one of the first, in fact, but he fell out with his partner and it was a bit of a mess.' Genie gawped, eyes wide as saucers. Then she nonchalantly flicked her hair over her shoulder and tried to act as if it was an everyday occurrence to be talking to someone who'd lived the life Ada had.

'We moved around a lot with Ned's work after that and the kids got the bug. They love to see new places and Cal does too. I worry about them all, but they've done well. Cal wanted to start small with his cookery and own a little restaurant, but it snowballed and he became a celebrity in his own right. Too much partying and not enough keeping an eye on suppliers and investors meant they bled him dry. I've offered to help him set up somewhere else, but he refuses. He wants to lick his wounds and for some reason decided that now was the time to visit his old gran.'

'He thinks I'm fleecing you,' said Genie.

Ada laughed so loudly that a nearby seagull squawked and flew away. Genie fleetingly wondered if it was her evil seagull, he seemed to follow her around these days. 'I know! I thought that from the moment he appeared. He's such a silly boy. If anything, I conned you.'

Genie's eyebrows shot up into her hairline. She was about to ask, *what the hell?* when Ada put out a hand to stop her. 'I now have a partnership in a beautiful little business that I love and I get to keep busy and swan around all day, while you do all the work. Yes, we have staff, and we have Cal now, but it's pretty much on your shoulders.' Here, she gently nudged Genie's arm. 'I do appreciate you and have no intention of trying to separate you from your heritage. I love that you love *Genie's* so much. You are the business, Genie. Without you, it doesn't exist.'

'But what about Cal? You just said that you want to set him up with a small business.'

Genie could see that Ada was trying not to laugh again. 'I'm not being insulting, Genie, but when I said small, I meant something probably four or five times the size of your restaurant. Cal's old business was too big, but a seaside place isn't for him. He's a fine dining chef.'

Genie bristled. The warm fuzzy feeling she'd had earlier was ebbing away with each wash of the waves on the shore. 'Why's Cal still here then? Surely he can see that the business is flourishing, and you aren't being separated from the contents of your wallet?'

'I was wondering the same thing myself, but perhaps he hasn't worked that out yet, or he's enjoying the anonymity of working in a small kitchen, and having space to experiment again?'

Hearing the word experiment made Genie think of her grandad. He'd finally picked up the phone and told her he was having an amazing time. He'd sounded more like his old self. She had a feeling he would grow bored and come home soon, though. He was already moaning about the size of the sandwiches in the cafés he'd visited. Sandwiches? What about experiencing different cultures? She was surprised that he hadn't asked the onboard kitchen to make him a packed lunch each day. Her lip wobbled. She missed him so much and her heart ached every time she spoke to him.

'I love what I do,' said Ada, snapping Genie back to the

present. 'I want Cal to start his own family legacy again one day and I hope I can help him, the way I've helped you. You shouldn't have so much responsibility at your age, but as you do, then I'd like to make it easier. If my being here helps in any way, then I'm happy.' Ada patted Genie's shoulder as if she was a pet dog and then realised what she was doing. They both grinned and any remaining tension flowed away on the breeze. 'You know, I've come to love you like one of my own,' Ada said softly.

Genie hugged her quickly again, but there were still a few unanswered questions. 'Why would Cal come and work for us for minimum wage? He could get a job in a top restaurant and make his money back in no time.'

Ada turned and looked back across the road at the restaurant, where Cal had just appeared. He was pacing up and down. He hadn't spotted them yet, they were tucked away, but he'd see them if he looked a little harder.

'Someone would recognise him if he did that, and he'd be hounded again,' Ada explained. 'He couldn't go anywhere near where he lived and, much as he loved his home, he was used to moving around and needed time to recover.'

Ada stood up and brushed down her trousers. 'Here he can play with food, which he loves, and he also feels he is keeping an eye on my behaviour and making sure you and I don't corrupt each other.'

Genie laughed. She did feel sorry for Cal. She knew from hard experience that a food business was tough to run on any scale. Knowing his bravado and cockiness, he'd probably brought his misfortunes on himself.

Her business brain began whirring and she thought of ways in which she could use Cal's expertise for her own benefit, before he got bored and decided to move on and annoy somebody else.

CHAPTER THIRTY-SEVEN

*G*enie woke up bright and breezy the next day and called a staff meeting with their tiny crew. Everyone pulled up chairs and turned to face her. Cal was wearing a short-sleeved T-shirt moulded to his chest and had sunglasses perched on his nose. He put his feet up on the chair next to him and looked like he was there for a photo shoot, which annoyed the hell out of her. She stared pointedly at his feet until he sighed and put them down.

'Okay, I've decided we need to change things up a bit. At the moment we are getting new custom, but I want to streamline the menu. I'd like us to be known as a sweet café, with healthier options.' She showed them her ideas to make them feel like they had input, in the hope that they would work more efficiently and start to understand what customers needed.

'I think we should have a small selection of gluten free, vegan and allergy options. Especially for cheese; lots of people are allergic to that these days.'

Everyone rolled their eyes, poking each other in the ribs,

sniggering. Genie's cheese aversion was well known. Genie ignored them. 'I don't want huge menus that confuse people. I want to keep costs down and maximise profits, which you will all share in, as I'll be able to pay you more. What do you think?'

She handed out her list of ideas for the new menu. There were five breakfasts, five lunches and five desserts. In addition, there was a sandwich section, with cheese and tomato right at the bottom, in the hope that people would have found something they liked before then. Genie had also designed a big ice cream menu, which was separate. Everyone scanned the paper and murmured their consent.

Cal put his hand up to speak and she lifted her eyes to the heavens, sighing. 'You don't need to put your hand up, we aren't in class.'

Everyone sniggered again. He grinned and she couldn't help but grin back, even though she really didn't want to. She was feeling much better that day and was determined to put a brave face on having him sticking his nose into her business. If he was here, she was going to work him to the bone.

'I suggest we make our own cones for the new ice cream bar,' said Cal. 'It'll make us stand out and we can add nuts, chocolate flakes, crushed meringue, grains, flavours and natural colours to the outside to make them really enticing.'

Genie felt her pulse ramp up a notch as she pictured her bag of crushed walnuts. She'd already had the idea, but she hadn't thought about adding colour and texture. Cal was the ideal man for this job.

'An inspired idea!' she said, while he looked surprised at her speedy consent. Then his eyes narrowed and she winked at him.

He thought for a moment and she could almost see the cogs of his brain whirring. She knew him well enough by now to know he would push the idea as far as it could go until she snapped at him for being overbearing, but today she wanted those new ideas and was open to them. She intended to expand and, without knowing it, he was the man to help her.

'I think we should also make crazy wafers in different flavours, or mini patisserie to sit on top of the ice creams.' He had clearly decided to go all out and make the most of the fact that she was listening to him. 'We can have iced yoghurt and low-fat ice cream versions of your bestselling flavours, and we should be doing at least a couple of sorbets,' Cal added.

Genie looked around and saw how excited everybody was by those ideas. She tried not to show she was grinding her teeth and that she wished she'd thought of them herself. For now, she'd let him have the glory.

Ada stood up and clapped her hands excitedly. Genie winced. Who knew that a tiny pensioner could have such a loud clap? Bailey got up and gave Genie a hug and the rest of the staff followed suit, chatting excitedly about how much easier their lives would be now. Cal didn't hug her, but he watched Bailey under hooded eyes as he walked over to cuddle Ada. Genie slung her arm around Bailey's waist, resting her head on his shoulder, her cheeks flushed with pleasure at how well her first staff meeting had gone. Bailey hooked his arm around her waist until he saw Cal's glower, but he didn't let go, he just leaned in and whispered something in her ear that made Genie laugh out loud and Cal stomp into the kitchen.

～

*G*enie's body protested at the hours she was working. She spent her days serving customers in her restaurant and nights working closely with Cal. She explained her own ice cream chocolate bar idea and, although her attempts were messy, the flavours were inspired. She'd almost given up on making the little ice cream squares that she had wanted to sell with the coffees, as she hadn't worked out how to mass-produce them.

Cal suddenly came up close and pressed his thumb to her lip, where a stray drop of chocolate had escaped from her mouth, and she gasped at the sudden intimacy. The heat in the room escalated. They'd been testing flavour combinations for hours. She was exhausted. All the same she found she had the energy to blush, and daubed a dollop of molten chocolate on his nose from the plate in front of her.

He grabbed her hand and licked another drop of chocolate from the inside of her wrist. Her eyes dilated, and she stared into his as they both suddenly froze and realised what they were doing. He could so easily have tugged her hand and eased her body towards his, and she was shocked at just how willing she would be. Once again, Ada wandered into the kitchen at exactly that moment to see how their ideas were progressing and they sprang guiltily away.

Genie bent head to try and refocus, but Cal's hand slid along her leg and he squeezed it gently before standing up and offering to make them all coffee, leaving Genie speechless and her skin tingling, bereft of his touch. She felt like someone had opened a furnace in the room and she had to fan her face with her hand to cool down.

She stood up and made room for Ada to taste some of the new flavours that hadn't melted and peeked Cal's way. He was whistling with a smug nonchalance, which annoyed the hell out of her and made her feel mutinous. She was damned if she was just going to roll over and be his next toy.

She enjoyed kissing him, and was pretty sure he would be a good lover from the way he touched her. He practically made her drool for more, which was quite embarrassing. She needed to shake it off and get him out of her system, before he decided he'd had enough of playing house with them and packed his things to return home.

CHAPTER THIRTY-EIGHT

*G*enie slumped down onto the sofa in the lounge and thought back over the last few days. Cal had been surprisingly acquiescent and had done her bidding without question. She'd almost felt like crying when he'd presented her with his first samples. They were perfect! The cones were crispy and flaky, the ice cream bars were small but beautifully constructed and the wafers were delicate and colourful. She wanted to eat them all. Added to her ice cream range, they had enough to ram the place with customers. Now she had Cal and the new waitress on board, they could easily cope with the added orders.

Cal had been generous with his time and worked the same long hours she did, even when she had told him to clock off and go home. He would sometimes sit sipping a black coffee and watching her do her usual routine of checking everything was in order for the next day, then he would stand up, go and rinse his cup and take the keys from her to lock up and walk her home. After the first day, he'd given up asking for the keys when she'd stared at him mutinously and pointedly stared at the beautifully written sign above the door that said her name. He'd smiled infuriatingly and dropped his hand, scooping hers up into his warm palm as soon as she'd slipped the keys back into her bag and lacing his fingers with hers before walking companionably home with her, as if his hand wasn't burning a trail of lust up her arm.

It was all muddling her mind and she was finding it hard to concentrate on anything else. She was sure that this was his plan. She was going to have to fight back, she just had to work out how. He'd gone out with his new friends a few times, but was pretty evasive about the finer details – not that it was any of her business, she supposed. She hated the way she felt territorial over him, when really they were just roommates who held hands.

When had they become so cordial? She didn't know, but she couldn't fault him now. He was a hard worker. He'd even begrudgingly agreed to begin giving Bailey lessons in pastry-making, as the younger man had shown a real interest and was willing to learn. Both she and Cal were aware that he couldn't stay there forever, so it was a necessity that they found a back-up plan. It would take years for anyone to reach Cal's standard, but Bailey learnt fast and they found he had an affinity with desserts. Cal still growled at him from time to time, though. She wasn't sure why, as Bailey was so eager to learn.

She knew she was working them both hard, but it wasn't as if she was swanning off for long lunches herself. She worked just as many hours, if not more.

Now she looked up as the doorbell pealed and dragged her aching limbs to answer the door. It seemed Cal must have dozed off in his room, and Ada was out. Then she came face to face with Toby.

She gawped a little and her pulse ramped up a notch. The last time she'd seen Toby had been on their date. But Cal had wiped her memory clean of that, and she felt colour rise to her cheeks.

'Toby! How lovely to see you.' She backed away from the door and welcomed him in, her smile wobbling slightly as she darted a glance at Cal's door, but it remained resolutely shut. Toby leant in to kiss her and she inhaled a heavenly aroma of sexy man and a musky fragrance she couldn't place. She turned to offer him her cheek, but he caught her face and kissed her gently on the lips. Sparks flew around her stomach and she grinned genuinely this time, taking his hand and leading him to the breakfast bar to make them a coffee. 'What are you doing here?'

He smiled and brushed a tendril of hair from her face, then looked out across the beach as the sun dipped and the sky turned darker. 'I was thinking about you and my legs brought me to your front door.' Genie felt her skin grow hot again. Men didn't usually talk to her that way and it was a revelation.

'Well, I'm glad they did. Coffee?'

'I'd love one. I know you've probably had a long day at the restaurant, but I miss your company.'

Genie hung her head. 'Sorry I haven't had time to text or call you much. Building a new business, even if it's a new *old* one, is hard work. I barely have time to wash my hair or eat.'

Toby's eyes slid over her figure and he accepted the coffee from her, whilst he used his other hand to tug her into him. His lips met hers before she had a chance to move away. She squeaked unattractively and then decided she was actually quite enjoying herself. She didn't feel fire in her belly like she did when Cal kissed her, but it was pretty hot none the less. She knew that Cal could leave at any time and go back to his old life. She needed someone who was here to stay.

She had cheekily asked Cal for some recipes, assuming he'd knock her back, but he'd generously written them all down in his big slanty handwriting and handed her a file of all of the dishes he'd made for the restaurant. That book must be worth a fortune, as they were all his own inventions, but he'd given it to her as if it meant nothing. She hadn't waited for him to change his mind, she'd grabbed them a bit ungraciously and hidden them in her room for after he left. She would really need them then.

She'd assumed he wouldn't share the secret of how his creations tasted so amazing, but maybe he wasn't worried as he was such a pastry magician. Maybe he assumed anyone else who tried to recreate his dishes would be useless at it.

She'd have to advertise for a proper pastry chef when he left if Bailey couldn't step up. All the signs were pointing towards him managing admirably, though, so she was keeping everything crossed that it worked out and they wouldn't be left scrabbling around trying to keep their customers. She'd worked so hard. It was her ice creams they came for, but she had to admit that Cal's bespoke cones and pastries lifted them up to another level.

Now she heard Cal's door open and tried to spring away from Toby, but he held onto her and pressed her hip into his own. She smiled brightly at Cal who frowned and then slapped on a smile to greet Toby, walking over to shake his hand which made him let go of Genie. She quickly moved to make more coffee for Cal. Cal jumped up onto the stool next to Toby and turned to face her, his gaze blazing. She couldn't meet his eye and grabbed another cup, taking the most time ever to pour water into the swanky coffee machine and offer him milk when she knew he drank it black.

She asked them to join her on the couch, thinking Cal would go straight back to his room. He elected to sit with them, though.

They had a pleasant evening chatting and reminiscing about the opening night and, as Cal hadn't looked like he was ever going to move, Toby had eventually given in gracefully and they had organised another date night. She'd walked him to the door. Cal hadn't followed them, which meant Toby had grabbed a quick kiss before he left that left her lips plump and Cal decidedly grumpy.

Over the next few days Cal begun walking around half naked again and she couldn't help her eyes following him everywhere. It was making her jumpy and frustrated. He kept coming out of the bathroom dripping with water. In the end she'd thrown an extra towel at his head, but he'd just laughed and walked into his room, closing the door behind him.

Ada had been out with Ralph a few times and it looked as if they were enjoying their friendship. Ralph often popped by and asked how *Genie's* was doing. She loved talking to him about her latest business ideas as the man's knowledge was encyclopaedic. He'd given her a few smart tips about cutting costs and complimented her on how the business was flourishing under her watchful care, which made her chest puff out with pride.

Her own parents were too busy with their new life to pop back and see how things were going. Genie felt the usual pang of regret, but it didn't hurt as much as it had before. She was learning to keep her tears to herself, lying in bed thinking about her old life. She might be successful now and have more excitement, but nothing could compare to her parents' arms around her and the whiskery face of her granddad.

She missed her old friends too. Although she did occasionally speak to Fae, she didn't have anyone to confide in. She had such a fear of failure that followed her around. In a funny way, Cal was one of the few people who might understand, as he'd lost his own business. *Genie's* was growing fast and she was scared about supply and demand. She was determined not to let Ada and Cal see how weak she was. They would be horrified to see her red-rimmed eyes and snotty face most mornings. It was why she got up extra early and blasted herself with a cold shower each morning. She often had to shower twice now that Cal was making her so annoyingly randy, but she was determined that was something else he'd never know.

CHAPTER THIRTY-NINE

*G*enie woke up and rubbed her eyes, easing her limbs out of bed. She was tempted to start walking round half naked too, to play Cal at his own game, but she wasn't confident enough about her body, even with her newfound waistline and firmer thighs.

She'd spent the evening tossing and turning in bed, imagining running her hands over Cal's glistening body, and had woken herself up many times with all the thrashing about.

She hadn't had time to indulge in her love of sweets or eat junk food for ages, so her body was tightening up. She still had a generous bust and wide hips, so she'd never feel like the models in magazines. She was seeing more women with curves in advertising, though, and it made her want to jump up and down with happiness to see a woman with a shape like hers look amazing in a designer outfit or even something from the high street. It now felt a bit more attainable to wear glamorous fashion and feel good in it, if curvy models were being shown looking sexy too.

Not that Genie had a penny of spare cash for clothes, as it all went into paying her business loans to Ada, and on stock and staffing. She was making a small profit already, even with five staff, and keeping her head above water, which she was mightily proud of. Her new accounts books were showing a healthy rise in business and for the first time in years she could start to save a little for any emergencies the business might have, like the cooker conking out or the booths needing filling in where she'd kicked them so much. She was actually pleased that she'd managed to control her temper recently, too. Her life had changed beyond recognition in a short space of time. Now she was the boss and everyone stood quietly to see what she had to say. It was weird but empowering, in a very scary way.

Seeing Cal walk into the kitchen to make some coffee, she took a deep breath and crept up beside him, making him jump. She smiled in satisfaction. 'Where's Ada?'

'She's still in bed. I think Ralph kept her out late again last night and she's not used to working then partying all night anymore. She used to do it all the time, but she hasn't for years. She's become a bit of a recluse since losing Granddad.'

Genie rested her head on his shoulder sadly and he kissed the top of her head, before releasing her and handing her the coffee cup. She felt a little bereft and had the urge to snuggle on his lap, but restrained herself with difficulty. She liked the vulnerable side of his personality more than the sexy playboy he usually showed the world.

'She seems to be spending a lot of time with Ralph.'

Cal shrugged his shoulders. 'I think he's always been in love with her, but she was besotted by my granddad.'

Genie's eyes went wide. Why hadn't she seen it before? Now Cal had said it, her brained whizzed through images of them together. It was so obvious!

'Stop gawping, Genie,' he said, laughing and dropping a kiss on her lips when she shut them, leaving her even more stunned. 'I don't think she sees him that way, but who knows if that will change?' He wandered over to look out of the windows and then turned to face her with a rueful smile. 'It seems that once a Mallory falls in love, they stay with their partner forever.'

He was looking straight into her eyes and she felt like she couldn't look anywhere else. He frowned and shook his head to clear it before opening the sliding doors and taking his coffee out onto the deck. Genie didn't know if he wanted time alone, but felt drawn to follow him. She sat next to him at the outdoor table and stared out to sea. It was too early for families to be out, but there were a few stray joggers and a woman walking her dog on the sand. She was trying to keep up with the excitable creature which was jumping in and out of the sea with such joy that Genie couldn't help but laugh.

Cal smiled too as the woman put the lead back on the dog and it then dragged her ankle-deep into the sea. She walked out of the waves and laughed hard as it shook its coat out and soaked her again. *Oh, to be that carefree*, thought Genie.

'Tell me more about your gran and granddad. What was Ned like?'

Cal stared out to sea and watched the waves lapping the shore without speaking for a moment. 'Grandad was a real character. He was always smiling and told us he'd won the lottery when he met Gran. I was a bit jealous of the way they felt about each other. How selfish was that?'

'Jealous? In what way?'

Cal rolled his shoulders and took a sip of coffee. 'They were always so besotted with each other. I wanted all their attention. I was a demanding kid,' he laughed suddenly, making her grin and cuff his shoulder.

'No... I can't believe that...'

He jabbed his finger into her ribs, making her squeal and jump away. 'My parents have the same soppy expression when they see each other. They've been married for years and have had the same sex with the same person for ages and they still goof all over each other. I just don't get it.'

'Me neither,' said Genie sarcastically, jabbing him back in the ribs. 'Having mind-blowing sex with a red-hot superstar or supermodel every day of your life must be soooooo boring…'

Cal looked thoughtful for a moment and then confused. Genie laughed and picked up their cups before going to rinse them in the sink. Cal's eyes followed the movement of her hips as she went and she turned just in time to see him lick his lips and stand up. The man was just so damn sexy. She couldn't imagine ever being bored in his company, but she guessed he must have a short attention span with women. She'd seen photos of him with several different girls when she'd searched.

'You've got plenty of time to find the love of your life, Cal. You're not exactly ancient.' She tried to stem the sinking feeling in her stomach.

'That's just it. Everyone in my family seems to meet that person when they're young.'

'Your granddad was much older than your gran,' she said reasonably.

'She was the one who set the trend, and since then it's happened to everyone who is old enough. I'm the black sheep as usual.'

Genie frowned. His cheeks were slightly red and he was looking at the floor and knocking his foot against the side of the kitchen cupboard. 'Look, it's still really early,' she said. 'It doesn't look like either of us got much sleep. Do you want to tell me about your past? You aren't a black sheep. Your family adore you. Ada's so proud of you.'

She walked over and took his hand, leading him to sit back on the couch, but he pulled her into his room instead and shut the door behind them with his foot. The little chrome clock beside his bed told her that it was only five thirty in the morning, so she didn't need to worry about work, but her heart was racing at being in Cal's room, even though she'd been in there before. The air was suddenly charged with electricity and her breathing became shallow. 'Cal?'

He turned her to face him and picked up her other hand, rubbing his thumb across her palm. 'I don't want to talk about my past. Maybe another time. What I do want is to kiss you and erase the thought of any other man from your mind,' he said honestly.

Genie began to shake a little. She licked her lips, not really knowing what to do. His eyes watched her tongue dart in and out and he bent to capture her mouth with his. He gently tugged her hands and her body melted into his as she sighed. He released her so that she could wind her fingers into his hair. He growled under his breath and scooped her up into his arms, carrying her to his bed where he heatedly kissed her lips before moving to the sweet spot just under her ear. He began to trail kisses across her neck and dipped lower while his hands glided along her skin and set a trail of fire wherever he touched.

She tried to clear her mind but his hands were pulling her hips into contact with his and she slid her palms under his shirt and pushed it up over his head, her eyes filled with lust and feasting on his glistening skin. She trailed her fingers under the edge of his jeans and dipped low, making him groan and catch her hands, placing them over his beating heart.

He stared into her eyes to make sure she knew what she was doing, but she released them and hooked her thumbs over the loops of his jeans and pulled them down, making him grin and rush to help her, opening the buttons and easing them from his hips. As he reached across her to slip on a condom from the bedside drawer, she almost cried in awe at the beauty of him, but he was already kissing her again and her mind turned to mush as his fingers laid a trail of fire across her skin. He raised her arms and slid her clothes from her body, and made love to every inch of her being. She revelled in the way he made her feel like a wanton goddess and she rode wave after wave of ecstasy before falling into a deep and dreamless sleep.

CHAPTER FORTY

*G*enie was in a world of confusion. Sleeping with Cal had been a revelation, but now her body craved his touch and although she was trying to play it cool, she was failing miserably.

Ada had asked her a few times if she was all right and had looked at them both oddly, but eventually she'd shrugged her shoulders.

Ada carried on with a supply check, so Genie could move a couple of their tables around for a big booking they had for lunchtime that day. They were finding that instead of the walk-in clients they'd usually had, people were now beginning to book in advance and requesting their favourite table. Cal had said this was usual for a new and popular restaurant, but as Genie had been running the place for years the same way, it was a big learning curve to juggle all of her new responsibilities. It scared her a little. Her dad had offered some advice, but this was her business and she'd do it her way.

Cal was often smiling these days and she'd had to swat his hands away from her a few times. He'd 'dragged' her into his lair every single night since that first time, and she'd guiltily snuck out early every morning in case Ada found out. She could imagine the look of disappointment on Ada's face when she saw them together. Genie knew Ada trusted her and Genie had broken that trust.

She'd thought about taking a day off, before they got the big booking, and had reached out to Fae and Una. Neither had picked up the phone, listened to her pathetic messages asking for them to call, or bothered to call her back.

Fae had finally sent her a text that morning saying she was sorry but things were hectic at work and with a new guy she fancied at the local bank, so she didn't have time to pop round, but she'd try to call Genie the following week to meet up. She did say she'd heard through the grapevine that her parents' restaurant was doing really well again and she thought that was great. *Her parents' restaurant!* Genie had almost thrown the phone out of the window when she'd heard that, but she was worried it might hit an unsuspecting seagull flying past. Genie had a weird affinity for birds, it seemed. Evil pigeon had turned out to be a girl! She'd tried to make a nest in the roof of Genie's grandad's shed but hadn't quite succeeded. There was straw and lolly sticks everywhere. Genie and Cal had set up a roosting box for her to lay her eggs in, which she had promptly moved into and seemed happy sticking her head out so she could keep an eye on Genie.

Genie was furious that Fae had attended her opening night and seen the rebrand, but obviously still thought the success was mostly down to her parents. Genie wondered how many other people thought this locally. Surely they all knew her parents had moved on? Her stomach ached and she sniffed. She rubbed her back, which was aching from an athletic performance in bed with Cal that she was actually quite proud of, but had no one to tell about.

Her mum still called almost every night just after closing time and they chatted about their day. Milly sounded much brighter these days and said she had some exciting news to tell her, but wanted to do it face to face.

Apparently it was nothing to worry about, but Genie thought it could only be that their move had been successful and they weren't coming home, which ripped her heart in two. She was grudgingly happy, though, that they were managing to take a few days off and spend time as a couple.

Her dad sounded less stressed too, although he kept asking questions about Ada and Cal and how she was running the ice cream bar, as if he couldn't quite believe her stories about it being a success. She knew he wanted her to do well, but he had admitted that when they'd first moved, he'd wanted her to fail and move to Cornwall with them – even if it meant her losing money, which she couldn't believe from someone who counted every penny like her dad did. She supposed it was because he'd had the worry of making enough money to support his family and staff for so long. She was just beginning to realise how hard this was, even though her restaurant was doing well.

She shoved the next set of tables together and sniffed the air appreciatively. Cal was baking again. He'd suddenly started making new recipes in the last few days and the kitchen was full to the rafters with his experiments. It reminded her of her granddad, and she'd even wondered if she should clear out the shed in the back garden to make room for supplies. It didn't seem her granddad would need it any time soon, with his new globetrotting ways and exotic lifestyle. She could have never imagined clearing out his beloved shed a few months ago. Now it seemed like her whole family had moved far away from the cosy life they had built together. The bonds that had held them close for years were stretching and swaying in the breeze, ready to snap at any time.

Genie saw Bailey watching her from the back door, and smiled back at him. He was such a handsome man, she was sure half her clientele came in just to watch him weave his way through the tables. They'd become good friends, but she was aware she was his boss and tried not to cross boundaries, which was pretty ridiculous when she thought about the fact that she was technically Cal's boss too.

Cal worked far more hours than she paid him for and he had been cooking up a storm at home too. Her stomach lurched when she thought of the penthouse as home. She looked up behind the restaurant to where her old family home had been. A new family was renting it now and she'd seen two small children skipping out of the front gate with a pretty blonde woman one day. She'd brushed away the tears that had sprung to her eyes and marched purposefully past. It had been her own fault, for wandering up that way to be nosy. She'd rushed back to the flat, crept into her room and cried under the bedcovers.

Nodding her head towards the beach and calling to Bailey that she was just popping out for ten minutes, she checked everything was organised in the restaurant, sweeping her gaze over it all. She quickly turned to cross over the road and jump the barrier that separated the pavement from the sandy beach below. Feeling the soft grains beneath her feet, she eased her flip-flops off and sank straight down onto the warm surface, leaning her chin on her knees and running her fingers through the sand as she stared out to sea.

She thought about Cal and how he would surely go back to America soon, then about Bailey and the prospect of him taking over Cal's role. Not the one with her – although she did get the feeling that he had a soft spot for her too. He was always joking and smiling around her and he'd spent a lot of time telling her about Liam.

She was used to Liam and his gran popping into the restaurant and she often let the little boy sit on the high stool behind her precious ice cream bar and sneak samples of the gooey confections while his dad wasn't looking. Instead of the sadness she'd thought the memory of sitting there with her own grandma might bring, it made her heart soar like the wind at the joy in his little round face when he held out his hands for another taste. She would tickle him and make him laugh and Bailey told her that Liam took his role as chief ice cream taster very seriously. She could see why Bailey adored him so much. She loved him too. It was hard not to. How could his mother have left him, however young she might have been? It must have been devastating for Liam.

Bailey had told her more about how frightened Liam's mum had been, giving birth at such a young age. Genie's heart went out to her and she wondered if she'd ever regretted the decision to let her son go. If she ever tried to get Liam back, she'd have a fight on her hands from Bailey. She knew it was something he worried about constantly, but he had an even bigger family at *Genie's* to offer him support now.

Cal found her sitting on the beach five minutes later. He leaned over the balustrade and looked up and down the sands before spotting her right beneath him. 'You ok?' He jumped over the barrier and landed on the sand beside her, sending grains flying in all directions.

'Who's running the shop?' she asked in alarm, turning around and about to get up. He settled her back down with a smile that made her insides melt.

'Your staff. They're more than capable of coping without us both for five minutes. I've only popped out to come and find you. The queues for our new ice cream and cones have finally died down.' He grinned and he slid his arm around her shoulders, as there was no one else on this part of the beach.

'Our ice cream?'

'Yes. Our. We made them together,' he said simply.

'What do you want from me?' she asked, trying to look into his eyes, but having to shield her own from the sun's glare.

'Nothing you're not willing to give,' he said, reaching down and placing the sweetest kiss on her lips while he pushed himself up, brushing down his sandy jeans and straightening his soft white cotton short-sleeved shirt. Giving her a cheeky wink, he offered her his hand and she reached out and let him pull her up, their bodies making swift contact before it was broken and they looked around guiltily to see if anyone was looking for them. 'Come on. Let's get back to work.'

CHAPTER FORTY-ONE

*C*al wasn't quite sure how to tell Genie where he'd been going for the last few Mondays. He hadn't exactly lied to her, but he hadn't told her the truth either. He was enjoying being around her and working in the restaurant, but he was becoming restless. He could easily lose himself in her every single night, but he'd begun to back away and he knew she was confused. He could have kicked himself for not handling this better, but when the call had come, it had been hard to turn down.

He missed the buzz of his old life, creating masterpieces and feeling the glow of pride when people appreciated his skill as a chef. Working in the kitchen at *Genie's* and being around her tireless energy and enthusiasm for her family business had reignited his passion for cooking. Now someone was offering him a chance to shine again and he wasn't about to let that opportunity pass him by. He owed so much to his own family and had to build on his skills and repay them for the time and investment they had given his career. Plus, he was seriously broke and the new offer was beyond his wildest dreams.

He'd barely had time to rest lately, what with work, practicing recipes and trying to persuade Genie to sleep with him at every opportunity. How Ada hadn't noticed, he couldn't fathom. Perhaps she had, and was keeping out of it. She usually had an opinion on everything, though, so he'd be surprised.

He and Genie tried to act naturally around everyone else, but his hands itched to touch her all the time and he was finding it hard to concentrate on work, so he'd had to avoid her a little. He'd travelled to London on the train for the first meeting, but he'd felt uncomfortable, even though no one knew who he was. It had been a stressful few weeks, and he'd had to keep it all from Genie and his gran. He didn't want to upset them before he knew what was happening.

He'd cursed when he'd been spotted by a local journalist and had to meet them and persuade them to keep quiet. The only way he could do it was by offering an exclusive interview about his new job. The one he'd already started each Monday. His upper lip began to sweat and he rubbed his hand distractedly through his hair, making it stick up on end. He thought of the shiny new hire car he'd just signed the paperwork for and how he'd explained to Genie that he needed a car as he'd decided to travel to London once a week to check out the latest food trends. She hadn't believed him, he could tell by the way she'd raised her eyebrows and shrugged, but turned away from him. He understood that she felt he was being distant, but the job he'd been offered was too good to turn down. It would mean he could pay off all his debts very quickly and have a healthy income again. Surely Genie should understand that?

He'd put her name on the car insurance too, even though she'd said it was unnecessary, and he'd persuaded her to give it a try. She'd passed her test years ago, but had never really needed to drive or had the money for a car.

They'd had a few interesting days out, where he'd let her take the wheel. She ended up loving it so much that she asked to drive to work each day, even though it was a few hundred metres up the road. He grinned as he remembered her driving him to a secluded spot and telling him it was a great place to watch the sun set. They'd spent two minutes looking at the horizon before hastily shedding their clothes and exploring each other's slick bodies on the back seat.

He could have stayed there all night, but she'd got cold and had snuggled into his neck, placing tiny kisses all around his collar bone before he was rock hard and he drove home as fast as he dared before racing her upstairs and into his bed, where he ravaged her once again.

He couldn't seem to get enough of her and that worried him, too. He was becoming too dependent on her and if he moved to London, or back home, he knew she'd never leave the business. She'd separated from her parents for it, after all.

He watched her bend across a table and whisk a cloth over the surface, exposing a tiny glimpse of flesh at her waist as her shirt rode up. Even that was enough to make his blood boil. Noticing Bailey looking at her longingly too made Cal shake his bad mood off.

He had some decisions to make. Perhaps it was better if she was with someone like Bailey. He had a ready-made family with his young son, whom Genie adored, and he was a good guy, even though Cal hated him. Cal hated anyone who looked at Genie the way Bailey did. Perhaps it would be better for Cal to be far away from the temptation she offered him, so she could settle down with someone who could stick around. The thought was like a punch to the guts. There was no way he was going to walk away and let Bailey step into his shoes without a fight.

The job he'd been offered was for a television show. They wanted a celebrity chef and had heard he was in town. They didn't seem to care that he had a failure in his past, once he'd shoved his ego aside and admitted to his mistakes. The television company loved that. A phoenix arising from the flames, they'd said. They believed people would relate to him not giving up, and the pilot they had made was all ready to go out. Then people would know who he was – and he'd have to tell Genie before that happened.

Ada would cope. She was used to a press frenzy, but he didn't want that for Genie. It had destroyed all of his previous relationships, even though most of those women had been in the media spotlight themselves and liked the fame. Genie was different, and he was scared that it would change everything.

CHAPTER FORTY-TWO

*G*enie was tapping her fingers on the table, outside on the deck at Ada's flat. Cal had asked them both to meet him and they had discussed between them how weirdly he was behaving.

Genie had finally given in and told Ada about their relationship and, instead of being angry, Ada had smiled the widest smile Genie had ever seen and hugged her hard, with tears glistening in her eyes. Genie had been relieved initially, but now she was embarrassed. She felt like she had a lump of wood in her stomach.

Cal had been so jumpy and restless lately. He couldn't quite look her in the eye. She was expecting the worst. She guessed he was bored with her now they'd slept together, even though he still couldn't seem to get enough of her.

He'd told her often how she made him feel like he could conquer anything and how beautiful she was to him. That always made her cringe as she knew it wasn't true. He was probably sleeping with her because he hadn't had time to meet anyone else and she was literally in his pocket, with a bedroom next door.

She'd been living in a bubble of ecstasy and she knew it had to burst at some point. He was far too gorgeous and sexy to be interested in her for long. For a while he'd had her believing him, but recently she'd known something was wrong and, with her track history, it was probably her.

She'd removed herself from the situation by being too busy to see him. Obviously she'd had to see him at work, but she'd gone out a few nights and, although he'd asked her where she was going, he'd been distracted and didn't really seem to care.

Two of the nights she'd babysat for Bailey, so that he could go out for dinner with his parents. They had tried to refuse, but she'd insisted. She hadn't a clue how to look after a small child, but Liam had curled up on the sofa next to her and watched a kids' movie and then fallen asleep in her arms both times, so she'd carried him to his bedroom and settled him into bed. When Bailey had returned home, she'd sat with them all chatting for ages and it made her homesick for her own little family. She knew that her grandad was coming home soon and she desperately missed him still, but she had changed since he'd left. They all had.

She jumped as Ada took her hand to stop the tapping and Genie looked at her worriedly. 'He's leaving, isn't he?'

Ada let out the breath she'd been holding and sighed, her shoulders drooping. 'Honestly... I don't know. Something's not right. Have you two argued?'

Genie flushed and looked down at their interlinked hands. 'No. We don't argue. He tells me what to do and I ignore him. It works perfectly.'

They both burst out laughing and Cal walked in right then with three glasses and a bottle of red wine. Genie stopped laughing and looked at his face, her smile dropping. She tried to straighten her shoulders and look tough. She'd already been deserted by her family and one more person she

215

cared about wouldn't break her, but she sagged in defeat and waited for the inevitable.

Cal kissed both women on the cheek, forcing Genie to look at him for a moment and giving her what he assumed was a reassuring smile, then he pulled up a chair and poured three huge glasses of red wine. Genie slugged back a huge mouthful and then almost keeled over. She was used to £2.99 bottles of plonk, but this was a rich and fruity vintage and the flavour burst into her mouth and made her cough. Cal reached over to rub her back but she shrugged him off.

Ada stared at them both and then rolled her eyes heaven-ward. 'Right, you two. What's going on?'

'I told you…' began Genie once she'd managed to grab a breath.

Cal's head shot up. 'You told her?'

Ada brushed his comment off. 'Oh, I've known from the very first night.' When both looked aghast, she laughed and slapped Cal on the back as he almost chocked on his wine too. 'You two are awful at secrets.' Her piercing eyes met Cal's. 'Well, that's what I thought until about ten minutes ago. Now, what have you been up to?'

Genie's eyes crinkled in mirth at Cal being told off by his gran. She hadn't heard a cross word between them before. Ada always let Cal get away with everything, even if it meant him filching the last biscuit. Then her stomach sank again and she looked out across the sea, ignoring Cal's attempt to take her hand.

Ada looked at her sternly. 'Genie, don't be petulant.' Genie's skin flushed and she looked up defiantly, taking another sip of wine and managing not to choke on it this time. She turned to face Cal.

'I've been offered a job in London,' he said quickly, taking another sip of wine and placing his glass back on the table. His eyes implored Genie to understand. 'There is a regular cooking slot on daytime television and the current host has decided to move abroad. They're frantically doing screen tests with new chefs.'

'So that's where you've been every Monday?' asked Genie, a slight edge to her voice as she took another mouthful of wine and felt it burn the back of her throat. *Another one bites the dust.*

Ada was trying not to look too excited for him, but clapped her hands and gave him a warm hug. Genie just stared at him.

'They liked your screen test?' asked Ada, smiling widely, then looking worriedly at Genie. The smile slipped from her face and her eyes lost some of their sparkle.

'They want me to start filming next week. The pilot they did was well received with test audiences. A local journalist spotted me and I had to agree to an exclusive to shut him up. I've managed to stave him off, but it will be all over the papers next week.'

Genie pushed her chair back until it fell over and she grabbed the bottle to refill her glass. 'So you wouldn't have told us if it wasn't going to be in the paper?'

'Of course I would have told you!' Cal stood up and faced her. 'I was going to tell you both. I didn't mention it before in case it didn't work out. I need to make a proper income, Genie.'

Ada bit her lip and then rubbed her forehead with her hand, brushing a wisp of hair out of her eyes. 'I told you I'd help you out if you needed money, Cal.'

'I don't want your money, Gran.' He leaned over and gave her a hug, but he was still looking at Genie. 'I want to be able to pay off my debts and perhaps I could invest in *Genie's...*' Genie gave him a dark look. 'Or perhaps not...'

'It's fine. Bailey has been practicing a lot and he can take over. He might not be anywhere near as good as you yet, but he's got talent.' Genie turned her nose up at him and stared at the undulating waves of the sea, lit up by the streetlights along the promenade.

'No!' said Ada and Cal in unison, so that Genie almost jumped out of her skin and sloshed some of the wine on her jeans. She put the glass down and rubbed ineffectually at the stain, frowning and starting to feel a bit drunk. She was trying to quell the panic that was rising in her stomach. Cal was leaving.

'I'll only be in London three days a week and back here for the rest of the time. I can easily bake enough for the restaurant on those two or three days. I just dragged it out because I liked being there.' He realised his mistake when Ada grabbed his arm and Genie turned to face him with fire in her eyes and fists bunched.

'You mean I've been paying you for five days a week when you could have done the work in two?'

Cal flushed and held up his hands. 'That's not what I meant,' he tried to soothe her, but she just batted his hands away when he tried to touch her. 'I mean that I will work into the night on the days I'm home to make sure the restaurant has enough stock. I wouldn't leave you if I didn't think you could survive without me.' Genie almost bent double as his words punched her in the stomach.

Ada winced and gave him a pitying look which he clearly didn't understand.

'I can easily survive without *you*,' growled Genie, grabbing the wine and marching towards her room. 'I don't need my family and I don't need a gigolo who's just around for a while. I'm a survivor,' she called over her shoulder, and slammed her bedroom door shut without looking back.

CHAPTER FORTY-THREE

'You wally,' said Ada, patting Cal affectionately on the shoulder. 'Come on, grab another bottle of wine and tell me all about it.'

Cal looked at Genie's closed bedroom door and began to stride after her, but Ada caught his arm and shook her head. 'Leave her to cool down for a while.'

'Why is she so angry? I can still help out at the restaurant when I'm here.' His heart was pounding in his chest but he also felt crushed that Genie hadn't listened to him, or let him explain.

Ada rolled her eyes at him and sat back down, waiting for Cal to collect a fresh bottle of wine from the kitchen and join her. His forehead was creased with worry and his hair was all mussed up. 'Didn't you just hear her say that everyone she loves leaves her?'

Cal's startled eyes met hers and she took his hand in her own. 'It's in the genes,' she said sombrely, then gave him a cheeky wink.

'What is?'

'Falling in love so quickly.'

'Genie isn't part of our family.'

'No… but you are,' was all she said. He digested that piece of information while she sat drinking her wine. Then he caught his breath and began to tell her of his plans.

'I need to start building a life again, Gran.'

Ada took his hand and rubbed some warmth into it. 'Plus, how you feel for Genie scares the hell out of you?'

Cal shrugged and rubbed his tired eyes. He hadn't been sleeping much lately, and Genie being too busy to spend many nights with him was making him grumpy and his groin ache. Perhaps she'd like it if he left, and eased the way for Bailey to step into his shoes. The thought made his blood boil. Perhaps that was why she kept brushing him off. He pictured Toby's eager face, too, and his mouth drew into a thin line. That woman was too popular by far. Everyone else could back off. The problem was that he wasn't going to be around as much and he might even have to go back home at some point. What chance did he have of persuading Genie that long distance relationships could work?

He shook his head to clear it, as he hated the thought of her in a different country to him. He wasn't even completely sure how he felt about her. She was argumentative and bossy, but she was also soft and delicious and loyal. She was different from any other woman he'd met and he loved that about her. He took a gulp of wine and looked into his grandmother's knowing eyes. She was no fool and she knew him better than he did himself.

She nodded her head and tilted it towards Genie's door. He pushed himself out of his chair, kissed the top of his grandmother's hair and strode purposefully towards Genie's room. He wasn't about to let Genie decide what was best for them both and he knew that from now on, his life would include her.

~

*I*t had been two weeks since Cal's bombshell and he'd tried to use every inch of his charm to persuade her to give him and their relationship a chance, but Genie kept repeating the fact that he would be leaving soon and it was better to cool it off now.

It astounded him how much he wanted her to give in to him. He craved her like a drug. He finally understood his dad's obsession with his mum and the way his grandad gazed adoringly every time he saw his wife. He couldn't keep his hands off her.

One night he'd found her crying in bed. He'd just meant to comfort her, but he wasn't made of steel. He'd tried to turn away and talk to her instead, but his rejection had made her cry even harder and his defences had broken like a dam. Their lovemaking had been almost feral, the way they just couldn't get enough of each other, as if they both thought their bliss might end soon.

Now she was trying to back off again and he was determined not to let her. He wasn't running away like her family had, like he had admittedly when his own problems with his business got too much. He could relate to her parents' misery but still hadn't had the courage to tell Genie that he knew why they had gone.

His first TV programme had gone out and the article in the local press had caught the attention of the national papers. People had discovered where he worked and *Genie's* was now bursting at the seams with old and new customers.

They sat long into the night trying to decide what to do. They didn't actually need more custom, *Genie's* had become so successful anyway. Now the extra footfall was becoming a headache.

Seeing Genie so stressed and knowing he was the cause

of it broke his heart. They had tried to ride the experience and enjoy the attention, but he could see it was making Ada nervous in case anyone realised she was here too and her quiet life was shattered.

Both of the women in Cal's life were miserable, and so was he. He could give up his new job, but he actually enjoyed the challenge. This whole situation was really testing his ability to stay put and not run and hide.

CHAPTER FORTY-FOUR

*G*enie sat slumped in one of the chairs in the restaurant, with her legs pushed in front of her at odd angles. She needed to stretch out her aching muscles, but her legs had other ideas. They felt like jelly.

She should be euphoric, she'd had her busiest day ever, but now people were getting grumpy with her staff if they couldn't find a chair or get served by Cal. They asked her so many questions about him and some even requested his number, which she thought was cheeky. She'd been tempted to accidently-on-purpose stamp on a few toes.

Cal wasn't her property and could date who he liked, but she didn't like other women mooning all over him in front of her. Not that anyone knew they'd been seeing each other, if you could call it that. They'd never actually been on a date and spent most of their lives working or hidden away in his bedroom. Perhaps he was just using her to scratch an itch. Then she felt disloyal, as he'd never made her feel that way.

She'd always known he'd leave her, though. He was far too gorgeous to want to hang around with someone as unglamorous as her. He might have been entertained by her for a while, but he was becoming more and more distracted by his new television show.

The TV company was putting more demands on his time and his new personal assistant, Penelope, had even 'accidentally' called her a couple of times asking for Cal, sounding proprietorial, as if Genie was his secretary down here or something. Genie had been tempted to tell her that he was in the shower after some mind-blowing sex, but that would have been a lie, as they barely saw each other these days. He was more likely to be having sex with Penelope than Genie. Genie had seen a picture of her on Cal's phone when her number came up with a work text. She was leggy and a glorious redhead. The bitch. It was just Genie's luck to fall for someone so gorgeous and talented.

Why couldn't she like a normal man, who lived nearby and loved her, despite the fact that she was bossy and a bit temperamental at certain times of the month... ok, most times of the month. Genie hadn't exactly given Cal much to work with, she thought glumly, rubbing her tired eyes and seeing Ada come into the restaurant.

'You ok?' asked Genie.

Ada shrugged and pulled out a chair, plonking herself down, which was so unlike Ada, who would usually sit demurely with her legs crossed at the side, nibble a sandwich and sip her tea, while the rest of the staff all ploughed in and stuffed their faces with any leftovers, having had no time to go home and eat, or take a lunch break.

Ada frowned and her eyes flashed. 'I want to come back to work. I know Cal loves his new job,' she said. That fact was like a knife to the heart for Genie and she winced. 'But I love my job too,' Ada continued. 'Half of our customers are press now, hoping to catch a glimpse of him. If they find out

I'm here too, you'll never be able to serve another customer again. I'm so sorry, Genie.'

Watching them, Bailey brought over two steaming and frothy mugs of hot chocolate. Genie smiled as it reminded her of the first time she'd sat down and spoken properly to Ada. It was the day that *Genie's* had been born. She smiled her thanks at Bailey and asked him to grab a mug of his own and join them. Everyone else had finally gone home.

While Bailey walked back to the kitchen to get one, she turned to Ada. 'Look. We both knew Cal wouldn't be here long term. He's pretty much taught Bailey how to run the patisserie side of things and Bailey wants the job. Perhaps Cal should just stay away now?'

Ada looked down into her lap guiltily as if she'd been thinking the same thing. 'How can we tell him to stay away when you're here, Genie?'

Genie's forehead creased and she tried to think what Ada could mean. 'I'm pretty sure he doesn't think I'm fleecing you anymore, Ada. Plus the business is in profit. We could try and make more of his celebrity status, or yours, but the restaurant is too small to cope. I don't need or want to expand to bigger premises. This place is my dream.'

Ada shook her head, as if Genie was missing the point completely and then sighed, rubbing her temples with her fingers. Genie sipped her drink as Bailey returned and sat down. 'Do you think you could cope in the kitchen if Cal left?' Genie asked Bailey. His eyes went wide and he stopped with his drink in mid-air, then put it back on the table.

'Honestly? I'm nowhere near Cal's standard, but he's taught me all the basic recipes and I'm willing to keep learning.'

'How about if we sent you to night school one day a week?' asked Genie. 'Could your parents look after Liam? I know you don't like being away from him, but we could find out if there is a course at the local college. It's only fifteen minutes up the road.'

Bailey looked from Ada to Genie, as if to see if they were joking, and grabbed Genie's hand in excitement. Genie knew that no-one had given him an opportunity to have qualifications before. Ada nodded. 'It's a great idea. We should do that anyway. You have shown such talent, Bailey. You'll be building a solid future for your family.' She looked so sad for a moment as she stared at their interlinked fingers.

Genie noticed and quickly put her hands in her lap, taking a long sip of her drink and surfacing with a cream-covered nose that broke the tension and made them all laugh.

'I think you should come back to work, Ada,' she said. 'We need you here to charm the customers, especially the pushy new ones. We can't make more space, but we can capitalise on the custom we have. I've been going over and over this idea in my mind. Let's hire two more part-time staff and offer delivery services to the beach.'

Genie explained her idea excitedly. 'People can place their order here, then grab a ticket and go and sit on the beach, or even order via an application on their phones. It's the end of the summer now, and still warm. The beach can be our extended restaurant with an even better view. Our new staff can take the orders across in cooler boxes. Gramps made me a couple when he was having one of his invention phases. He told me to go and sell ice cream on the beach if I was so passionate about it. Perhaps he was right! He made cone holders to stack inside. They would fit our coffee and tea cups too.' She jumped up and started waving her arms around trying to envisage how this could work, enthusiasm rushing through her veins, then whacked her arm on one of the booths and swore colourfully in Spanish, making Ada and Bailey jump up to see if she was ok.

She hugged them both. 'This could work, couldn't it?'

Bailey and Ada hugged her back hard, and she dragged them into the garden to show them the cooler boxes. Her grandad's lattice invention inside was lightweight and removable for easy cleaning. 'You granddad made this?' asked Ada in awe.

'Yep. I should have listened to him, but he always made it seem like he didn't support me following my ice cream dream. I thought he wanted to shut me up and get me out of the restaurant, so I sulked instead.' Genie hung her head and Bailey pulled her into a fast hug, resting his head on the top of hers. They heard a noise behind them and the little group turned to find Cal standing at the restaurant back door, watching them all. He looked tired and she wanted to run to him, but stood her ground. Bailey's grip on her tightened for a fraction of a second, then he let her go. Her smile dropped and she locked eyes with Cal.

Ada smiled widely for the first time in days and went to bring Cal over to join them. 'Genie's just had an idea. Let's all go back and make ourselves a late dinner of leftovers and we can sit and decide where we go from here.'

Cal eyed Bailey over the top of Genie's head and followed them back indoors. Genie had picked up the two cool boxes and Cal took them from her and peered inside, his hands brushing hers, making her skin spark so she almost dropped the boxes. She gripped them harder before placing them on the floor.

'Don't you have to be back for Liam, Bailey?' asked Cal.

'It's ok. Mum's there with him,' answered Bailey, with a chilled edge to his voice. 'He's exhausted today. They took him to his first playcentre.' He paused for a second. 'Now I'm earning a full-time wage, I can treat him a bit more and support my family. He knows I'm always nearby.' Cal took the dig to the ribs, but stood straighter and followed Genie.

She hoped Cal felt bad for trying to make Bailey leave. He worked so hard and was an integral part of their team now. She needed him more than ever at the moment. They'd become close, she thought of him as one of her best friends.

Fae and Una had begun showing up at the restaurant in the last couple of weeks too and had brought their gang along. It was like an out of body experience. Genie had dreamt of them wanting to spend time in her restaurant and with her, but now they were demanding more and more of her attention, she zoned out. She smiled politely, answered their questions about her business and Cal, shook hands with their new friends, agreed with Una that they were besties.

Of course they could come to the restaurant any time they liked, and spend time with her, she'd told them, before mostly avoiding their tables with every fibre of her being. If Fae looked disappointed that the owner was too busy to sit and chat with their noisy crowd, then Genie bit her lip and hardened her heart. She had real friends to talk to and spend time with now.

They might have come from the most unusual of circumstances, but Cal, Ada, Bailey, and even Ralph and Toby were all there for her, as she was for them. Toby hadn't quite given in when he'd learnt from Ralph about her and Cal. He still sent her texts and popped in for coffee now and then, but she knew he'd met someone new and half did it to wind Cal up, and half because they really got on well.

Genie enjoyed having such hot and interesting friends. Toby often walked into the restaurant and kissed her on the lips in front of Fae and Una, because Genie had confided to him about them. Cal would growl from the kitchen doorway and then shake Toby's hand a little too forcefully, but he also knew why Toby was doing it and couldn't openly kiss Genie himself, however much he told her that he wanted to. The journalists still dotted around would love to witness this. She sometimes wished he would declare some sort of affection for her, but he'd probably be embarrassed to be linked publicly to a little dormouse like her. She longed for Amazonian legs and flowing blonde locks, but she had big eyes, big hips and big boobs instead. How could she compete?

Genie waited for them all to sit down and unwrapped plates of cold meats and cheeses and placed a baguette on the table with some cutlery. She'd added the cheese with a fork, and kept it well away from the meat, but she was actually able to be near the stuff now. Her parents leaving, and the evil pigeon dropping the stuff all around her, had half-cured her cheese phobia. She supposed that was something to be grateful for.

She thought they'd all be famished and dive on the food, but everyone was subdued and waited for her to speak. She faced Cal. 'We need to change it up. Our regulars are being pushed out. I've been thinking of having a priority booking card for regular locals only, and offering an ice cream and coffee delivery service to the beach.' Cal seemed to be listening carefully, but didn't comment, so she continued. 'We need to use the hype about you in some way, but you being present might be difficult for a while.' Her gaze implored him to understand.

He looked directly into her troubled eyes and sat back in his chair, clearly taking in how tired they all were. Genie knew that he was under more and more pressure to base himself in London and she was giving him an easy way out. She'd survive. She felt a protective wall begin to build itself around her heart and she tried not to betray the fact that it was breaking.

'It will be easier for you if I'm not around?'

Genie hesitated a fraction too long and Ada winced. 'Of course it won't be easier. It will be hard on all of us,' said Ada.

She gave Genie a look that dared her to defy her. 'Especially Genie. You two have become so close.' Genie gulped and looked at Bailey, who digested that bit of information, his face flushing as he looked between her and Cal. Genie didn't know why Ada had felt the need to lay their private life open to the world, or to Bailey anyway, and she couldn't quite meet anyone's eye, she just hung her head and let her hair fall across her face.

Cal leaned over and brushed the hair away tenderly. 'If it is easier for you, I can stay in London during the week and visit you in secret at the weekends.'

Ada looked like she wanted to shake him and Genie lifted her head with fire in her eyes. Even Bailey shuddered at his stupidity.

'That's been the problem all along, hasn't it?'

When Cal looked clueless, she ranted on. 'You never did want anyone to know about us. Why would you want to be seen with a mousy local girl when you could have two supermodels hanging off each arm. You just pottered around here checking that I wasn't after your inheritance, then got a better offer.'

Cal pushed his chair back, so that it fell with a clunk to the floor. He stood looking at Ada for help, but she was tight-lipped. Cal's skin flushed red and his fingers bunched. 'What the hell? I'd have happily taken you out if I'd thought that was what you wanted. I assumed you didn't want the staff to know about us.' When Genie tried to shout back, he spoke over her, his voice level and clear, but with an edge that made her shut up and listen. 'You told me that you were my boss and you didn't date the staff.'

Both Ada and Bailey gawped but didn't interrupt.

'You seem happy for me to be near you at home, but as soon as we are here you act like I don't exist. I tried to teach Bailey to help you out as much as I can, and as much as you love this place, I love what I do, too. If I could follow my dreams every day here like you, I would, but me being here causes chaos now. It will be worse when they realise my gran has invested in your business.' His face flamed but he looked at his fists and made himself take deep breaths and release them. He stood facing her, both of their eyes spitting fire.

'You're the one that's been making the rules here, not me.'

Genie opened her mouth to scream at him, but suddenly all the adrenaline left her and her shoulders sagged. 'I didn't mean to make you feel that way. I'm sorry. I thought you were embarrassed by me.' Cal took her hand and Bailey and Ada backed away and took the plates and cups to wash up in the kitchen. Bailey's shoulders were drooping slightly and Genie realised he must be wrung out from all of this, too.

Genie looked down at their entwined hands, then up again at Cal. 'I don't know what the answer is.'

'I don't either, but pushing me away won't solve anything. I can work in London during the week if it's easier for you, but you won't keep me away at the weekends.'

Genie moved to rest her head on his chest and listened to his heartbeat, as he pulled her whole body into contact with his own. Her heart began to race and her hands crept around his waist as if they had a will of their own. 'I don't want you to go, but I don't know what else to do.'

'Well, that's a good start,' he smiled down at her and she ran her hand through his hair, kissing him gently on the lips. Hearing someone close a cupboard in the kitchen, they kept their hands linked and wandered in to see if they could help.

'Where's Bailey?' asked Genie.

'I told him to go back to the flat to get some sleep,' said Ada. 'I thought you two might need some privacy.'

Cal went over and hugged his gran tightly until she squealed to be let go. Genie kissed her soft cheek and they locked up and walked back to the penthouse arm-in-arm. As soon as they stepped through the door Ada bid them good-night and took a glass of water and a headache tablet with her. Cal swept Genie up into his arms without a word and carried her into his room, kicking the door closed behind them.

CHAPTER FORTY-FIVE

*G*enie picked up her phone and put it back down again. She'd had countless annoying messages from Fae and Una asking her to join them on a night out. If they'd have done that months ago, she'd have jumped at the chance and even now, she felt the pull to join them. They were her oldest friends.

She kind of wished she could be carefree and pretend to be the girl she'd been before her parents left. But every spare moment she had now was spent cooking and replenishing her ice cream stocks. Her body literally drooped with exhaustion as she walked these days. She'd had to buy a huge storage freezer and set it up in her granddad's shed. She'd felt sad, moving some of his inventions out of the way, but she'd tried her best not to disturb too many things. His most recent phone calls had been quite frequent and she guessed from his tone that he was feeling homesick. She half expected him to just turn up one day and surprise her. She didn't want everything to be so different that he'd run away again.

She quite liked having Fae and Una back in her life. It was

a bit like a comfort blanket, although this one had prickles inside, as if you'd dragged it along the forest floor. The funny thing was, now they wanted to be around her, she was genuinely too busy to see them. This time it was because she was successful, not just a loser.

She realised that she hadn't really been much fun before. She'd been so obsessed with her family and probably a bit of a bore. She wondered if she'd have dumped them if they'd been going through what she had, but decided that that train of thinking wouldn't get her anywhere. They couldn't wait to see her now and she should be grateful, she supposed. She understood what Ada had meant about being hounded by the press, as a few local papers had asked for interviews with her about the fact that Cal had worked at *Genie's* for a while. She'd laughed and brushed it off, saying he'd been on holiday and had begun popping in to use the kitchens. Then he'd offered to train her staff for a couple of weeks before he went home, as they were friends. The story was so boring that they'd left her alone after that. She was a bit in awe of how Cal and Ada survived real press onslaughts.

There had been so many staff meetings lately. Cal was trying to make it work by training Bailey as much as he could, coming home at weekends and hiding in the back of the restaurant. She could see the bags under his eyes and the way his smile didn't quite reach his eyes. Holding down two very demanding jobs was becoming increasingly difficult. Genie tried not to think of him in glamorous hotels and bars, or relaxing after a day of filming with Perfect Penelope. It made her foot itch to kick something, preferably Cal's balls.

Cal didn't fit into her life any more than Ada did, really. They were probably just flitting in to sprinkle some magic over her, then they would fly back home to America. Genie felt proud of the part she'd played in helping them both to heal, as they'd helped her, but it was like a double whammy to lose her parents and now Cal and Ada.

She feared the press would turn its attention to Ada soon, too. If they found out she had invested in *Genie's*, then all of their hard work would be overshadowed, and her family and friends would probably think she'd had this golden opportunity handed to her on a platter. They'd ignore the blood, sweat and floods of tears it had taken to get to this point. Genie had never worked so hard in her life and was starting to get a bit fed up with people underestimating her. She had built this business back up with her bare hands and she'd continue to hold it up, long after her superstar friends had gone home.

She sat down on the mattress in her bedroom and looked round at the familiar muted grey walls and delicate little dressing table and gilded mirror. Even the plant pots were so beautifully made that Genie felt they had been crafted just for this room. The minute you stepped over the threshold you immediately felt calm. The bed was so inviting, with its view across the sea. It was hard to feel unhappy there. She thought back to her messy bedroom at home, with the same sea view, and craved her mother's arms and words of comfort. Milly always stood up for Genie when anyone upset her, with her dad behind, silently backing her up. Tears squeezed out of Genie's eyes and plopped onto the duvet and spread out onto the fabric, making a dark stain. She sniffed, wishing her mum could see her now. Not with a runny nose and a red face, but as the owner of their family business. The person who had made it flourish again. If Ada and Cal left, then she would make it her mission to bring her parents home.

Glancing up, she noticed that one of her plants was looking a bit droopy. She gave it some water from the glass by her bed. She could sympathise with its state, as her own limbs were feeling decidedly heavy too. She needed a drink of something a bit stronger if she was going to be able to get to sleep herself, so she padded to the kitchen in bare feet, grey jogging bottoms and a deep red vest top. Her hair was swept back in a hairband. She noticed her nails needed painting; she had a slight chip on one finger. She berated herself for letting her standards slip and went to switch on the kettle, then veered left and grabbed a glass and a bottle of wine instead.

Filling her glass generously, she sat on the couch, looking out across the water. She tucked her legs under her bottom and leaned back into the welcoming material, allowing her muscles to relax for the first time that day. She was too restless to sleep and had a strong urge to call her mum. She glanced at the clock on the wall to her right and realised it was after midnight.

She'd been calling her mum a lot more lately and Genie felt Milly sounded happier and more settled. She was enjoying owning the café and was working fewer hours, but there was always an edge to her voice when Genie enquired about her grandmother's health. Genie could imagine Lucille as one of those dastardly gangsters that ruled the roost from her armchair, barking out orders to her minions, with dark glasses and a secret bunker built under her house. Genie smothered a giggle at the mental picture of her grandparents running a crime empire from their suburban bungalow in Cornwall. Her grandmother would make her 'hired muscle' wear flowery aprons and brush their hair until it shone. One stare from Lucille was enough to make grown men weep.

Milly had asked Genie so many questions about her life and the business that Genie had laughed and begged to surrender! Perhaps she was more like her own mother than she realised? Genie hoped not. She loved hearing how proud

Milly was of her, though, and they had booked in a visit to each other soon.

Milly had subtly enquired about Ada, Cal and even Bailey. She'd sounded sad for a moment when she asked how serious it was with Cal. Milly hated being so far away, but she promised to jump on a train and come home for a visit to meet him soon. Genie just hoped she managed it before he left again. Milly had said that Cal sounded like a dreamboat, and they had both giggled like schoolgirls.

Genie asked her mum about her relationship with her dad, but Milly had brushed it off, saying they were fine. Genie had been too tired to push the subject, but when her mum arrived in a couple of weeks, she wouldn't let her go back to Cornwall and her demanding mother, before Genie had all the facts.

Genie's grandma was still playing up. It seemed like she'd had an argument with Milly about something, too. Milly mentioned it in passing, but there was more to that story, Genie knew it.

Genie had told her mum that all the restaurants along the parade were flourishing now and had mentioned that Trudie had popped in to ask after her. Milly had gone silent and then changed the subject, so Genie thought perhaps their friendship had changed since her mum had left, or they'd had an argument about Milly leaving Genie. It would be just like Trudie to stick up for her, but was a shame as her mum and Trudie had been close friends for years. Genie hoped her mum wouldn't drop her now life was more exciting, the way Genie's friends had dropped her.

Milly and Genie often video-chatted while Genie made up huge batches of ice cream at night, but they hadn't had time today as the restaurant had been full until late. Genie frowned as she recalled that she'd never actually seen her dad in the background and felt bad that she always forgot to speak to him, too. But they often exchanged news via text. She took a big slug of wine and felt adrenaline kick in her stomach. Something wasn't right, but she couldn't put her finger on what it was. She racked her brain to think of how her dad had sounded the last time she had actually spoken to him, but he'd been fine… hadn't he?

He'd told her how proud he was of her and she'd told him to come back. There was plenty of custom for all of them now, and she needed her parents' support more than ever after all that had happened. Genie was so much stronger than she had been six months ago, but without her family, there was a gaping hole in her happiness. Only they could fill it.

CHAPTER FORTY-SIX

*G*enie was attempting to rally her nerves. Her new delivery service had been a big hit and it had eased the load for the staff. Her delivery girl, Cindy, was amazing. She was just out of college and was taking some time off before starting a job in London.

Cindy had wandered in for an ice cream and began chatting to Genie. By the time she'd left Genie had offered her the job. Genie knew it probably wasn't professional and she should have asked her in for a formal interview, but that wasn't how she worked. She had checked the references Cindy had emailed over, though, and the girl had started work a few days later. She was a natural with customers and everyone was sighing with relief.

Bailey was flourishing in the kitchen and she let Liam sit in with them some mornings while they were setting up, so that he could spend time with his dad. Liam's chubby little face was full of smiles and he automatically reached out for Genie as soon as he saw her now. He'd melted her heart and she loved him. She'd taught him how to fold the napkins for the tables and he had his own little plastic table in the restaurant garden so that he could sit and draw. Two of his masterpieces were proudly displayed in Genie's room and they lifted her mood every time she saw them. She knew Bailey was nervous about Liam's mum coming back into their lives, but for now they almost felt like a little family.

She still craved Cal's touch, but was trying to distance herself from him by working herself to the bone and immersing herself even more in the progression of her business. Ada's skin was glowing and Genie wondered if she had been seeing more of Ralph. She had one of those secret smiles that made you wish you had some of what she had.

Cal had asked Genie out to dinner a couple of times, but he'd had to cancel each time as his filming schedule had changed. It was good that he'd actually listened to her, but she still felt like a dirty little secret. She'd seen him photographed out with Penelope in London, so he obviously could find time away for the right person. The thought made her insides burn, so she smiled when Fae and Una beckoned her over to their table and went to see what they wanted. There was a group of them tonight, girls and boys. They were all tanned and sexy and she felt decidedly out of place.

As she drew near, Fae pulled her into a hug and insisted she squash into the booth next to her, even though there was barely room. A tall stool sat at the end of the booth that she could have perched her bottom on, but that had just been taken by a good looking man with mischievous eyes. Another sandy-haired man was watching her with interest from the other side of the table, and reached across to shake her hand and introduce himself. Genie looked around at her bustling restaurant and very capable staff and decided to let loose for once. She caught one of her waiters' eyes and ordered herself an iced cocktail, feeling pride when it arrived back within a few minutes, looking delicious and tasting sublime.

Everyone asked to try it and several more were ordered. Genie sipped her drink, which went straight to her head. She grinned as Bailey had obviously added a double measure of liquor. She smiled at her friends, happy that they were happy. Una leaned across the table and touched her arm to gain her attention. 'So come on, Genie. Give us the gossip. How the hell did you get Cal to work here? Didn't you know who he was?'

Genie flushed and hid her face behind her drink. She was actually used to these questions now, but it felt different coming from her friends. She used to confide everything to them, but things had changed. The man opposite was grinning at her and had moved his leg closer to hers under the table.

Fae's eyes were sparkling and she gave Genie a sloppy kiss on the cheek. 'How did you concentrate every day with a hunk like that in your kitchen? Mind you, make that two hunks, with Bailey here all the time now. Did you know he's got a little son? I thought it was his kid brother.'

'We'd have been here all the time, too, if we'd known they were there, wouldn't we, guys?' Una giggled at the other girls in their party. Genie felt a twist of sadness, but kept smiling. 'You're so lucky Cal ended up here. Look what it's done for your business.'

Genie looked around and bit down on her lip, refusing to let the tears fall in front of the crowd. The man across from her touched her hand again to regain her attention, just as she was swept up into the air. She squealed in protest, as hot lips nibbled at her ear and strong arms curled around her waist. She was glad she'd let go of her drink and didn't dare look up, but her body instantly recognised its mate. She tried to jump away from Cal, but his arms were holding her firmly and he snuggled her into him.

'I've missed you,' Cal whispered into her ear, sitting down

in her place and taking her with him, and she sighed and relaxed her body into him, perching on his knee.

Everyone seemed to have been struck mute, then chatter burst all around her, although her own table was still stunned into silence. She wriggled round and locked eyes with him, and it felt like they were the only ones in the room. He kissed her gently on the lips and then turned to face their guests. 'Are you going to introduce me to your friends?' he said in a louder tone. Genie gulped. He already knew full well who Fae and Una were, as he'd seen photos of them in her room. She flushed and turned to face the sea of faces, who were sitting agog at the scene in front of them.

Cal stared pointedly at the man whose hand was rapidly retreating back across the table and then smiled brightly at everyone. 'Uh... um... this is Fae,' said Genie, as Cal leaned over to take her hand and kiss it, making her giggle coquettishly and flush, eyes as wide as saucers.

'I'm Una,' said Una, pushing her hand across for Cal to kiss. It couldn't quite reach, but he nodded his head and said hi, encompassing everyone in the group and making them sit back in awe.

This must be what it's like to be a celebrity, thought Genie. Everyone just sat there feeling stunned. It was a bit like the Queen had arrived at their table. She giggled into Cal's neck. She felt a bit tipsy from the cocktails and began to see the funny side of the situation. Cal wasn't about to let her off his lap. She silently thanked him for what he was doing in front of her old friends, but wished he really felt that way about her.

Bailey came out with more drinks, saw her sitting on Cal's lap and eyed her thoughtfully. She knew it was unprofessional, but she was fed up with always playing by the rules. Una tried to drag Bailey into their group, but he backed off, telling them he was at work and that he might call Una later.

Genie was surprised that they were close enough for that, and wasn't sure how she felt about them dating. It was none of her business, but she was protective of Bailey and Una would eat him up and spit him out. She hated kids too. She was always telling Genie how they just got in the way and made a lot of mess and noise.

Cal saw her looking at Bailey and stood up, taking Genie with him, and carefully putting her down so that her feet met the floor. 'Can I steal Genie from you for a moment?' he said, not waiting for an answer but grinning at them all conspiratorially. 'I haven't seen her all week and I need to say hello properly.'

Fae and Una's mouths dropped open and one of the other women almost spat out her drink, then started giggling. Genie didn't have time to react because he grabbed her hand and dragged her through the throng of people and into the shed in the garden. People craned their necks to see where they were going, but Bailey shut the garden door behind them.

The minute the shed door was closed, Cal rammed her up against the wall and plundered her mouth as if he was downing. 'Cal!' she gasped when they came up for air.

'I'm fed up with hiding. I don't care who knows about us. If I want to come here, I want to come here. People will just have to get used to seeing us together, Genie.' He drew in a deep breath and let it out. She watched the rise and fall of his chest and placed her hand on his heart, her lips plump from his kisses. 'Things are organised enough here for you to be able to come and visit me in London now, and we can even go up and visit your parents.'

Genie was at a loss for words, but her heart was racing. 'I don't understand what you're telling me. You want to meet my parents?'

'Of course I want to meet your parents.' He threw his

hands up in frustration. 'You're my girlfriend. I don't want to have to keep second-guessing your feelings for me. Either tell me you want me in your life, or tell me to leave.'

Genie's face flamed and she looked around for a way out. She'd thought he was the one pushing her away. It had never occurred to her that he felt the same. Had she made him feel insecure? She hadn't meant to. She took his face in her hands and gently kissed his lips, his eyes, his neck, until he held her hands and pushed her away. 'It has to be more than this, Genie. I want a commitment from you. I know you have Bailey and Toby and God knows who else sniffing around you, but when you're in my arms there's only you and me. Tell me what you want. Tell me you want me.'

Genie stood in shock with her hands at her sides. She didn't know what he was going on about with Bailey, and she hadn't seen Toby for ages, unless he popped into the restaurant for a coffee and a chat with her and Ada. Her hands crept up and around his waist and touched the bare skin beneath his shirt, making him catch his breath. She leaned on his chest and heard his heartbeat. His arms wound around her and he held her tight.

'You're all I've ever wanted,' she sighed. 'The business means the world to me, but you are my universe.' Before she could say anything else, he turned her to face him and kissed her with so much longing that it almost took her breath away. Hearing Bailey call her from the restaurant, they looked into each other's eyes and grinned, before Cal took her hand and led her back inside. He walked her straight to her friends, ordered them all a round of cocktails on the house and spent the rest of the evening charming them into submission.

Genie waved them off home, way after closing time, promising to meet up with them again soon. Cal waited for her to lock up, before they walked home as fast as their legs would carry them. She pushed him through his bedroom door and straight onto his bed, where she climbed above him and ran her hands over every inch of his body, discarding clothes as she explored. He groaned and buried his head in her hair and then flipped her onto her back and nipped and tasted her slick skin until they both forgot what day it was and lost themselves in ecstasy.

CHAPTER FORTY-SEVEN

*G*enie had woken up to a hot man nuzzling her neck and had never felt so desired or free. She couldn't quite believe that this gorgeous hunk of maleness wanted her company and so obviously desired her like crazy, but she wasn't about to dissuade him.

She was going to grab this with both hands and enjoy every moment. She was fed up with feeling second best due to her family and friends. Recently she'd realised that she was a strong woman who could run a successful business and date pretty gorgeous men who actually liked her, phobias, evil pigeons and all. She wasn't boring or stupid.

Her staff liked working for her and told her often, Ada was much happier since she had met Genie, and Cal was stronger too. He was the happiest he'd been since she'd known him. It was like the weight of the world had been lifted from his shoulders and they'd talked into the early hours of the morning, after making good use of the time alone in his bedroom first, of course. Her muscles still ached from their enthusiasm.

They'd decided that they would both take one day off

during the week to spend together. He was keen to show her around London. He said she could make good contacts through the television show and that they were really trying to help him fit his new job around his life with Genie, as he'd told them that they were a team. Her heart had soared at this. She'd never been part of a proper couple where someone was nice to her before. It was a revelation.

Who knew that hot men could be such good boyfriends? *Boyfriend…* Even the word made her happy. Cal was officially her boyfriend. She literally wanted to get up and jump up and down on the bed, shouting it out of the open window, so that the whole world would know.

Cal had insisted that she have a lie-in and he'd offered to go in and open the restaurant for her that morning. Ada had peeked round the door and blown kisses to them both when Cal had announced they were a couple. Her eyes had shone with happy tears and Genie had blushed and hidden under the duvet.

Hearing the door shut and sinking into the soft covers, Genie gazed out to sea and watched the thin curtains flutter in the slight breeze. She could smell the salty air from the beach and decided that she'd make a picnic and insist that they sat on the beach, their toes in the warm sand. She stretched out like a lazy cat and enjoyed the ache in her muscles. Cal had promised her a massage later and she wasn't about to turn the offer down. She moved her legs over to the side of the bed and slowly sat up and gazed out to sea. She wondered if her parents were sitting and looking at the water too. Her eyes misted over and she decided that today was the day that she would work on her plan to lure them back to the Essex coastline.

Ideas had been whizzing around her head, but she would persuade them to keep the manager they'd hired in Cornwall, and to spend half of the month helping her to expand *Genie's*.

There was plenty of work for everyone now and they could even retire in a few years if they wanted to spend more time together.

They could come back with their heads held high at having made a success of their new venture, and bring back the family element that was sadly missing in her own business. Genie wasn't quite sure how they would manage with her owning the business now, but she pushed that idea aside, as surely all they wanted was to have more time away from work, but to be making money. Genie had solved both of those problems. Her chest puffed out in pride and she grinned.

Who'd have thought, all those months ago when her parents had said they were leaving, that fate would have brought Ada and Cal to her door? She ran her fingers over the pure Egyptian cotton sheets she was sitting on and pressed her toes into the plush carpet around the bed. She noticed the indent Cal had left on the pillow and grinned even harder. Who knew that life could be this good?

Deciding to stop being lazy and to get up and make that picnic, Genie glanced around for her dressing gown and remembered dropping it on the floor, or maybe on the desk where Cal had kissed her senseless. She should have been ashamed at her wanton carelessness, but she wasn't.

Padding towards the window, she stopped momentarily, unsure if she should be in his room when he wasn't around. Then she had a flashback to the previous evening when he'd been licking the inside of her thigh, and she decided with a smile that those boundaries had already been crossed. He'd also told her to have a lie-in and that was exactly what she'd done. She scanned the room. Her dressing gown wasn't hard to spot. It was a wisp of soft grey fabric that she'd treated herself to after the opening of *Genie's*. It was strewn across the masculine metal and wood desk that sat beside one of the large windows.

Reaching out to pick it up, she noticed a large envelope with papers haphazardly stuffed back inside, some crushed at the edges. She picked them up to straighten them, not meaning to pry, but the words at the top of one of the creased pages caught her eye and she froze instantly. Blinking rapidly she tried to focus and understand what she was seeing. She turned the envelope and looked at the address on the front. Cal's name was emblazoned across it, at this address, so it was something recent.

Turning back to the untidy papers hanging out, she gulped in some air, looked around furtively to make sure no one else could possibly see what she was up to, and pulled them free of the envelope. Scanning them, leafing from page to page, her stomach dropped and her skin turned pale. She started to sweat and pushed her hand through her hair in confusion. Soon it was sticking out all over the place, but she didn't care.

She pushed her way out of Cal's room, using the walls and door for support. She still had the damning paperwork crushed into her hand and her face was a river of tears. How could Cal do this to her? How could her parents? Her whole world was crashing down around her and everything she had ever known about her parents now seemed a complete fabrication.

The words from the simple pieces of paper swam before her eyes and she pushed open the door to her own room and threw the documents on the bed. She sat down with her head in her hands and sobbed and sobbed. Then she curled up into a protective ball on the bed and howled. When she had no more tears to cry, she felt anger overtake the sorrow.

Had her grandad known about this? Thinking back to how

he had given up his family business for the sake of his son, she now understood how hard it would have been for him if he did know. He'd given everything up to encourage them all to move on; to help them stay together as a family, and she had messed that up. Her heart broke for what her granddad had done for his only child. She wanted to punch her dad in his silly face and had mixed feelings about what her own mother had done. How could Milly have lied to Genie for so long?

Genie's stomach turned over and she rushed into the bathroom and grabbed a washcloth to wipe across her forehead. The cooling water immediately soothed her, but she leaned her palms on either side of the sink and looked at her reflection. Gone was the happy girl of an hour ago. She looked wild. Her hair was mussed up from running her hands through it, her face was flushed and blotchy and her eyes were red and watery. It was enough to scare birds from the trees.

She went back into the bedroom and picked up the crumpled papers, scanning them. Cal's betrayal was almost as bad as her parents'. Had Ada seen this? Tears swam in her eyes again and she clenched them shut. Pushing herself up from the bed and looking out across the sea, she didn't know what to do next. Every single person she had trusted had lied to her. She didn't know the circumstances of what had happened to her mum, but the years of untruths and false smiles cut into Genie. Had they all been laughing at her? Poor old Genie, who was too useless to fend for herself or too thick to be able to understand who her parents actually were.

Her phone buzzed with a call from her granddad and seeing the name lit up on the screen made her pick it up and throw it into the bin, where it landed with a satisfying crack. Spurred into action, she jumped up and opened her wardrobe. She picked up a gym bag that she'd never actually used. Fae and Una had only invited her to join them once, when they knew she was working. She'd bought it in the hope that they'd ask her again, but they never had. Whisking in some tops, shorts and some underwear from the drawers, she thought about fishing her phone out of the bin, but decided that there wasn't a single person listed there that she could turn too.

She fleetingly pictured Bailey's face, but dismissed that thought. He would want to punch Cal as much as she did and whatever was going on now, she was more determined than ever that her business would grow stronger. She wouldn't let this ruin her new career. She'd need it more than ever. She was the one who had built it back up and she would be the one to keep it going, no matter what. She had a great team around her and they could survive a few days without her.

They would be wondering where she was by now, at the restaurant, but Cal and Ada could try running it, if they wanted the business from her so much. Were they going to blackmail her? Had they always planned to sweep in when she was vulnerable? She couldn't think of another reason why a man like Cal would look at a loser like her. He'd investigated her and then seduced her. She was such an idiot. What had she been thinking? She hadn't been thinking, that was the problem. She'd let a firm set of abs cloud her judgement. She would never make that mistake again.

Checking the train times and calling a cab, she threw her bag over her shoulder. She couldn't be bothered to take much with her, but she didn't know how long she would stay either. Her parents had some hard questions to answer and she wanted to be staring them straight in the face when she asked them.

If they thought that they could lie their way out of the fact they had broken up her family and tried to sell her business from under her, they were sadly mistaken. She thought again about the contents of the letters and she ground her teeth. So many wasted years.

Slipping her favourite pair of flip flops onto her feet, she picked up the landline to call the restaurant. Her luck was in and Bailey answered, so she told him in a wobbly voice that she was unwell and he would need to close the restaurant and talk to Ada about covering for a few days. Hurrying downstairs, she left the building without a backward glance.

CHAPTER FORTY-EIGHT

*C*al looked up from the tray of macaroons he'd just piped, put them into the oven and set the timer. 'She's what?'

Bailey looked confused and Cal could understand why. Genie hadn't had a second away from the restaurant since its opening – and now she was sick? She had seemed fine earlier. He tried to stop the smug grin from forming on his face in case Bailey saw it. It would make him look happy about Genie being ill.

Cal assumed it must be something mild, and hoped she'd come in later. He liked being around her in the kitchen, as it gave him a chance to steal a few kisses and touch her silky-smooth skin. He tried to concentrate on what Bailey was telling him, but his body was still warm from her touch.

'She's not well and asked me to tell you to arrange cover for a few days.'

Cal's head snapped up. 'A few *days*? She can't be that unwell, surely? She's never had a day off since I've known her. She was fine this morning.'

Bailey frowned and shrugged his shoulders. 'I'm just the

messenger. Do you want me to run up and see if she needs anything?' he asked with a hopeful tone that Cal really didn't appreciate.

'No!' said Cal a little too forcefully. Bailey gave him an odd look, then turned and asked their new waitress to pick up the food order for table three. Cal peered around the kitchen helplessly. He couldn't leave the half-made pastries he'd begun earlier and, if Genie wasn't there, then they needed all hands on deck. They hadn't had to do anything without her before.

Cal was fine, he'd run his own restaurant, but he didn't want to upset Genie by doing something the wrong way. She was soft and dreamy in his hands, but he knew from experience that she had a temper that could erupt at a moment's notice. Something must be seriously wrong for her not to be at work. He wondered how to get her a doctor's appointment and tried to think of ways to help.

Grabbing his phone, he called Genie's mobile, but she didn't pick up. He was just about to go and ask Ada to check on Genie when the oven timer went off. Cursing under his breath, he pulled the tray out and almost burnt his hand. Swearing again, and placing the confections on the cooling trays, he bit his lip in frustration and rolled his eyes heavenward.

Ada stuck her head around the kitchen with a frown and he assumed the bush telegraph had been working. 'Bailey's just told me that Genie's not well. Shall I go and check on her? She was fine this morning. It must be bad, for her not to be at work.'

'That's what I thought,' said Cal, taking his apron off and handing it to Ada. 'Can you manage without both of us for half an hour while I check on her? You just need to cover the rest of the batter mix and place it in the fridge. Once the tray has cooled, they need cream piped into the centre, and that's ready in the fridge.'

Ada looked like she was about to argue, but she was probably as worried as he was and she took the apron. 'Of course! I'm sure she's just exhausted…'

She gave him a knowing look and he had the good grace to blush. Was it not possible to have a single secret from this woman? It seemed not. She didn't look too unhappy about it though, as she flicked his backside with the end of the apron and told him to hurry up.

As he pushed open the door to the penthouse, he knew straight away that something was wrong. Genie always played 80s music at full blast when Ada was out of the flat. He teased her about how quiet his gran thought she was when she was actually a bit of a soul music freak. Today the flat was deathly quiet. He left the door ajar and walked quickly to her room. The bed was made, but the cupboard was half open, and there were clothes on the floor. He frowned and backtracked into his own room. He saw some crumpled sheets of paper on his desk and it took him a moment to realise what they were and what that meant.

His heart sank to his toes and he slumped down onto the edge of the bed. She'd hate him now. She'd never understand that he'd been trying to protect his grandmother, not pry into Genie's life. How the hell was he supposed to have known what her parents had been up to? The point was that he wouldn't have found out, if he hadn't hired a private investigator to look into her family's past. They could have begun a regular relationship like normal people.

Now all that was destroyed. She knew what her parents had done and she'd never forgive him for not telling her as soon as he'd found out. But how could he have told her that her mum had given away a baby at the tender age of sixteen, and that her dad was having an affair with her mum's best friend, Trudie? He assumed that was why her mum had suddenly decided to move as far away as possible from her 'friend,' and why Genie's dad had agreed to go with her.

Cal guessed that her granddad knew, too. Why else would he give up a business he had built up with his beloved wife, however slow trade was? They could have ticked along for years and still stayed in business, but he'd given in for the sake of his son's marriage. What no one had expected was that Genie would refuse to move with them, and would then turn their business into a roaring success. It meant they still had ties here and they would have to visit, no matter what. It was a mess.

Cal wished he could be as selfless for those he loved. He'd rushed here because he'd thought Genie was conning his grandma, but when he looked at his own actions, the press had begun to hassle him again and he'd wanted to get away. He'd used his own family as an excuse to come here and he'd lived rent free and earning minimum wage, because he wanted sex with a hot brunette who owned a local business.

Genie challenged him in every way and each day his feelings for her grew stronger. The thought that she wouldn't be able to look at him without wanting to be sick spurred him into action. He went into Genie's room. Opening her drawers he tried not to feel indignant at the delicate lace that he hadn't seen before. Noticing the bin next to the drawers had toppled over, he straightened it and saw her broken phone nestled inside. Picking it up and turning it over in his palm, he tried to control his breathing and not panic.

He pulled his own phone from the back pocket of his jeans and explained to Ada what had happened. She told him that she was appalled at his behaviour, but he sensed that she'd already known about Trudie. She didn't shout or call Trudie names as he'd expected, though. She silently listened and told him to go and sort out the mess he'd made, telling him she would call around and find some temporary staff to cover the restaurant if they couldn't manage, but she was happy to step back into her role and welcome guests. She told him she would wait tables if she was required to and asked him to stop fussing, when he tried to tell her what to do.

He hated leaving her with such a long list of instructions, but he couldn't abandon Genie. He was going to be there to support her whether she liked it or not. Throwing some things into an overnight bag, he grabbed the rental car keys and slammed the door behind him. Once in the driving seat, he sat back and took a deep breath before tapping the address of Genie's parents' new business into the satellite navigation system. He almost baulked when it said how long it would take him to drive there, but he put his foot on the pedal, eased the car out into the traffic, and headed towards Cornwall.

CHAPTER FORTY-NINE

*G*enie eased her tired body forward in the seat she'd found. She was glad there was a small bar area on the train. She'd trudged along to it four times so far and each time she'd bought one of those mini bottles of wine that you hung upside down when it was empty and wondered where the rest of the wine was. They didn't sell big bottles, or she'd have grabbed one of those.

She was welded in between a big man with terrible body odour and a teenager who was playing a very noisy game on his phone. Noticing someone vacating their seat further along the carriage, she found a tiny spurt of energy and pushed herself up and walked on slightly wobbly legs towards it.

The train had been full when she'd got on, but gradually people were getting off at the bigger towns. The sky had turned to an inky black and Genie felt it suited her mood well. The place where her parents and grandparents now lived was almost at the end of the line, but after hours of sitting, drinking and having to try and block out the words she'd read earlier, she'd finally had to face facts, or the facts as a private investigator employed by Cal had told them. She slumped down in the window seat and was grateful that Fae and Una weren't around to mention how puffy her face was or how red her eyes were. She hated her family right now. She hated everyone.

How could they? All of them! How could they have kept this from her? No wonder Genie's mum had suddenly decided to move. Her best friend was shagging her husband! No wonder her cheating scumbag of a dad had agreed to give up his family legacy. It was probably either that or have his balls chopped off by her mum. How her mother had managed to look Trudie in the eye and not push her in the sea was beyond Genie. Then she remembered her mum's own lies and her insides began to boil. They were both as bad as each other!

Her mum had got pregnant when she was sixteen and had given her baby away. Genie thought of Liam, and how Bailey had fought to keep him, and she scrabbled in her bag for another bottle of wine. Her parents had told her they met when they were both sixteen, and they had brought her up as an only child. Did her dad not know her mum had had a baby when they were supposedly dating? Had she slept around? How had she kept that a secret, or was it her dad's child too and had they both deserted the baby? So many questions came and went through her mind and she wrung her hands in her lap, and tried to focus on the beautiful scenery that sped by the window. Was her sibling still alive? Had they met her parents?

Genie's pulse began to pick up and she glanced at her watch. She would be coming into the station soon and she wasn't about to face her parents looking a mess. They would know she'd found everything out and she'd have no advantage over them. She needed to see their faces when she accused them. She needed to know the truth.

Taking some foundation out from her handbag, she slathered it on and hoped it covered the bags under her eyes. Spritzing on some perfume and straightening her clothes, which were crumpled from sleeping fitfully in her cramped seat, she got ready to leave. She'd taken this route many times when visiting her grandparents and, as she got off the train, she knew with absolute clarity that her grandma was somehow involved in all of this. She was so controlling that there was no way Genie's mum could have had a baby without Lucille knowing about it... was there?

She wanted to get a cab straight to her parents' new restaurant, but her hands were shaking. She wished she hadn't smashed her phone, so she could at least have checked they were there. She delved into her bag, but her hands just came into contact with the empty wine bottles. She chucked them into the nearest bin, giving an evil look to a woman with big hair who was raising an eyebrow at her. Nosy cow.

Seeing a coffee shop in the station and feeling her tummy rumble, she realised she hadn't eaten anything all day. She grabbed a takeout coffee and a biscuit. Then she decided her stomach couldn't cope with food and handed it to a man with a dog who looked homeless, crouching outside the entrance. Wincing when he seemed confused, she realised he had simply been bending to tie his shoelace. She motioned to his dog and muttered that she thought it might like a treat, before rushing towards the taxis with her head bowed.

Jumping inside a cab, she peeked over at the man, who was still standing there with the biscuit in his hand, staring after her in surprise. She gave the driver the address and shoved her bag onto the seat next to her, sinking down further into her seat.

She closed her eyes and wondered why she always managed to get herself into a mess, then remembered the papers she'd picked up earlier and realised that it was all her parents' fault. She'd grown up surrounded by half-truths and false smiles.

She tried to hold back the tears that threatened to push past her eyelids. She didn't want them to see the gibbering wreck they'd abandoned all those months ago. She would confront them as a confident business owner, a woman who could stand her ground without erupting. If she chanted that in her head enough times, she hoped she could get through this first meeting without strangling one of them.

Her parents would expect her to start screaming at them. That girl was gone. She was a woman now and she would stand before them and demand to know what the hell they had done. She wanted answers – and she wasn't leaving without them.

CHAPTER FIFTY

*G*enie stood in front of the building that housed her lying, cheating parents. She had no idea how long she'd been there and really wished she could have another glass of wine for courage. It was dark outside, with just the lights from other shops giving off a faint glow. The train journey had taken forever, the taxi ride had been long too, and her feet ached, even though she'd spent most of the day on her backside. Her limbs felt like they were full of lead.

She took in the pretty exterior of the new café. It was surreal to be at the place that had stolen her parents from her. The last time she'd visited, with her grandmother, she hadn't really paid attention. Lucille had waffled on for ages about the merits of the venue and staff until Genie had tuned out.

The frontage was compact and pretty. The sign was beautifully painted and had little flowers swirling around the lettering. Hanging baskets overflowing with scented blooms hung either side of the sign so that the flowers trailed lazily to the ground in a riot of colour. It looked as if it fitted seamlessly with the other shops along the small parade. She could see the beach just further along the road. It wasn't the main seafront restaurant her parents used to own, but it was newer, easier to manage and it also seemed totally without any history. This café could have been anywhere in the world and it would have blended in. Unlike *Genie's*, with its surfer look and watery murals. Her place stood out now. It was beautiful, and it was hers.

Her stomach growled at her and she remembered giving her biscuit away. It felt like she had a family of ants trampling around inside her now. She glanced up and saw movement in the upstairs window. It was her dad. He'd just opened a window and was staring out at the sea. He seemed to have aged, even from this distance, and she took a deep breath and urged her legs to carry her to the front door. Each step was like wading through treacle. Her dad must have sensed that someone was there as his gaze searched the pavement and met hers. She winced as his eyes lit up. He rushed down to open the door for her, hugging her hard, drawing her indoors, putting on the lights and giving her a tour – before turning to see how slumped her shoulders were and apologising.

'Sorry, darling. I was so excited to see you that I wanted to show you everything. Why are you here? Not that I'm complaining, but I thought you couldn't get away for another couple of weeks?' he was babbling and Genie's eyes narrowed. She took in the pristine interior of the café and saw nothing of their old style, their plastic tablecloths and big menus. Here, everything was refined and gorgeous. Just like she'd wanted their family business to be, before her parents had run off.

'Change of plan,' was all she said for a moment. They stood looking at each other in the silence and his skin began to tinge red.

'You know, don't you?'

Genie didn't answer for a minute, but left him to squirm. 'Where's Mum?'

'Uh… um… she's been staying at a hotel down the road for a while.'

'What?' Genie dumped her bag on the floor and placed her hands on her hips, forgetting her earlier promise to herself to stay calm.

Her dad hung his head and pulled out a chair for her. She gratefully sank into it, her muscles protesting as they were so wound up. Her dad switched on the machines behind the little counter and began to make them a coffee, his solution to a crisis. It took all Genie's willpower not to get back up and demand answers. He handed her the steaming coffee and a slab of coffee cake and she sniffed both appreciatively. Even the cups were pretty, made of delicate china with a gold rim. She was surprised that her dad hadn't broken her cup with his big bearlike paws.

'Tell me what the hell is going on.'

Her dad sat down and gave her one of his stares until she took a sip of the coffee and ate a mouthful of cake. Her stomach rumbled appreciatively, but she knew his game. 'Stop putting it off. Tell me.'

'Don't you want to look round?' He shuffled his chair back slightly and gestured to the café.

'Dad. Tell me.'

He stood up and seemed to make a decision. 'I'm pretty fed up with all this and to be honest, I think your mum should tell you, or we both should. I didn't know half of it myself until recently.'

'Tell me about Trudie?'

Her dad's skin went white and he leaned on a chair back for support. 'Who told you about that? Did she tell you?'

Genie's eyes flashed a warning. 'If I ever set eyes on her

again she'll be sorry,' she slurred slightly, making her dad frown.

He tried to take her hand, his eyes pleading for understanding, but she shook him off, eyeing the rapidly cooling coffee and wondering if she could get away with throwing it at him. He followed her line of sight and sighed. 'Nothing happened with Trudie and me... well, nothing much.'

Genie rolled her eyes. 'Either something happened or it didn't.'

Her dad ran his hands through his hair. He pulled out the chair again and sat down. Her eyes never left his and she picked up the coffee again, then picked up the fork and broke off another small bite of cake. It was like heaven in her mouth. Whoever had baked it was worth their weight in gold. She fleetingly thought of asking for the recipe, then her dad coughed and she put her fork down. 'So. What happened with Trudie?'

He shifted uncomfortably in his seat. 'It was my fault. Your mum was always angry for some reason. She wouldn't talk to me. It was as if she had so many secrets...' he said, suddenly banging the table with his fist and making her slosh coffee everywhere. He kicked the chair next to him, and she finally understood where she got that habit from when he yelped in pain and rubbed his toe. 'The loss of my mum seemed to hit her harder than anyone, even your granddad. I knew they were close, but I just couldn't reach her. I didn't know they'd had this secret between them for years.'

'Grandma knew?' Genie couldn't help the dagger that just sliced into her heart. How could her beautiful kind grandma have kept something as big as this from her only child and granddaughter? Then she remembered that she wasn't the only grandchild and winced. She pictured her gran's smiling face and then the picture twisted into something she didn't understand and she had to take in a sharp breath to ease the pain. 'How could she keep it from us?'

Her dad was gazing off into the distance and she didn't dare speak. What she had wanted to do when she'd arrived was to slap his silly face, but he was her dad and she loved him with all of her heart, even though she hated him a little right now.

How could he hurt her mum? She'd been loyal to him after they became a couple, hadn't she? Genie remembered her dressing up a bit more and taking time with her appearance, and Genie thinking she had a secret man, but now she understood that Milly found out about Trudie and was going into battle. How she'd not fallen apart was beyond Genie. Then she remembered that her mum had been hiding her own secrets, and her heart hardened towards her too.

She tapped the fork on the table until it began to annoy both of them, so she put it back down.

'Trudie was always there to listen. She kept complimenting me,' said her dad. Genie slapped her forehead with her palm. He held up his hands. 'I know, I know! It was stupid. I felt such a loss after Mum died and none of us, or the business, really recovered. Milly was distracted. You were our only shining light, Genie.'

Genie sat back in surprise. 'I was?'

'Of course. You wouldn't let us fail and you kept trying to tell us how to change, but we wouldn't listen.' He reached across to take her hand and her body sighed at his touch. She'd missed him so much. She wanted to go and sit on his lap and rest her head on his shoulder like she had as a child. She moved her hand from under his and put both in her lap, primly waiting for him to go on.

'Your mum could barely look at me and one night I walked Trudie home and she kissed me. I didn't stop her and for a moment, I kissed her back.' He hung his head and started playing with the edge of the pristine white tablecloth.

'And...'

'And... what? That was it. I pushed her away and went home and told your mum. She went mental and said Trudie's body would be washed up at sea the next day, if she ever saw her again. I didn't know what to do, so I told Trudie to keep away. She packed up and went abroad for a while for some 'training'. Mum saw that as a double betrayal on my part.'

Genie remembered her mum crying and saying her own mum was ill and rushing to throw some clothes in a small case. She'd been gone for a week, which was the longest she'd ever been able to stand being in the same room as her mum for, and when she'd come back, she was calmer. 'So she left you and went to Grandmother's?'

'Yes.' Her dad still wouldn't meet her eye. 'When she came back I promised I'd do anything to keep her by my side. She's the love of my life. I made a stupid error of judgement. Trudie kept hassling me via text and when your mum said we'd have to move away or split up, I had no choice but to leave my family home and go with her. I didn't know that she was moving here for another reason until later.'

'Because she wanted to get away and tell you about the child she'd had?' Genie tried to calm her beating pulse – and the urge to vomit on her dad's shoes.

'It was our child, Genie. You've got a full biological sister.' Genie was lost for words and staggered back a little. *Surely the day couldn't get any weirder?* She looked around for some wine, but just saw tea cups and a coffee machine. 'Your mum told me just before we first got here. I was in a complete mess trying to make up for my mistakes and then wham... she told me she'd always lied to me. Literally since I'd known her. I can barely look at her now, but we have to continue here and try to build a life. It's not easy.'

Tears escaped from Genie's eyes and she wiped them away with the back of her arm. Her dad's eyes were shining with unshed tears too. She squeezed his hand and felt the coffee cake swirling round and round in her stomach.

'Where is the other child?' She couldn't quite bring herself to say sister.

'We found her, well... Lucille did.' Her dad almost snarled. 'She's in Cornwall. It's why we suddenly decided to move here. We would never have gone without you if we hadn't been backed into a corner.' Genie sat in stunned silence for a moment, trying to understand what he was telling her, but her brain was so tired it couldn't compute what was going on.

Her parents had been through hell and her heart broke for them. Her mum kept her pain to herself and shielded Genie from her dad's betrayal, but then she'd hurt them all with her own secret. Why hadn't she told them? Genie still wanted to kick her dad, but it seemed like he'd tortured himself enough. 'So you got her pregnant and deserted her? How could you not know she was pregnant? She was sixteen!'

Her dad put his head in his hands. 'I didn't know the baby existed. Your mum made sure of that, by hiding her pregnancy from me.'

Genie felt bile rise up at the back of her throat. She couldn't help herself from getting a little dig in for her mum before she screamed at her dad for letting her mum have a baby on her own. How could he not have known? Seriously?

'Trudie keeps coming into the shop. She asks about Mum, though, not you.' Genie almost spat her old friend's name. Just saying the word made her want to smash something. Her dad needed to know what kind of woman she was.

He laughed bitterly. 'Yes she's texted and tried to call both of us. She misses your mum's friendship! Can you believe that? After all she's done to her.'

'All you've both done to her,' scolded Genie. 'Mum was a good friend to Trudie. No wonder Trudie misses her. The stupid cow. Sorry Dad, but you'd have been a ten minute wonder. She likes flashy men with big wallets. What a waste of a good marriage.'

Her dad took the hit and didn't argue, his skin just tinged red. He reached for her arm and she let him draw her hands into his. She didn't snatch them back this time. 'I was an idiot. Your mum still hasn't forgiven me, but now there's more to it. She kept my own child's existence from me. I moved here for her. I gave up my family home and business for her. I'm just hoping we didn't lose you in the process?' His eyes pleaded with hers. 'Our intention was never to come without you. We didn't for one second think you'd be stubborn enough to stay. It's been a nightmare for all of us. This wasn't an easy decision to make, but I thought your mum was worth it. It was why Grandad went abroad. He wanted you to come with us and thought you'd never agree if he was around.'

Genie's heart broke a little more. 'Does he know about my sister?'

'He does now. He was devastated that your grandmother and Milly kept it from him. His anger made him want to get away from us all, but he hated leaving you. He shouted at us for deserting you, but with Trudie there and your sister here, we had to make hard choices and he did understand.'

Genie let out the breath she'd been holding. 'Grandad's coming home soon.' She pictured his whiskery face. 'He vowed never to leave Essex once. Look at him now.'

They both grinned and her dad pulled her into his side and squeezed her to him, kissing the top of her head and resting his face on her hair. She angled her face up and eyed him warily, but he was still her dad. He was an idiot, but she loved him, whatever his mistakes.

'This place looks nice,' she gazed around and was at a loss to find anything linking the place to home. She'd been sure they would make it a little replica of their seafront business, failings and all, but they seemed to have moved in and moved on. The square tables and wooden-backed chairs with plump cushions sat perfectly in surroundings full of teapots and pictures of cake. Rather than being twee, the photos were modern and made your mouth water. The cakes really were a work of art.

'Who makes the cakes here? You? I've never seen you go to extremes like this before.' The strawberry cake pictures oozed fruit and cream and had several layers dusted with icing. Another picture was of a chocolate cake that was almost indecent! It was so chocolaty that Genie wanted to get up and lick the picture. She quickly scooped up another forkful of coffee cake and sighed as the soft buttery sponge hit her taste buds. Her mouth immediately salivated for more.

'Your sister, Fern.' said her dad, making her drop her spoon with a clang. 'I didn't lie when I said I'd be stepping back. She's the manager who came with the shop. She's brilliant like you are, Genie. She could work anywhere, but her... adoptive parents owned this place and she couldn't afford to keep it on her own,' he flushed, looking down into her eyes as if pleading for understanding. 'Your grandmother set us all up,' he said bitterly. 'But you'll love your sister. I can imagine you both sitting heads together discussing ice cream and cake flavours.'

Genie put a hand out to steady herself on the nearest chair back. 'What the hell?' she raged. 'Does she know I exist or who you are? Isn't it creepy that you've bought her parents' shop?'

Her dad rubbed his face and she could see just how much he had aged since he'd left their little seafront restaurant. The most he'd had to worry about, before the whole Trudie business, had been balancing the books. 'I would have said the same, Genie, but after I learnt that she existed, I'd have agreed to any of Lucille's hairbrained schemes to meet my other daughter.' Genie's skin prickled at the mention of this girl Fern and she wasn't sure how she felt about sharing her parents with a stranger.

Suddenly she pictured a huge cake made out of ice cream and noted that in her memory banks to try out later. She thought of sharing the idea with Cal and fire flared in her eyes again. Luckily her dad didn't notice. He was trying to change the subject by babbling on about the flat upstairs and how she'd love staying there, even though he'd been conned into buying it.

'How is Gran involved in all this?'

Her dad's head snapped round. 'She's evil.'

Genie couldn't argue with that. 'I know that. What's she done?'

'She's always been evil.'

'Dad! How's Grandmother involved? Didn't she support Mum when she was pregnant? How could you not know? Did you run off and leave Mum?' She closed her eyes and tried to picture Lucille helping a scared sixteen-year-old, but however hard she tried, she couldn't do it. Genie pushed herself away from her dad and hated Cal even more for causing all of this upset. She put her hand on her dad's arm to turn him to face her. 'If Mum had a baby when she was sixteen, why didn't you help her? You can't have been that blind.'

'I didn't know! How did you find out anyway?'

Genie silently reached into her bag and pulled out one of the crumpled sheets she'd taken from Cal's bedroom and handed it to her dad. He scanned the page and then sat back down with his head in his hands. 'Who did this?'

'Cal. He's Ada's grandson. He wanted to see if I was conning his gran,' she tried to keep the edge from her voice and failed. Her dad's eyes narrowed.

'How dare he accuse you of anything! You're about as honest as they come.'

'He didn't know me then,' she said automatically, then wondered why she'd bothered as this was all his fault. She really wanted another glass of wine.

Genie pictured Bailey and Liam and her heart almost broke in two. What might have happened to Liam if his dad hadn't known about him? Was Genie's dad really even the father of this Fern girl, or was Milly still lying to them all? He'd been so young, too. Genie suddenly wondered if she shouldn't have said that out loud or should have looked into this more, instead of grabbing a bag and jumping on the first train. It seemed like she'd inadvertently caused even more heartache for her parents. She gritted her teeth and tried to feel sorry for them, but to be honest, they'd brought the whole sorry mess on themselves and she wanted some answers.

Her dad stomped up the back stairs and she heard him moving about. She just picked up her bag and turned towards him, when he pushed past her and headed for the door, his coat thrown over his shoulder. 'I'm going to find your mum. She told me not to worry about you as Cal was around. How stupid is that?'

Genie bristled. *Why did everyone think she needed someone else to look after her?* She ran after him, then quickly turned and checked that the door to the café was securely shut, before picking up speed in the direction he'd headed. For a big man he was fast!

Huffing and puffing after him, she caught up with him as

he stood and looked up at the window of a small hotel, just down the road. He paused for a moment and then strode inside. Genie rushed after him and heard the smart woman by the little reception desk tell him that Milly was out for the evening. Fishing into his coat he pulled out some car keys and Genie mutely followed him to a little red car that was parked opposite the hotel and got in the passenger side.

'Dad... Dad! Listen to me.' She turned in her seat and put a hand on his arm. 'Shouldn't we both calm down a little bit first? Where are we going?'

He kept looking straight ahead and ignored her hand. 'To your grandmother's. That old witch knows everything. I'm sure she isn't ill and Milly has refused to see her since we came down, even though she keeps turning up at the flat. I thought the whole point was to see more of her, even though it's not what I want. Milly wouldn't tell me why, but just said she'd done something unforgivable. For the first time I kind of felt an affinity with Lucille and let her stay for a while at the café.'

'She was best friends with your sister Fern's adoptive parents. They passed away recently and that's why the shop came up for sale. Your gran dotes on her. It's a bit creepy to be honest.'

Genie frowned. She had a very bad feeling about all of this. She rubbed her tired eyes and tried to clear the fug the wine had created in her brain, then gave up and watched the lines of buildings speed past as they wound their way to the bungalow – and some answers.

CHAPTER FIFTY-ONE

*H*er dad swung the car into her grandparents'
immaculate drive and gravel sprayed everywhere. Genie should have told him to slow down, but was
quite gratified to see the mess he'd just made. Half of the
stones were now scattered on the manicured lawn. It had
literally been a two-minute drive, and neither of them had
spoken. They were both trying to catch their breath.

Her dad leapt out of the car and was striding to the front
door before she could reason with him that perhaps this
wasn't the best idea. Her grandmother would probably keel
over from a heart attack and actually die of shock at a family
member that stood up to her. Not that she'd ever really
considered James to be her family. He was more of a blot on
the landscape.

Milly stood at the open front door as they approached,
her face white. 'James, Genie? What's going on? I heard the
car.' She pushed past James and wrapped her arms around
Genie, inhaling the scent of her hair before ushering them
inside.

She glanced from face to face, clearly trying to work out

what had happened to bring them there, but she couldn't hide her happiness at seeing her daughter. She closed the door behind them and hugged Genie until she wriggled free, then saw the fire in James's eyes and backed off slightly.

'Milly, who is it?' came a strong voice from the lounge. Genie cringed. That voice could make a bird drop out of the sky mid-flight in shock. Genie had often hidden in the branches of the big tree at the bottom of her grandparents' garden and she could attest to the fact that birds flew away when her gran was near. How she used to wish for wings of her own so she could join them.

'It's James and Genie,' said her mum, her voice going cold.

'Bring them in. What are you standing dithering out there for? You'll let a draught in.'

Milly went to turn away, but James caught her arm and she winced. 'Is Fern mine? Have you been telling me more lies?'

'No!' said Milly, her face filling with colour for the first time as she looked at her daughter in horror and realised that she knew what they were talking about. 'You told Genie? I know we don't communicate well now, but I thought we agreed to do that together!'

Genie touched her mum's arm. 'Dad didn't tell me. I found out about Trudie and Fern on my own. It's why I'm here.'

Tears sprang to Milly's eyes. 'I'm so sorry, darling. I didn't want you to find out from anyone else, but I didn't know how to tell you.'

'You didn't even tell Dad?'

Her mum cringed and flushed, brushing tears away with the sleeve of her lightweight jumper. 'I didn't tell anyone. The only person who knew for years was my mum.'

'You told Grandma Vera too,' said Genie, an edge to her voice.

Milly glanced up at James and she pulled a tissue out of her jeans pocket and noisily blew her nose. 'She caught me at a weak moment. I've cried on my own for years. It's never got easier, but I've managed to hide it better, especially around your or Fern's birthdays, when we should have been celebrating together. Vera found me one year. I swore her to secrecy. It was torture for her and very unfair of me. I can see that now. But I think she understood that I'd never had anyone on my side.'

Genie was appalled and rushed to hug her mother. 'I've always been on your side!'

Milly brushed Genie's hair from her face and leaned her cheek against her daughter's. 'I know that, darling, but this secret was too heavy to share. I would've had to face the look of disgust that you and your dad both have now, years ago. When you were younger I didn't know how to tell you. With your dad, every minute of the day, the lies got worse. How could I tell him? I believed he'd deserted me.'

'What?' James was rubbing his chin with his hands and moving around restlessly. He looked a sight and Genie's heart went out to him too. 'I didn't desert you.'

'I know that now. But I didn't then.'

'Come into the lounge,' demanded a voice from the other room. James took both their hands and led them to face his mother-in-law.

'What did you do?' he demanded to know.

Genie looked from her mum, to her dad, and finally to her grandparents. Her grandad was asleep in his chair, but the commotion woke him up with a start.

'Tell them what you did,' said Milly. Genie glanced round, spotted an open bottle of wine and poured herself a glass, looking to her parents to see if they would join her. They didn't, so she topped her own glass up. Her grandmother looked on with a sour face, but didn't stop her, for once.

'I don't know what you're talking about!' said Lucille, colour rising up from her neck and spreading across her chest. She started fussing with the patchwork blanket that was laid across her legs.

Milly kept looking straight at her mum. 'Tell them what you did.'

Lucille huffed and made a fuss of straightening the blanket, then looked into James' eyes and then at Genie and sighed theatrically. 'Sit down, all of you.' She waited until they all threw their hands up and sat down. 'I don't know why Milly is making such a fuss about this.'

Genie thought her mum looked like she was going to throttle her own mother and quickly scooted up next to her and held her hand. Lucille spoke directly to Genie. 'Your parents met when they were sixteen. It was most unsuitable.' Genie's eyebrows shot up and she prayed her dad didn't explode, as he was gritting his teeth. 'Your dad wooed your mum and then left her.'

'I didn't leave her!' James jumped up and began pacing the room. 'I was sixteen too and I had to go home with my parents. I called regularly and came back every year after that, even after you told me Milly had moved away to live with your sister.'

Genie gasped and felt the sickly white wine swirl round in her stomach.

'That's the bit Mum didn't tell me,' said Milly with real sadness in her voice. 'I was pregnant and alone. Mum and Dad wouldn't support me and Mum told me you hadn't been in contact. She sent me to her sister's to give birth and told me I had to give the baby away or I couldn't come back. I had nowhere else to live.'

Genie's mouth hung open as she looked at her grandmother as if she'd grown two heads. 'You made her give the baby up?'

'Oh, for goodness sake! She was sixteen. He was sixteen. They weren't responsible enough to use protection, let alone look after a child.'

'I came looking for you,' James said sadly to Milly.

'I know that now.'

Milly stared at Genie with glazed eyes and rubbed them with the back of her hand, smudging her mascara and leaving a trail across her cheek. 'It gets worse.' She tilted her head towards Lucille. 'I can barely look at her.'

'What happened?' Genie demanded of her grandmother, whose eyes flitted around as her hand went to her throat. 'Don't you dare say you feel ill or tell a lie. This is your chance to make amends.'

'She can't make amends for what she's done,' said Milly, getting up and going to stand next to James. His arm automatically went around her and she leaned into him, her body sagging until he propped her up.

'I don't know what all the fuss is about. I did the right thing.' Lucille peered down her nose at them and they all stared back, even her husband looked shiftily away.

Milly sniffed and looked at James. 'She told me you weren't interested and that I'd have to give up my child. She sent me away to her sister's house where I was left to give birth on the bathroom floor. Then someone came and took my baby away. I barely got to hold her.'

James went to say something, but she stopped him and stared at her mother. 'She told me she'd found a suitable family far away, but here we are with Fern down the road. Mum gave her to her best friend. She lives in Tindle Street. I grew up so close to the child I pined for every single day, and she let my heart bleed. I searched for Fern for years and Mum knew that. All the time she had a friendship with her grandchild. She was known as 'auntie' Lucille and she was

Fern's godmother. That was part of the deal.' James roared in pain and both Genie and Milly jumped up to restrain him.

'You evil bitch! No wonder Milly didn't tell me what had happened, if she grew up with someone like you. You made her feel abandoned and ashamed. I only wish my other daughter had got off so lightly and didn't have to know you.'

'Dad!' cried Genie, but she had to agree with him.

Milly was openly sobbing now. 'She only told me about Fern because her best friend died and Mum felt we'd be a good fit for the café. She wanted someone to keep an eye on Fern and was worried about her. If they hadn't passed away, she'd never have told me. I'm eternally grateful to them for looking after her so well, but they were complicit in my misery. They wanted to foster or adopt a child and were willing to play by Mum's rules to get one. Private adoption was a fuzzier subject back then.'

'Oh Mum,' said Genie, hugging Milly hard and wanting to cry for all of the suffering her mother had endured. Giving her grandparents a disgusted look and grabbing both of her parents' hands, she led them to the front door. 'She doesn't warrant any more of our time.' Another car pulled into the drive as they stepped out and Genie shielded her eyes. Opening them and knowing full well what she would see, she came face to face with a worried-looking and rather crumpled Cal.

CHAPTER FIFTY-TWO

'*M*um, Dad, this is Cal,' was all Genie said before walking round him, getting into her parents' car and slamming the door shut. James eyed him warily, then followed Genie and got into the driver's seat of the car without a word.

Milly stepped forward and gave Cal a hug, which he appeared grateful for by the warm smile he gave her. 'Have you come all the way from Essex tonight? You must be exhausted!' She put her hand on his arm and frowned at Genie and James's rudeness. She guessed Cal and Genie must have had a row, or he knew what had happened and he'd followed her here. Either way, he was here and Milly was glad of the distraction. It was late now and she was fed up with living alone in a tiny hotel room. She was going back to the flat tonight and if James didn't like it, then he could leave. It was her home too.

She couldn't think about her old home and friends without her heart ripping apart, so she was trying to make the best of what she had. Meeting Fern again had gone a long way to healing the hole she'd felt when they'd parted, but at

280

the same time Milly had lost Genie, then James. It was almost too much to bear. Making a quick decision, she called out to the others to go home and jumped into the passenger seat of Cal's sleek car, telling him to get in too. James immediately started the engine and roared out of the driveway.

'It's lovely to meet you, Cal,' Milly said when Cal had buckled his seatbelt. 'I don't know what's happened between you and Genie, but she's told me you're dating. It's been a long day for all of us and we should go and sit down at the flat. I need you to park at my hotel and wait outside while I pick up a few things first. Is that ok?'

Cal appeared like he wanted to say something, but he started the engine and carefully drove out of her parents' driveway, listening while Milly briefly filled him in on how much Genie had been through that day, what they'd all been through.

Milly recalled her mum's angry face as she'd stood up and tried to defend herself against the onslaught of her daughter's words, but it had been a long time coming. It had been the reason that Milly had gone there tonight. Lucille knew how much Milly had pined for her firstborn, but she'd decided that she knew what was best for everyone.

Vera had told Milly once that she and Gus would have brought up the baby with James, and that had been the hardest thing to hear. They had both cried for hours and hugged each other. Milly might have been young, but she, James and the baby could have made a little family.

Vera had tried to reason that they might have broken up under the stress and not had Genie, but Milly had argued that as a couple, they were strong, until recent events had proved her wrong, of course. James had cast her aside through his own pain, not knowing about of the years of suffering she'd shielded him from.

'It's just down here.' Milly pointed to a street to the left and a building with a red and blue neon hotel sign swinging in the evening breeze from one wall. 'I'm sorry to dump all of this on you when you probably came down to sort out a silly tiff.'

Cal turned in his seat and Milly frowned at his flushed face and tired eyes. He must have driven for hours and hours to follow Genie here. 'I made a mistake,' he said, hanging his head, making his sandy hair flop over the front of his face.

Milly pulse began beating faster. What else could life throw at her tonight? She really couldn't take much more, but she knew the voice of shame. 'What have you done?'

'Genie hates me.'

'I'm sure she doesn't…' then Milly pictured her daughter's flashing eyes and her lips set into a thin line and bit her own lip.

'Before I came to Essex, I'd lost my own business. I over-extended. I got cocky. So I hid for a while, licking my wounds. Then my mum called me and was worried about Gran… Ada.'

Milly digested all of that information and wished she wasn't so tired that her head was a big foggy. 'Ok.'

Cal looked up and Milly could see the pain he was in. He appeared like a man in love and her heart soared for her daughter. Milly hoped he knew what he was getting into, as her beautiful, feisty girl was a bit of a handful at the best of times. She smiled gently at him and took his hand. 'I'm sure that whatever you've done, it can't be half as bad as all of the things she's learnt about me and her dad tonight.'

'That's just it. It was me who told her. Inadvertently.'

Milly sprang back into her chair. 'What! How?'

'My family are pretty wealthy. I'm the black sheep. My gran was a famous actress and my pops a celebrity photographer.' He named his parents and Milly's mouth hung open unattractively. She snapped it shut again, her eyes as wide as saucers.

'Wow, ok... but if you know Genie by now, she's not at all interested in glitz and glamour. She's obsessed by the family business. Even being apart from us couldn't drag her away. That was a shock when we realised it meant more to her than we did!'

Cal turned and smiled at her this time. The smile lit his face and it was as if the sun shone down on them. Milly gazed in awe. *No wonder Genie was smitten.* 'It wasn't about that for her. She was devasted when you left. She cried for weeks, apparently.' She saw Cal immediately realise his mistake and winced.

A tear escaped from Milly's eye before she could brush it away. She really was a useless mother to both of her children. She'd got everything wrong.

'Ada filled a gap in her life but I thought Genie might be conning her. I didn't know Genie then. I set a private investigator to find out more about her.'

Milly's mouth formed a big O. A few more things made sense now. Poor Genie! Milly felt her hackles rise on her daughter's behalf but Cal held up his hands. 'I know. I know. I'm an idiot. As soon as I knew her better I realised that wasn't the case, but by then the report was in the post. I shoved it on a shelf in the desk in my room and didn't think of it again. It was as if it didn't exist and I hadn't betrayed her. I was so confident about us that I didn't even hide it. I pretended I hadn't done it and moved on.' He sighed and rubbed his temples.

'She found out?'

'She found the papers. It had everything about you both, Fern and Trudie on it, written in black and white for her sit and read on her own.'

There was a bit of censure in his voice and Milly took

that hit too. 'I should have told them. I just didn't know how. I pushed James away and it got harder each year to try and pretend my past didn't exist. I tried looking for Fern, but her surname was different and my parents kind of gave the baby to their friends on the understanding they could see her regularly.'

Cal drew in a sharp breath and Milly really wanted to get out of the car and kick something. It always seemed to work for Genie and James. She opened the door. 'Stay here while I get my things and we can go back to the flat and sort this sorry mess out once and for all.'

Milly got out of the car on trembling legs and paused for a moment to gain strength. It was really late now and she hoped there would be someone in reception to let her in. It was a small hotel and they locked the doors at eleven every night. Luckily she'd got to know the night manager and he'd probably be snoozing in his chair by the door if she knocked quietly. Knowing she was going to have to face all of the mistakes of her past or ruin the future for her two children, she straightened her shoulders. She'd made one mistake and spent her whole life paying for it. She'd been a child who'd been dominated by her parents, but no more.

It was up to her to sort this mess out and the first thing she would do was move back into the flat, try and forgive her husband for his moment of weakness with her ex-best friend and start to build a new level of trust with her daughters. *Daughters.* Just the word filled her with hope and she smiled a genuine smile for the first time that day.

CHAPTER FIFTY-THREE

*C*al wanted to rest his head and sleep for a week. He hadn't realised how gruelling the drive to Cornwall would be and the sky had turned from cornflour blue to a deep dark grey whilst he drove. It had felt ominous and his hopeful mood crumbled the nearer he got to his destination. He'd stopped twice for a quick coffee but he must have been running on adrenaline. He'd called the restaurant a couple of times from the hands-free car system. Ada and Bailey had been desperate for news about Genie. They were the only people who really knew what was going on. To everyone else, Genie was unwell and Cal was looking after her. They'd had to confide in Bailey as he was an integral part of the business now. Cal hoped Genie wouldn't hate him for that, but they'd had to trust Bailey if they wanted him to step up and run the place in her absence.

Cal had always been wary of the close bond Genie had with Bailey and his son. He wasn't stupid; he knew what might happen if he wasn't there. The problem was that it was Genie's choice. She'd have an even bigger connection to

Bailey now, as he'd been through a similar situation with Liam, from what Genie had told him.

Cal admitted that he kind of liked the guy, but he couldn't relax around him when Genie was there. Cal had never felt jealous in his life, but if Bailey looked at Genie, Cal was spitting fire! It was getting embarrassing. She didn't need either of them and Cal was at a loss to know what he could offer her that she couldn't get for herself. He knew they lit up the sheets in bed, and the thought of another man touching her silky skin brought out the Neanderthal in him. He wanted everyone to know she was his girl, especially Bailey and those girlfriends who'd neglected her until she was a success.

Genie had problems to deal with, but Cal was sure she could handle them with or without him. Her mum looked like a tough cookie, too. She was taking back the reins of her life. Cal wondered if Genie would forget his part in all the drama. He sighed and rolled his shoulders, which cried out in protest. It had been a long few months, helping Genie alongside his new job on the cookery show. People knew who he was again now, and that in itself brought new issues.

Seeing Milly lugging two cases out of the hotel, he jumped out of the car to help her. He lifted them up then staggered at their weight, putting them in the boot.

'What the hell have you got in here? The kitchen sink?'

Milly laughed and brushed a tendril of hair out of her eyes. Genie obviously got her big blue eyes from her mum and the dark colouring and long sooty lashes from her dad, who still had a full head of thick dark hair. Cal hoped he still made Genie want to fight for him when they had been together so long.

'I was so annoyed with my mum that I took a suitcase round and scooped everything I could out of the two boxes of my things she'd always kept in the back room. It's mostly old school books, they weigh a ton!'

She grinned and he grinned back. They drove the short distance and then Cal found an extra ounce of energy to start to drag the bags from the boot to the café. They stood side by side in silence, staring at the little place. 'It's beautiful,' said Cal finally, after catching his breath.

'It is. It was what's inside that brought us here, though. Mum finally told me about Fern and her adoptive parents dying and I felt an obligation to help her any way I could. I originally thought we could all charge here and take care of her. Well, that didn't happen,' she said sadly. 'Genie messed that up.'

When he was about to object, she held her hand up and he noticed that her nails were painted in the softest pink colour. It was the exact same hue that Genie wore most of the time. His guts turned over as he looked at the café door.

'I know it was my fault,' said Milly. 'When we arrived here it was horrific, as we had to tell Fern who we were.'

'How did she take it?'

Milly held her breath for a moment as if the memory scalded her. 'Not well. She felt betrayed by my mum and her parents. She knew she was adopted, but her parents had told her I'd died in childbirth.'

Cal was stunned to silence.

'She wants to meet Genie, but asked us to give her a while to digest everything beforehand. It's been agonising not being able to talk to Genie about it. Now it's too late,' said Milly sadly.

Cal winced and moved the bags as far as the front door. A light came on in the café and James appeared. He seemed calmer. He looked at the cases, but didn't comment. He just picked one up as if it weighed nothing more than air and sloped back inside. Cal flushed and picked up the next case, trying to pretend it didn't feel like a ton of bricks, and followed Milly and James indoors.

Genie was sitting at the table with a coffee in her hands. She looked up at Cal with scorn on her face. He didn't know what he'd been expecting, but he was hoping she'd had time to think about his motives on her journey from their little seaside restaurant. Then he kicked himself as it wasn't anything to do with him and the restaurant certainly wasn't 'theirs'.

Milly and James stared at each other for a moment and then Milly suggested they grab a coffee themselves and take it upstairs to talk. He nodded his head and they all waited in an awkward silence while the water heated up and he frothed some milk, ever the restaurateur.

Cal was relieved when they took their drinks at last and headed upstairs, but not before James had pulled out a chair opposite Genie and set a steaming drink on the table for him. He almost groaned out loud. All he wanted to do was scoop Genie into his arms and then sleep for a week. His phone buzzed with a text from Ada, but he ignored it.

He sank into the chair and took in his surroundings. There were wooden tables and chairs, the sleek coffee machine and empty cake domes on the little counter at the back of the shop. The walls were a cool grey and the photos of cake made his stomach rumble. Genie looked up when she heard the noise and gave him a wry look. 'Have you eaten today?'

'No.'

'Me neither. Dad gave me some cake earlier, but I couldn't stomach more than a bite or two, even though it was heavenly.' She got up and went into the pristine kitchen behind the counter. Opening the fridge and almost disappearing inside, she came back out, holding a plate of cheese. She snagged a bag of crisps from the display on the counter and brought it to the table. 'Cheese and crisps will have to do.' She opened the crisp bag and folded it out flat so that they could share.

'Cheese? You hate cheese.'

'I've decided that I need to get used to it now I own my own restaurant. I've been working my way up from eating a tiny morsel to a whole slice.'

Cal grinned. 'You're going to eat all the crisps first, though, aren't you?'

'Yep.'

'I'm sorry, Genie,' he said, reaching across and taking her hand. His fingers itched to stroke her soft arms, but he daren't. 'I didn't know you at all when I hired the investigators. Then, when I did know you, I forgot I'd even spoken to them. The file arrived and I was confused about what to do with the information. I didn't want to know your parents' secrets. I just wanted to protect my gran.'

Genie pulled her hand away and looked into his eyes. There was fire in hers. 'Why didn't you tell me then? Why not show me the papers when you did know me?' She got up and began pacing the room, the food forgotten. She kicked the wall and then yelped in pain. He jumped up and pulled her into his arms, sitting down again with her on his knee. She was trembling.

'Because I thought this would happen. You'd run away from me and not listen to the reason behind it. I know you wouldn't con my family. If anything, you've helped us all.' He rested his head on her hair and felt her take a wobbly breath.

'My family are so messed up,' she mumbled, glumly. 'I don't know if my parents can save their marriage and I thought I was an only child. What if I hate her? This sister?'

Cals arms tightened around Genie and she snuggled into his chest, before she seemed to realise what she was doing and pushed away. He held his breath in case she decided to jump up. When she didn't, he spoke gently to her.

'You won't hate her. In fact it seems you're eerily similar. Your mum told me she bakes incredible cakes, a bit like your gift for making ice cream. She runs a café and lives by the sea.' He kissed her nose and couldn't resist stealing a kiss from the nectar of her lips. One kiss turned into two and before long she was pliant in his arms. She tasted of red grapes with a hint of coffee, and he wanted more.

'Uh… I guess you two have made up…' came a voice from the bottom of the stairs. Genie hid her embarrassment in his chest and he had to face her mum, her face flushed but much happier than the last time he'd seen her. They smiled at each other and he got up and eased Genie to the floor where she stood next to him but wouldn't take his hand.

'What about you two?' asked Genie, her face lifting to stare at her mum.

'I'm moving back in and we're going to work on it. We want to try and spend half of our time here and half of our time visiting you and Grandad… and Cal and Ada… if you'll have us.'

'What about Trudie?' Genie almost spat her name.

'Trudie left this morning. Right after Ada payed her a visit,' said Cal.

Genie looked up at him in awe. 'Ada did that for us?'

'She did it for you, Genie.' He tried to ignore seeing Milly flinch at his words. 'Ada loves you – and Gus got back today and went with her.'

Genie turned to her mum in alarm. 'Gramps came back and none of us were there?'

'Ada was there and I'm sure she's taking good care of him.' Milly shrugged.

Genie frowned. Cal knew exactly what Milly meant. Ada and Gus had been keeping tabs on them both for months via text, and had developed a cute kind of friendship.

'I need to get back home. I've got a business to run,' said Genie, through a wide yawn.

Milly rushed over to hug her and stroke her hair. 'Can't you stay for a few days?'

'I can't,' said Genie with genuine regret in her tone. 'I'd love to be here for a while and see how you do things, but you're doing great and my business needs me.'

'I need you,' said Milly.

'You've got Dad,' said Genie simply. Milly looked like she wanted to object, but pressed her lips shut instead.

'What about Fern?'

'I think I need to get used to the thought of having a sister before I meet her.'

Milly looked like she wanted to say something, but held out a key that she'd been grasping in her hand. 'It's the key to my hotel room. I haven't checked out yet. Reception was shut. Use the room to get some sleep tonight and we can have an early breakfast here before you head home. Fern doesn't arrive until nine.'

Genie glanced from her mum, to Cal, to the key and then obviously decided she was too tired to argue. She kissed her mum goodnight, called out to her dad, and Cal took her hand and led her back up the road towards the hotel.

CHAPTER FIFTY-FOUR

*C*al opened the hotel bedroom door and looked around. It was small and fit the seaside theme, with little starfish on the set of reclaimed drawers and canvases of waves splashing against the shore on the walls. In the centre of the room, facing the window that looked out to sea, was a double bed flanked by two small side tables. There was a lamp on each. Their shades were pretty silver metal with tiny holes that sent spirals of light across the ceiling when he turned them on. There was a two-seater couch under the window and he dumped his bag on that. 'I can sleep here.'

Genie's eyes were glazed, but she closed the door behind her and went into the bathroom with her bag, returning moments later, completely naked. His eyes went out on stalks, but she seemed as if she didn't even see him. She just climbed into bed and then pulled the covers around her like a cocoon, falling almost instantly into a deep sleep.

Cal stripped off his own clothes. His body protested and he looked despondently at the couch. He was a tall man and he'd never fit on there without half of his legs and his feet hanging off the edge. He looked under his lashes at the bed, but couldn't do it.

'Get in,' said a sleepy voice from the bed. 'We need sleep.'

Not waiting to be asked twice, Cal very carefully peeled a bit of the cover up and slipped between the cool sheets, sighing in pleasure. He took care not to disturb Genie and within seconds he was asleep.

During the night something touched his warm chest and he woke up with a start, shaking his head and trying to work out where he was. He'd forgotten to shut the curtains. It was still dark outside. He looked down. Genie had turned and her arm was thrown across his chest. His movement made her open her eyes sleepily and instead of recoiling, her hands trailed down his chest and along his thigh. He drew in a sharp breath and then bent gently and kissed her. She responded by biting his lip and he groaned and rolled her onto her back, dropping kisses on her neck and across her chest as her hands crept around his backside and rested there. He'd missed her so much. He knew he should stop and they should talk, but his body craved hers and seemed to have a mind of its own. Her hands slid across the back of his legs and then up to his waist. He moved his body on top of hers so that he could explore every inch of her with his tongue and she cried out in ecstasy. The sound almost sent him over the edge, but suddenly she was kissing and licking his neck and face and he pulled her on top of him, moving his body with hers. He ran his hands along her sensitive skin and up to cup her breasts and they lost themselves in each other as if the world was going to end.

Sometime in the night they fell asleep and then woke to hungrily explore each other again with such love and passion that Cal drifted off with a smile on his face and his girl in his arms. Every fibre of his being was screaming in exhaustion, but he was happy. They could work this out. Their problems weren't insurmountable.

His dreams were full of her and as the sun streamed through the window, Cal shielded his eyes and blinked. Then he remembered the night before and turned to face Genie with a smile. Her side of the bed was empty, so he swung his feet to the floor and walked into the bathroom, flicking the switch on the little kettle perched on the set of drawers as he passed, to make them both a cup of tea.

Frowning and seeing the bathroom was empty, he noticed the sheets of paper Genie had found on his desk were lying beside the bathroom sink. His stomach sank and he picked them up and turned them over. On the back were six words that tore his heart in two.

'I can't do this. I'm sorry.'

Retracing his steps into the bedroom and grabbing his jeans and his phone, he dressed and tapped out Genie's number while he emptied his bag and located a clean T-shirt. Hearing the dial tone, he pictured the phone in her bedroom bin at the penthouse, lying on its side with a cracked screen. His temper rose. It wasn't safe for her to be running around without a phone. He hoped she'd just walked down the road to her parents' place, but he knew Genie too well by now. He threw the phone into his bag and grabbed everything else. He hadn't brought much with him.

He almost growled with frustration when his phone pinged again with another text. He was due back in London that day as they were filming tomorrow. He couldn't do anything about the schedule. The timing was appalling.

His ego had taken such a hit, thanks to Genie's note. A night with him obviously wasn't enough to make her stay in his arms. She must have woken up and regretted it, which made his skin flush with shame. He should have pushed her away and made her sit and listen to him, but one look at those big sultry blue eyes, and when she'd licked her lips to moisten them, he just hadn't been able to control his body. He'd wanted to refuse her and to talk... a bit... then he'd wanted to kiss every inch of her skin. He missed being around her, even though it had only been a day. He hated fighting. And, for the first time in his life, he was scared that a woman might not want him around.

CHAPTER FIFTY-FIVE

*I*t had been a weird week since Genie had returned from Cornwall. She'd tentatively sent an email to her sister after finding the café's contact details on its website.

She hoped her mum was still as technophobic as she had been when she'd lived in Essex. Milly could never work out how to write an email, let alone venture onto social media. She often said she wanted to live in the real world and not one run by computers. The café did have an up-to-date website, though, so Genie assumed her sister had either paid someone, or ran it herself. When the first reply had come in, she hadn't wanted to open it, but now they spoke daily and having a sister actually wasn't that bad. She finally had someone in her corner.

She thought back to that first night in Cornwall. It had been tumultuous. Although she'd kissed Cal first, she hadn't quite forgiven him for breaking her heart. The restaurant here was busier than ever and her friends popped in and out every so often, so she hadn't had a chance to mull it over. She flushed when she remembered how brazen she'd been in that hotel room. When he'd stood by the side of her bed, all sexily tanned and glistening, she hadn't been able to insist he kept to the sofa. She'd tried to sleep, she really had, but her hands had a mind of their own when he was near. Her skin craved his touch. Her anger at him had subsided, but the hurt hadn't abated. All the people she loved had lied to her, except for Fern.

Her grandad was back and pottering about his shed as if he hadn't disappeared for six months and travelled the world. Evil pigeon absolutely loved him and sat on his desk eating cheese, which made Genie felt quite jealous. Her grandad wasn't as grumpy as he had been, but he wouldn't discuss what had happened, saying the past was in the past and was best left that way. It was easy for him to say that. He hadn't discovered his parents had had another child and then upped and deserted him for that child, after living in each other's pockets for the best part of twenty-two years! She'd spoken to them on the phone, but it had been awkward and stilted. She was actually glad now they were so far away. She sniffed and picked at a bit of sunburn.

Genie would never speak to Lucille again. The suffering she'd caused them all was too much to bear. Genie didn't even care if she was old and pretending to be frail. She was shocked that an such abundance of nastiness could lurk under an unassuming exterior. The old woman looked kind and harmless, but then she would strike at the heart.

Genie's phone had been fixed and she spent endless hours going over and over the texts Cal had sent her on that fateful morning, and every day since. He'd had to stay in London for work and in a way she was glad. She had enough to do, running her very busy restaurant and trying to keep her grandad out of the way. He literally poked his nose into everything and she'd had to ask him to invent a way to keep their ice cream teas chilled, to get him out from under her feet. He absolutely revelled in how busy they were and happily chatted to customers with Ada. It did warm her heart to see it, but he kept offering to help and then falling asleep on the job. He was used to afternoon snoozes on the cruise and it seemed to have become an annoying habit. He found their little booths a bit too comfortable.

In the end he'd come up with an ingenious idea of little cake stands with a deep metal plate underneath with a lid that they could unscrew and freeze after filling with water. They stayed chilled for hours afterwards and the little iced cakes she served with delicate sandwiches stayed intact and delicious. They were an instant hit in her new cream tea backroom and the restaurant became even busier than ever.

Genie signalled to Bailey that she was taking a break and walked across to sit and wiggle her toes in the warm sand for a moment. She looked out to sea and watched the waves lap against the beach. Bailey had been a revelation. He now took charge of their kitchen and he'd spent hours sitting in the booths with her after they'd closed and talking about how it felt to have a child at such a young age and the responsibility that came with it. He sympathised with Milly. Genie suspected it had actually helped him to come to terms with his own past and to forgive Liam's mum for not wanting a child at sixteen.

Liam came into the restaurant all the time and now had his own stool and apron. He loved helping her decide which ice cream ingredients to use next. He had a flair, even at his age, and she thought there might be another family business starting one day between father and son – as soon as he got over his phase of sticking crisps with everything.

She smiled as she watched a seagull pecking at a discarded ice cream cone and coming up with a pink beak. She opened the shoulder bag she'd brought with her and rested it at her feet. She pulled out the first of the parcels and unwrapped it again. It had arrived at 9am that morning and she'd had a delivery on the hour, every hour, since. She turned the seashell over and felt the weight of it in her palm. It had been wrapped in blue paper and ribbon and had a simple tag attached to it with a pink heart at the bottom edge. She'd been confused at first, but as morning turned into afternoon and the parcels kept coming, she was more and more touched by each sentiment. The shell symbolised the beach where they lived. The next delivery had been corn-flowers, her favourite. She remembered telling Cal one night how much she loved them and hadn't thought of it again.

The next two gifts had been a bottle of her favourite wine and some macaroons coloured with tones of the sea. He had teased her because the wine she liked was pretty awful, but she adored the design of the label as it reminded her of a summer sky. She remembered the first time she'd been in the kitchen, interviewing him for a job, and he'd made maca-roons that she'd kept filching while he'd teased her that he wouldn't be able to finish if she kept eating them. She knew it was a skilled job to make them and she'd never seen colours like this on food before. It was art. The bases of the macaroons were dusted with some kind of sherbet that made them look like they were gems nestled in the sand.

When the courier had arrived with the next gift, she'd blushed to the roots of her hair. Ada had raised an eyebrow and Genie had rapidly stuffed it back in its packaging, side-stepping with it behind her back until she got into the staff toilets and locked the cubicle door. Her heart was beating fast. She drew out the wisp of blue silk and reverently held it up to her body, the colour of the material reflecting the sparkle in her eyes. She didn't know what to feel about this gift as it was so sexy and suggestive, unlike all the other presents Cal had sent. Her stomach churned constantly for the next hour, but then she'd sat and laughed when a pair of fluffy bed socks were delivered to go with the negligée. Genie loved to tease Cal by putting her cold toes on his legs in bed and he often jumped, which made her giggle until he kissed her to the point where she forgot her own name.

The latest gift had been one of the little starfish that had sat on the chest of drawers in the bedroom they had stayed in at the hotel in Cornwall. Memories of how wanton she had been that night made her skin flush. She'd made him think that all was right with his world, and then she'd left him. He'd made mistakes, but who got through life without some of those? She certainly hadn't.

She looked at her phone and was sad to see no calls or texts from Cal, or anyone in her family that day. She inhaled some of the calming salty sea air and listened to the waves again, enjoying the feel of the sun on her skin. She didn't want to admit it to herself, but she was clock-watching. She wanted to be back in the restaurant before the next hour was up, in case another gift was delivered. She placed the little seashell back into its wrapping and picked up a similar one from the sand, nestling them both together.

A shadow fell across her legs and she shielded her eyes and looked up. Cal was standing before her, looking tanned and gorgeous. Her heart leapt into her mouth. Her hands started shaking, then she noticed he was wearing a blue cotton shirt that moulded his muscles and her mouth went dry.

He reached for her hand and she took it, letting him pull her up into a hug that she never wanted to end. The sun was still in her eyes. When they pulled apart, he grinned and kissed her on the lips, making her lick them and want more. But he stepped back and she saw that someone else was standing behind him.

All the air was sucked out of Genie's lungs and she gasped. There, standing on her beach, next to the man she loved, was her sister. She'd have known Fern anywhere. She had the same big blue eyes, although with more of a green tinge to them. Both had long lashes and dark hair, although Fern was slightly taller and slimmer than Genie. She obviously hadn't inherited their paternal grandma's curves. Genie didn't speak, but when Fern reached out for her, she flew into her sister's arms until they were both sobbing happy tears and didn't want to let each other go.

Over Fern's shoulder, Genie watched Cal walk back up to the restaurant and go and shake hands with her dad, who was standing like a proud peacock outside. Then he leaned in and hugged her mum, who was laughing at something Ada had said. Her gramps was standing just beside her. Genie moved back and took her sister's arm in hers. 'Come on. Let's go and taste some of my ice creams. There's one of our gran's that you might be able to turn into a cake. It's full of boozy apples and cinnamon. I'll give you the recipe.' Feeling Fern hug her to her side, Genie enjoyed the warmth that suddenly filled her soul, right the way up from her prettily painted pink toenails.

They were just about to cross the road when Genie pulled back and stopped short. 'What the hell?' Her grandad and Ada were standing next to each other with their hands almost touching as they spoke to Cal, big smiles on both their faces, their chemistry apparent to anyone who was looking.

Fern giggled and grabbed Genie's arm again and the sisters walked towards their family. Cal scooped Genie to his side and planted a kiss on the top of her hair as soon as they arrived, and he handed her the ice cream he'd been eating which had melted and run down his fingers. He licked some of the cream away and her eyes followed his tongue, making her moisten her lips, wishing she was kissing him.

She gazed across to the sea and the families playing

happily in the surf, and then back to her wayward bunch of hoodlums and hell-raisers, but she wouldn't have it any other way. This was a new beginning for them all, whichever way it turned out. Gazing up into the eyes of her very own gigolo sex god, she couldn't be happier.

She smiled and waved to a couple of regular customers as they left the restaurant, and then ushered her family inside, out of the blazing sunshine and into *Genie's*. Hearing their words of appreciation as Cal gave them a tour of the new place went a long way to healing any damage to her heart. She fully intended to let Cal and her parents grovel for a little while longer, but having her sister here and seeing everyone so happy, with the restaurant full to bursting with replete customers, well, it made up for some of the pain.

Observing her mum ask Bailey for a quiet word and then go and sit out in the back garden, heads bent together, she hoped that he might be able to ease some of her mum's guilt for not standing up to her parents. It wasn't her fault, she'd been young and under terrible pressure. Genie hoped she would one day be able to see that. It must have been so hard for a teenager to make a decision like that alone. Genie fully intended to be there for her now and to let both her parents know they could have two independent children, see them regularly and be involved in both their lives. She was determined to make it work.

Genie was a business owner with a hot boyfriend and she wouldn't tell them yet, but she also had big plans. She wanted to brand her ice creams and ship them to Cornwall and to do the same for her sister's cakes and bring them here. The idea could expand rapidly, but for now she was content just to think it through. Her parents could run that side of the business and travel to sell the cakes and ice cream elsewhere.

She had a feeling that her grandad and Ada might suddenly decide to book the same cruise later in the year.

Meanwhile, Cal would be travelling to work, but be home on weekends. She might even let him be her chief ice cream taster beside Liam, and make him his own apron. She giggled at the idea of the toddler and Cal standing side by side tasting ice creams, then pictured a sandy haired child, like Cal, and shook her head before her insides began to melt.

Fanning her face with the menu she'd just collected from table five, she noticed that Fae and Una had arrived and were looking for a seat, but were having to stand in line. Genie's face lit up with a wide smile and she turned in the opposite direction and left it to her staff to seat them – eventually – while she laced her fingers with Cal's, and led him outside to join the rest of her family.

ABOUT THE AUTHOR

International bestselling author and award-winning inventor, Lizzie Chantree, started her own business at the age of 18 and became one of Fair Play London and The Patent Office's British Female Inventors of the Year in 2000. She discovered her love of writing fiction when her children were little and now works as a business mentor and runs a popular networking hour on social media, where creatives can support to each other. She writes books full of friendship and laughter, that are about women with unusual and adventurous businesses, who are far stronger than they realise. She lives with her family on the coast in Essex. Visit her website at www.lizziechantree.com or follow her on Twitter @Lizzie_Chantree

For more books and updates:
www.lizziechantree.com

I really hope you enjoyed reading The Little Ice Cream Shop By The Sea. If you liked reading my novel, please consider leaving a review. Many readers look to the reviews first when deciding which book to choose, and seeing your review might help them discover this one. I appreciate your help and support. Make an author smile today. Leave a review! Thank you so much. From Lizzie :)

'Books like this are the reason I love reading.'

'Rarely has a book held my heart in its hands the way If You Love Me I'm Yours has. An incredibly uplifting romantic story that has had me laughing and crying over and over again.'

'As always the main characters fizz and entrance, with underdogs and divas, harassed hunks and devilishly attractive but flawed rogues... The espionage aspect helps the seemingly workaday schoolyard environment along famously with catty cliques and beastly little brats, as well as adorable, yet still edgy kids.

If you haven't had the pleasure of reading one of Lizzie's books yet - treat yourself!'

'Loved the book! Lots of fiery, and glamorous characters, but there are some who are dealing with deeper issues. A book packed full of suspense. a riveting ending that made me want to keep reading. It's a romance novel, and it is about relationships, but it's also about the love a parent has for their child. Highly recommended.'

'I stepped outside my normal genre comfort zone of crime thrillers to read this book; it had been recommended to me and I had my eyes and heart opened. I laughed, I cried and had a precious insight into the life of people who on the surface appear, okay. I have bought another book from this author and started reading it immediately – such exceptional writing. I do not hesitate to recommend this book.'

THE LITTLE CUPCAKE SHOP BY THE SEA

Coming soon!

A seaside escape, filled with new beginnings and magical settings. Will moving to a sun kissed coast, lead Fern to love?

When a broken relationship takes Fern on a journey to find out more about her family, it's a chance to put heartache behind her. She quickly falls in love with a beautiful cove and adjoining shops which awaken her dream of a cupcake and cocktail café by the sea, but an emotional revelation and a handsome but grumpy new tenant make her question her past decisions.

Genie is excited about the new shop by the sea, but is trying to balance the demands of a famous boyfriend and her unpredictable family.

Jessie wakes up one day to find he has a new landlady for his surf shop, which makes him furious. But the more time he spends with Fern, it's clear that they have a connection that neither of them can deny.

Can Fern find the courage to tell Jessie about her past? And if she does, will she get the lasting love she's been dreaming of?

The Little Cupcake Shop By The Sea is the second book in a series of seaside romance novels, by Lizzie Chantree. All of Lizzie's books are uplifting, heart-warming stories of romance, love, hope, second chances and new beginnings, featuring different characters in stunning locations.

IF YOU LOVE ME, I'M YOURS

ALSO FROM AUTHOR LIZZIE CHANTREE.

CHAPTER 1

Maud closed her eyes and prepared to jump off the emotional cliff she was teetering on the edge of. She shuffled forward until she felt sick with nerves, took a deep calming breath and waited.

'Oh, Maud...' her mother sighed. 'Not again.'

Maud cringed at the familiarity of those words, and in her mind, she stepped off into the void and plunged into the icy darkness without a whimper. In reality, she was still in her lounge, but being around her mother made her feel like an abject failure and the words she uttered sliced through Maud and filled her with doom. Her mum pushed her to the edge of reason on a regular basis. She wished that for once her mother could try harder to be nice. Surely it couldn't be that difficult to be grateful for the anniversary gift she had been given and to offer a smile, even a fake one, for the sake of her child? It was the same every year and Maud was finally ready to surrender and stop trying so hard to make them understand her and compliment one of her paintings. It was never going to happen, she realised with a heavy heart.

Maud didn't mind being boring, not really. She had a

sensible job, sensible clothes, a sensible love life... if you counted two overbearing exes and a one night stand who had thanked her, rolled over and was snoring before she even realised he had started! She was ok with not fulfilling her dreams or being outrageous and carefree, she just wanted her parents to pay her a compliment, just once, after years of disapproval and disappointment.

Maud knew that as far as her mum was concerned, she was the most amazing parent who encouraged her daughter to have a responsible career until she settled down and found a 'suitable' husband. Granted, Maud was a very good, well-liked and adept teacher's assistant in the local primary school, but every time she pushed against the boundaries set by her parents for their perfect daughter... *'Oh, Maud!'*

It was ridiculous, she was twenty-four, thought Maud. She wished she had a big glass of wine to slug back, but her mother would disapprove of that too, suggest in horror that she was a 'wino,' and hand her the number for AA, which she would have readily available in the little brown Filofax she carried everywhere in her patent handbag. The woman was a menace.

'You don't like the painting, then?' she asked. Her mother tilted her head to one side without a word, her lip between her teeth as she concentrated and her brow furrowing as she looked at the artwork in confusion. It wasn't the reaction Maud had hoped for. She had spent hours delicately drawing the lines of the little landscape painting of her parents' house and she felt salty tears scratch her eyes. She refused to let them spill out in front of her mother, though, and bit her own lip until she tasted blood. The painting wasn't Maud's preferred style, spidery black lines depicting beautiful animals, filled in with splashes of vibrant colourwork to bring them to life. She had hoped that by toning down her eclectic style and drawing such a personal space as her parents' home, her mother would finally see the little girl who desperately wanted to paint.

Her father coughed into his hand and looked at his daughter. 'Well...' Maud's heart almost stopped beating in her chest as she waited to hear his response to her work. She turned towards him with unshed tears in eyes shining with hope. He had seen this look so many times and she knew that he hated to disappoint her, but her mum would make his life a living hell if he encouraged her. Her mum saw anything creative as frivolous and a waste of time, and generally her dad agreed with her. He said quietly to her sometimes that he appreciated that Maud enjoyed painting, but her art wasn't exactly going to set the world ablaze with awe at her talents, now was it? The words had cut into her heart and she'd cringed in pain. She knew he felt that it certainly wasn't appropriate for a serious young lady who wanted to teach children and catch a husband. The thought of her attracting a layabout artist and spending her days smoking spliffs must horrify him, as he often left articles about wild artists who were living outrageous lives around the house when she visited. He must have gone out to buy the magazines especially, as her mother would never leave anything out on the table otherwise, she was such a neat freak. Maud sometimes wondered how many hours he must spend sifting through the shelves at the newsagents, as how many articles about wild and out of control artists could there be? Maybe he stored them in the garage in a cardboard box? She had never actually picked one up, as that would fuel their obsession. Perhaps he just recycled the same article? She'd have to pay more attention next time.

He moved to the edge of his seat to scrutinise the little work of art and scratched his head in obvious confusion. She hoped he could see it was quite pretty and that Maud had obviously spent much of her free time on it. She could imagine the thoughts in his head, like where would they put such a colourful picture on their mostly beige walls? He looked across at her and must have noticed the unshed tears in her eyes. 'I wish with all my heart that I could see what you do, but art is a complete mystery to me,' he sighed. 'I'm not one for artsy stuff. We have racks of your paintings in the spare room from when you were younger. I've put up shelves in there,' he paused and she could almost hear him add *to hide them away*, 'but we do appreciate the effort you put in and are grateful for this year's anniversary present, darling.'

Maud was sure he couldn't help but notice that she was almost hopping from foot to foot in agitation and her eyes were bright with questions. He looked pained, as if his guts had just turned over. She knew her mum would hide this little painting in the spare room as soon as possible after she had stepped through the front door at home, but hopefully he could see how much it meant to Maud. He gritted his teeth and her heart melted as his shoulders straightened and he stood a bit taller. She could see that he'd decided that for once he was going to stand his ground. 'It's pretty, love.' Maud let out the breath she'd been holding and rushed over to squeeze the life out of her dad in her excitement, until he was laughing and gasping for air.

'But...' interrupted Rosemary, getting up. Maud wondered if she had told her dad not to react when Maud gave them another painting and finally to talk her out of this most unsuitable habit. 'For goodness sake, Maud! You're a teacher with lots of other ways to fill your days. Why are you mucking about with paints when you should be trying to find a husband?' Maud's smile dropped from her face and her dad looked upset. She could feel the gloom returning.

'It's pretty,' he repeated firmly, making Rosemary sit back

down in confusion at his forceful tone. 'We can put it by the window in the kitchen so that we can look at it every day.'

Rosemary's face went white with shock and she looked like she might faint at the thought of that monstrosity in her pristine cream kitchen, but one glance at her husband silenced her protest. She lifted her face and saw Maud's slightly unkempt hair and wild eyes and her face softened slightly.

'I don't know why it means so much to you for us to have some of your pictures, but maybe we can find a corner for this one if it's that important. I'm not a monster. I don't know where you get this painting thing from, Maud,' she added, getting up and running her hands down Maud's soft blond hair to straighten out the kinks.

Maud dressed impeccably in neutral tones and her hair didn't usually have a strand out of place, as she tamed the unruly curls at the ends with hot hair straighteners every day. Even her bungalow, with its stark white walls and modern but functional furniture, was always immaculately clean, even if it was a strange choice of home for such a young woman. Maud's mum didn't really have anything to complain about, as Maud did everything in her power to please her parents, other than this one small thing. For some reason her mum had a deep rooted fear that Maud needed to be kept under control in case she started running around naked or dying her hair pink, orange and blue again, like she had as a child.

Rosemary often recalled the memory to Maud. She blamed her own older sister, Maud's aunt – whom she too often referred to as 'the annoying one' – for starting this mess by buying her then five-year-old niece a set of colourful finger paints. For the next few years it had been chaos. Rosemary said her stomach often turned over at the recollection. The beautifully clean walls of their three-bedroom terraced home were spattered with every colour of the rainbow, as Maud decided that they should be 'smiley colours.' Her clothes, which her mum spent hours laundering and ironing, began to be covered with pen and ink blobs and smears, which were the faces of their pedigree, non-shedding cat and his rather less salubrious neighbourhood friends. Every surface Maud could find followed suit.

Her mum had initially thought that it was a phase that Maud would grow out of, and yelled at her sister for being so bloody inconsiderate. She got haughty distain in return, and it explained why they still couldn't stand being in the same room together. As Maud grew up, she learnt not to paint on the surfaces of her home lest she invoke the wrath of her parents, but she began doing odd jobs for extra pocket money and bought paper, pens and an art folder to hide under her bed. Within weeks it had been full to bursting and her mum had wrung her hands in despair at the clutter and nearly kicked the poor cat as she constantly tripped over tubes of paint, which had escaped from the desk drawer. Admittedly, Maud's room was mostly tidy, but her home-work desk overflowed with art supplies and the smell of fresh paint now made her mum feel faint.

Over the years, Maud had realised that her art was a frivolity and she had gradually dwindled to painting only occasionally, until she had stopped altogether. Now she had her own private space, the 'phase' had begun again, and her mum was distraught. At least the mess was at Maud's own house and she didn't have much time to paint now she had a full-time job.

'You do seem to be happy here,' Rosemary sighed, looking around at Maud's home and mentioning that the kitchen cupboards needed rubbing down and repainting. She watched Maud as she leaned forward and hugged her dad again, dodging away from her mum's hands, as Rosemary tried to brush a speck of dust from her soft blue jumper and then tugged at the hem of her skirt to straighten it.

'Thanks, dad,' Maud beamed at him, generously turning and enveloping her mother in the hug too, making her blush furiously and shoosh her away.

CHAPTER 2

Dot straightened one of the five pigtails on top of her head and made sure they were sticking out at the right angle. She moved the chunky jewellery she was wearing to the correct spot on one side of her neck and patted down her checked skirt and sparkly blue tights.

She glanced around to assure herself that everything was in place and the paintings were lit properly. The drinks were all set out along the temporary bar, which was actually her receptionist's desk; glasses sparkled and surfaces shone with the elbow grease that had gone into making this evening perfect. Tonight was a big deal for her and the largest art show she had personally organised. Working as creative director for her parents and big brother was lively and inter-esting, but her soul cried out to be part of the inner circle of artists, rather than on the outside echelons as their manager. She knew she was brilliant at her job, but her family was a dynasty of talented artists and she was the oddity, the black sheep with colourful hair.

Dot adored painting, but unfortunately she was

completely atrocious at it. It was hopeless. She didn't just stink at painting; she was abysmal; a word she'd heard whispered about her work by a visiting uncle en route to his latest exhibition. The look of pity on her parents' faces when they scrutinised her painterly offerings, and the confusion in her brother's eyes when he tried to find a meaning in the splotches and swirls, were enough to make her hang her head in shame. As a consolation, and to make her feel involved when she was old enough, they had kindly offered her the chance to manage their work, as she had the advantage of understanding them all so well. She had taken on the role after much persuasion and a little emotional blackmail over their hurt feelings and she was determined to make everyone see she was one of them.

She dressed accordingly for someone who was part of the art community, with zany and outrageous clothes, and worked determinedly to ensure her family's art was seen all over the world and reached markets and customers they had never considered before. They had been suitably astounded as, satisfyingly, she was surprisingly good at her job. She handled their work with flair and was a real asset to them, but as a failed artist and family member, Dotty still felt that she had something to prove, however much they told her she was irreplaceable.

Anyone could sell art this good, surely? thought Dot.

Out of the corner of her eye she spotted a light above her brother's second piece of work flicker and die. All of his creativity was dark and stormy and the public went mad over his brooding good looks and grumpy demeanour. She loved him dearly… but what the hell was all that about?

She could see the appeal of his art; it was sublime, but her brother was not the best advertisement for relationships. Women flocked to his feet, but he could barely remember their names and left her fielding calls from the moment she arrived at the gallery each morning. The fact that he only gave them his work number should have alerted them to his intentions, but they all thought he was worth mooning by the phone for. Yuck. It was almost enough to put her off dating for life... almost.

CHAPTER 3

Maud reverently stroked the embossed surface of the invitation she was holding to a private gallery viewing later that evening. She'd visited many galleries over the years, but none so glamorous or exciting as this one. The Ridgemoors were world famous artists, and attaining a ticket to the preview show was like getting back stage passes to an Ed Sheeran concert and being allowed to snog his face off afterwards.

Maud's best friend Daisy had forced her to go alone tonight, which wasn't very kind of her. Maud had claimed one of the prizes in an art competition, which she hadn't even known she'd entered, as her friend was a common thief and had stolen one of her little paintings and entered it without Maud's knowledge.

When it had won, Daisy had plied Maud with alcohol at the local pub, which Maud should have instantly found suspicious as Daisy hardly ever bought a round of drinks, and then confessed to stealing her work. Maud was slightly mollified by the fact that it had won a prize and even she couldn't turn down the opportunity of getting so close to one of Nate Ridgemoor's paintings.

The prize for her winning entry was one precious ticket to the private view. She grudgingly accepted that Daisy thought she was helping her to get out and meet new people. Then her best friend had called her that evening and put on what Maud could only describe as the worst acting she had ever heard, coughing and spluttering that she couldn't drive her to the viewing, which was Maud's stipulation for accepting the invitation, even though Daisy had been perfectly fine earlier in the day at work. Daisy thought Maud's knickers were made of concrete as they were so tough to get into, and she was desperate for Maud to meet a man. She used every excuse to dump her alone somewhere, even if it meant her getting the train on her own at night.

Daisy was one of the few people that Maud had confided in about her own love of painting, although even she hadn't seen Maud's latest work. The art she had submitted on Maud's behalf was pretty enough, but it wasn't her usual style at all. Nonetheless, the turbulent seascape had won a prize and the expensive invitation in her hand had arrived with a letter saying her work had shown promise and that she had been one of five entries selected to win tickets to the private view.

Maud remembered how Daisy had danced around the simple room when they had arrived back at her bungalow and she'd realised that Maud wasn't about to dive over the table to strangle her for being so deceitful. She'd tried in vain to entice Maud to bring some of the vibrant cushions she had strewn across her hand-sewn bedspread into the lounge, to brighten the place up, but Maud had remained resolute that it was unnecessary and would give her mother a heart attack when she visited.

Luckily, Rosemary had never ventured into Maud's bedroom or seen the serene forest mural on the wall. Daisy said she thought this was strange, but Maud just shrugged, as if the fact didn't hurt, and mumbled that they didn't have that kind of girly relationship. Daisy often wondered aloud if Maud actually wanted her mum to poke her nose around the house and take an interest in the way her daughter expressed her true personality, with the vibrant colours and fabrics she had hidden away. Daisy thought she wanted to shock Rosemary, but anyway, the moment had never materialised, as her mum was too focussed on how neat the kitchen was or if Maud's clothes were ironed to perfection while she was wearing them.

Maud kept her bedroom door firmly shut and her mum never expressed an interest in staying too long, before busily pronouncing she had somewhere else to be. Rosemary enjoyed Maud visiting her own house, but only at the most convenient times, preferably when there was someone else there for her to brag to about Maud's teaching career, which made Maud cringe in embarrassment as she'd had the same job for ages now and hadn't bothered to apply for anything else. Maud wished she had a brother or sister to confide in, but that was her fault too. She had been so messy and inconsiderate as a child that her mother had told her that she couldn't cope with more children like her.

Maud slid open the door to her wardrobe and ran her hand along her collection of rich, textural fabrics hidden inside. Sighing heavily, she slid the door further along and grimaced at the rows of bland tops, skirts and dresses. Her fingers itched to grab something frivolous, but the vision of her mother's angry face and bugged-out eyes always stopped her.

Maud hated her magpie tendencies to buy beautiful, sparkly clothes, as she'd never wear any of them. She just couldn't walk past a shop window and not bring them home; she had to have them, even if it was just to look at. Reaching out and selecting a simple black dress, she stuck her tongue out at her reflection in the mirror in the en-suite bathroom and hung the offending dress up on the back of the door, before turning on the shower to warm the water up a little.

Towelling her hair dry after an invigorating shower, she plugged in her hair straighteners and watched the tiny light on the side turn green. She had to get up half an hour early every morning to tame her hair and tonight she needed to get a move on if she was going to arrive on time. She was the only person she knew with straight, curly hair. Her hair was completely poker straight until it reached just below her ears, then it sprung into unruly curls. What the hell was all that about? She was sure her hair was rebelling and wished she had the courage to do the same.

She couldn't have a perm as her hair wanted to be straight and it didn't take hold. The bottom section could be straightened, but as her hair was thick and golden-blonde, this took forever to get right. She grabbed the irons, narrowly missing scorching her hand, and began the laborious process of taming the curls into submission.

Available from Amazon.

ALSO BY LIZZIE CHANTREE

Romantic Fiction

The Little Cupcake Shop By The sea. **Book 2**

My Perfect Ex

If you love me, I'm yours

Ninja School Mum

Babe Driven

Love's Child

Finding Gina

The Woman Who Felt Invisible

Shh… It's Our Secret

Non-Fiction

Networking for writers